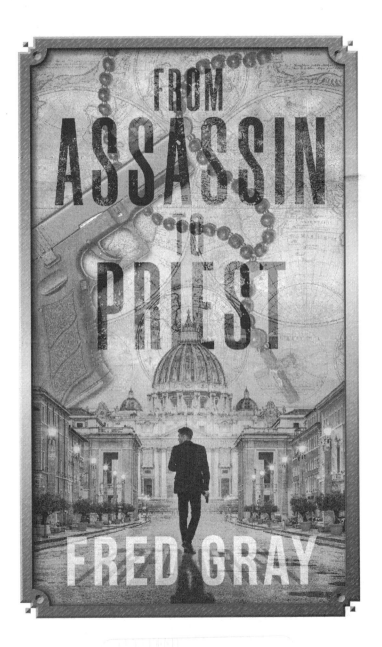

FROM ASSASSIN TO PRIEST

FRED GRAY

Published by Twin Press Publishing
2310 Gladiolus Lane
Mascotte, Florida 34753
ISBN: 979-8-218-11953-9

Cover design by 100 covers
Interior layout by Mike Butler, Torque Creative LLC.com
Edited by Marsha Butler, swmpwriter@gmail.com

DEDICATED TO GOD

My wife, Kelly—
For all your love and support

Mary Flynn—
Who carries the title of Best Friend

Glen—
My number one fan

My beautiful family,
all of you!!!

Acknowledgments

I would like to express my gratitude to the many people who helped me as I wrote this book; to those who provided support, read, discussed, offered comments and assisted in its design, editing, and proofreading.

To Kelly Gray for endlessly listening to me read and re-read and for her positive support throughout.

To Mary Flynn, special thanks for being my teacher, mentor, and, most of all, friend. Thank you for your infinite patience.

To my editor, Marsha Butler, for her endless patience and professionalism and all the common stories of life that we shared.

To Mike Butler, graphic designer, for his fine layout and formatting of the interior of both the e-book and the print version, and for guiding me through the machinations of self-publishing.

To Matt Stone and Jamie Ty and the team's fantastic design work on the book's covers and his friendly, prompt, and professional service. Many thanks, Matt, for being willing to go the extra mile with me.

To Professor Joseph P. Whelan, American Kenpo Karate sixth-degree black belt, for helping create fast-action, realistic fight scenes.

To all Beta readers, paid or not.

And, last but not least, I beg forgiveness from all those who have been with me over the course of the years whose names I have failed to mention.

ALSO BY FRED GRAY

—FICTION—

MIDDLE GRADE

CLOUD KINGDOM VOLUME 1

—NONFICTION—

TRAINING THE DUMB END OF THE LEASH

—SHORT STORIES—

BALANCE DUE—CHRISTIAN

SECOND CHANCE—CHRISTIAN

ARE WE EVEN YET—ONE NIGHT IN A DRUNK'S LIFE

Prologue

Sicily, 1988

The ICU room pulsed as if it were alive—a mixture of dark and luminous energy. His eyes blinked constantly, uncontrollably, allowing him to see only flashes of images, but never allowing enough light in to eradicate the dark and light shadows that were pulling at his soul.

The torment was more than any thirteen-year-old boy could bear. One moment, he felt terror, bewilderment, frustration, and despair; the next, love, peace, happiness, and hope. The pattern continued in a nauseating loop.

Nothing worked. His brain gave orders that his body refused to obey. His soul clutched at despair. The defining darkness devoured his thoughts, leaving him no way out. He felt utterly alone.

Horrific visions swirled deep within his mind—a tapestry of murder laid out before him. Blood and gore, the mutilated bodies of his beloved family.

Simultaneously, he could hear voices and feel the presence of people all around him, but he could not focus. Suddenly, all was silent, except for the squeal of the heart monitor. His body jerked as he heard a deep, resonating, angelic voice: ***Don't be afraid. You will not die.***

At the side of his bed, a nurse watched the redline on the

monitor go flat. "Doctor," she screamed, "he's flatlined."

Nine minutes later, the heart monitor beeped. The shadows of light and darkness were no longer fighting above the boy's bed. A gentle breeze had forced his essence back into his body. The boy opened his eyes.

"Order a brain scan as soon as he's stable," the cardiologist said. "Tell them I want it stat!"

"Yes, Dr. Marino."

Ninety minutes later, the nurse stuck her head in Dr. Marino's office. "They're up."

"Good work. Thanks."

What the…? Marino pulled the boy's CT images up on his monitor and pondered them. He'd never seen anything like this before. The cardiologist looked down from the computer monitor at his phone and hit the speed dial button for the neurologist, Dr. Romano.

"Romano," he answered on the second ring.

"Got a minute. I've got something I need you to look at."

"Give me ten. I'll be there."

Ten minutes later, Dr. Romano appeared in Marino's office. "Thanks for coming. Here, sit." He gestured toward his desk chair in front of his computer. Marino stood behind him.

"So, Sam, what do you see?"

Sam whistled under his breath. "I have never seen such brain activity in my life. Where did you get this?"

"Believe it or not, from that young patient I brought out of a coma this morning. We ordered this CT after he flatlined and had been brain dead for nine minutes and then woke up."

Sam held up his hand in a halting gesture. "Wait, that can't be. This isn't possible."

"I know, I know. But there it is."

"Bill, it's not possible that this kid can even be alive, much less that this can be his scan. His brain activity is on the scale of a genius. How does this happen? I can't imagine what this boy's mind has seen."

"I don't know. Most of the time, under these circumstances, the patient dies. For some reason, this boy lived."

Chapter One

—« PRESENT DAY

KRISTOFF SAT AT his desk in the world's tallest building in Dubai, United Arab Emirates. He loved the Neo-futurism design of the Burj Khalifa Tower—the feeling of constantly moving upward until you were at the top of the world and could see it all.

Kristoff ran the largest biochemical and nanotechnology company in the world. But today, instead of pondering advancements in nanotechnology—the science of assembling materials one atom at a time that allows complete control over the structure of matter—and the rage of Silicon Valley investors—he was pondering how he would become the new leader of the world's largest and most powerful cabal.

As he watched the clouds move quickly past the window walls of his office, he could almost see the creation of the lightning inside the clouds. As the sky turned a steel grey, the nucleus of the cloud surrounded by black with a pinhole of light, an overwhelming sense of the knowledge of all things filled him. The power that flowed through him could indeed move mountains.

Kristoff buzzed for his secretary, who appeared instantly. "I want division heads worldwide on a conference call in exactly twenty-eight minutes.

Thirty-five minutes later, his secretary announced that they were ready. Kristoff's office lit up with 212 monitors. Everyone was yelling their salutations and questions about what was happening at the same time. Kristoff stood in the middle of his office and raised his hands for silence. The uproar morphed into a murmur then into silence.

"I'm going to move the company in a new direction."

He introduced his secretary to his guests. His employees nodded in acknowledgment. Kristoff turned to his secretary. "How long have you worked for me?"

"Six years, sir."

"Any family?"

"Just my partner, sir."

"What time did I tell you to start this meeting?"

"In twenty-eight minutes."

"And when did it start?"

"In thirty-five minutes, sir."

"Thank you. Stay there for a moment."

Addressing the forum of division heads, Kristoff continued. "I will give you a new directive. As of now, I am taking over the cabal. I will be putting a team together to retrieve an item, that will bring us tremendous power.

Questions began to fly again. Kristoff raised his hands for quiet. An obedient hush fell over the room.

Kristoff motioned his secretary closer. When he was within reach, he grabbed the man by the throat in a stranglehold, raised him off the ground like a rag doll and shook him. His secretary clawed at Kristoff's hands as they cut short his life-giving breath. As the man gasped his last breath, Kristoff looked around the room at the hundreds of faces staring back at him from their computer monitors, then with the slightest hint of a smirk, he dropped his secretary's dead body to the floor like a crumpled piece of trash.

Bodies straightened in their chairs; eyes went wide.

Kristoff waited a few moments for the full impact of his deed to hit his employees before he broke the silence. "I took no pleasure in that, but I will not have my orders disobeyed. Thirty-five minutes is not twenty-eight."

Kristoff looked around the room filled with monitors. "Now, I want to draw your attention to the large screen across from you."

They all stared at the screen as it crackled to life. The image of a beautiful, black-haired Brazilian woman appeared.

"I'm ready, sir," came a sultry voice.

The scene of a mammoth castle stretched across a brilliant green mountaintop—a storybook scene, you might even say. They couldn't have picked a more picture-perfect day.

"This is the home of Louis Du Bois, the head of the cabal,

and the site of his daughter's wedding today. On their guest list were the twelve top men of the cabal. I was invited to this beautiful ceremony, but I believe in taking my business responsibilities seriously."

"Now, don't miss this little show I have planned for you." Everyone's eyes were focused on the lovely castle, perhaps hoping to catch a glimpse of a beautiful bride and her handsome groom vowing their eternal love for each other.

Kristoff nodded to the over-sized screen. "Now, Cersei." he said.

A stunning, blinding light appeared on the screen, and the next moment the castle disappeared, leaving only a giant crater where the wedding party and guests had been a moment before.

"As you can see for yourselves, with all of them missing or gone, my responsibilities are to take over. Any questions?"

A resounding "no" reverberated on screen from around the world.

"Thank you, Cersei. You may come home now."

Chapter Two

THE EVENING SUN was at half-mast. Vatican City's lights began to peek out, an odd glow surrounding them. Even the sculptures around Rome seemed to move in shadows. Gargoyles smiled. Angels appeared to turn into demons. Inside the Apostolic Palace, all was quiet until you rounded the corner to the Pope's quarters. There contentious whispers could be heard.

Two men hovered at the Pope's door, engaged in a hushed disagreement. The Pope's secretary was a tall, thin man—six-foot-one. His black cassock floated around his feet as he moved. With a harried expression, he gave no quarter. Opposing him, Cardinal Lintzinburg stood imperiously in a full white simar complete with a cape and zucchetto. Perfectly placed on his shoulders and head, they showed off his bulbous nose and double chin.

"We must wake His Eminence! The news must be brought to his attention immediately."

Cardinal Lintzinburg waved his hand. "Not yet. Let us

think on this."

"With all due respect, Cardinal, the Pope has been monitoring the events of all the spiritual signs in the last decade, looking for oddities pointing to the prophecy, and now these new signs appear. He must be told."

The Pope's secretary leaned into the door to listen and heard the Pope rustling about. He knocked.

"Enter."

"Sorry to wake you, Your Eminence," the secretary apologized as he opened the heavy, creaking door, "but I have news."

The Pope slid out of bed, waving him away. "I'll meet you in my private quarters."

Moments later, he sat behind his desk. "Summon the Cardinals of the Order of Mysteries," he commanded.

In the early 1500s, twelve of the Cardinals in Pectore organized and created their bylaws, which included creating the covert Order of Mysteries. Their charter was to look into the scientific world and search for any spiritual correlation or spiritual consequences that would have an effect on mankind in a questionable way. Each member's appointments were kept secret and known only to the sitting Pope, and the Pope who had consecrated him to the office of Cardinal. If one should die, the other were to have a unanimous vote for the new man.

In less than half an hour, the current twelve members of the Order had assembled in the Pope's office, each of them stoic and listening intently. "This is the event I have been waiting for. Evil is on the move, hunting for one of the Church's most sacred items." As the Pope spoke, misty rain, enveloped in a black fog, descended on St. Peter's Square.

Cardinal Lintzinburg stood, his large frame overbearing even in the size of this office. "What are you talking about?" he demanded.

"As the Cardinals of the Order of Mysteries know, there exists a letter of prophecy that states that in the 21st century, new technology will threaten mankind. I asked our science department to confirm or debunk my suspicion as to what this threat might be."

As the Pope walked about his office, he scrutinized each Cardinal, that they may fully appreciate the situation. "The reports and the evidence are now overwhelming. We now see that new technology using algorithms is targeting people, especially our youth, in an attempt to capture their minds, bodies, and souls with it's increased chemicals in the brain with dopamine being number one. It is an addiction of the highest order and as strong as any existing drug."

The head Cardinal of the Order of Mysteries declared that yes, nanotechnology, and these new algorithms unchecked, would have far-reaching consequences.

"If allowed to go unchecked, we will be dealing with a world of lost people." The Pope said. All but one Cardinal, Cardinal Lintzinburg, nodded in assent.

One of the members of the Order of Mysteries spoke up. "They now believe they can make it even more potent with the power of Christ by using a relic of his Passion."

Another stood and bowed his head and began, "The goal of nanotechnology is to replicate the perfect being. We all know who that was, Jesus Christ himself. With the relic of Christ's passion, they will try to bring forth their creation."

The Pope nodded. This foreshadows the coming of Satan on earth to retrieve what is believed to be the most valuable possession of the Church." Fear pervaded the room as the cardinals gazed from one to another.

Cardinal Lintzinburg looked around the room for confirmation of this highly dubious statement. He was met with faces set like flint. He saw not one blink of an eye from anyone. He whipped around and glared at the Pope, "Why have I heard nothing of this?"

"You do not belong to their faction," the Pope replied, "but I have brought you here for your support and advice on this matter."

Somewhat placated by the Pope's deferential words and silently reminding himself to whom he was speaking, Cardinal Litzinburg softened his tone. "Your Eminence, I thank you for your vote of confidence, but I feel I am out of my depth here."

"Nonsense, you will pick up on this quickly. I have instructed one of the Society to bring you up to date." The Pope looked around as he rubbed his hands together and addressed the small assembly. "I believe that God will send us someone to help us in this our time of need. Until we next meet." They took their leave in prayerful discernment. The Pope called back his secretary.

“Please find Vito Rosario for me,” the Pope said, stroking his chin. “He is one of the new graduating seminarians. I wish to dine with him in two days in my quarters.”

Chapter Three

CARDINAL LINTZINBURG'S ANGER made him tremble at his desk. He couldn't stop shaking as he drafted a letter to the cabal. He wrote in furious print.

Kristoff, we need to meet, I can no longer suffer the indignities of this old man. We must get rid of him. It is my time to reign. Spiritual warfare, indeed. He will bring the Church to its knees with his backward thinking.

His intelligent eyes scanned the office as if he could see the answers floating about. Moments later he hustled down to the Vatican Secret Archives—53 miles of shelving and 35,000 catalogued volumes. One needed to be 75 years old or older to gain access to these records. *Thanks to the old man's dispensation,* I'm in. Now cautiously optimistic, the Cardinal thought, *I need to control this situation and get ahead of him.*

He needed to get his hands on the letter the Pope had disclosed. If it was anywhere, it would be here.

Cardinal Lintzinburg nearly tripped as his weak knees and burly legs tried to hustle down a new aisle. He grabbed another box and rummaged through it. There, he found what he thought he was looking for: Scientific documents. He expeditiously examined the documents until he came upon one called Journals of an Abbott with an asterisk on it. He pulled it out and began to read.

Lightning from the late night storm-filled sky lit the monastery doorway. Brother Luke walked to the front of the choir area and stopped. He thought he had heard a faint noise muffled by the thunder and lightning. Through the dim candlelight the stone floor behind him looked polished by his robe, but only on one side, for his right leg was shorter than the left. Reaching the heavy, 15-foot-high double doors, he heard it louder. Someone was singing outside.

Luke pulled open the front door just as a flash of lightning raced across the sky again. The shadows of light from the candles danced across the walls. He stepped back to see a strange little man bellowing a tune.

"What are you doing out there?" Luke yelled above the storm.

The stranger sang loudly, his words slurred, "Danny is my name. For a swill of wine, I'll let you know a secret of mine."

"Get in here. You are going to catch your death. But please, keep quiet." Luke grabbed the small, ruddy man and tried to drag him in, but Danny proved to be a handful.

"Danny is my name. For a swill of wine, I'll let you know a secret of mine," he sang again, only louder this time. The large and drafty monastery walls seemed to magnify the sound like echoes in a mountain valley.

"You must quiet down if you want me to help you."

The drunk pushed Brother Luke away, looked him up and down, and said, "Kindly keep your hands off me, sir…I mean, monk."

Brother Luke took his hands away and sighed. "What can I do for you, sir?"

"I need money, my kind monk. So that I may get more wine."

"Come with me, let us see what we can do for you." Turning and spinning on his long leg, it looked like Luke glided in a half-circle. The drunk tried to do the same spin and fell on his ass. Luke marched back to Danny and cradled his arms under the man's armpits, yanking him upright. As he did so, the smell of wine and three-day-old body odor assaulted the priest's nose. The inebriated fellow went along quietly as he was led through the monastery.

"Where are you from?" Luke asked.

"I'm from England, and my family is from France."

Luke turned to face Danny. "Have you ever tried to quit your drinking?"

Danny stepped back and looked at him as if he had two heads. "Of course, I have. Every waking moment. But that resolve doesn't seem to make it. I just can't. Too much guilt and shame in my life."

Luke quickly bowed his head in apology. "Maybe I can help. Why don't you tell me about it?"

"If you want to help, just give me some money for drink, and I'll be on my way."

"Sorry, I can't do that, but I will give you something to eat and a bed for the night."

Danny seemed to consider the offer, but then his face lit up with an alternative. "Hey, I got something you might be interested in. It's a map."

"Let's get you cleaned up and something to eat and maybe some rest first."

"No, look! Here," Danny proclaimed as he swept away his long coat and dug deep into his soiled pants. "This is a map of my family's misdeeds. I have been trying to sell it all night, but no one wants to even look at it."

Brother Luke glanced down and saw a dank, yellow-stained paper crumpled up in Danny's hand. He shook his head. "Come, we'll take a look at it later."

Danny stepped around to face Brother Luke. "Only if you promise to buy it."

"We shall see."

"No, I need the money. You got to buy it."

"I won't promise you anything, but I will do something for you."

"You promise?"

The monk nodded. "Come."

Cardinal Lintzinburg looked up from his reading and smiled, triumphant. Oh my, this is better than I thought. I *have the vestige of a map.* His avarice grew as he continued to read.

Many hours after his arrival, the drunk awoke, looking for something to drink and wondering how he got to this place, whatever it was. He rolled out of bed, shuffled out of his room and looked right, then left. He could only see a long, deep hallway with many doors and minimal light. Being right-handed, he chose to head right. As he lumbered down the hall, shadows seemed to move with him. Cracked paintings hung from the walls and some doors had old crucifixes attached.

"What the hell is going on? Where am I?" Looking at one of the doors with a cross on it, he banged his leg on a side table that held a dimly lit lamp, knocking the lamp over. He caught it before it could clang to the floor and placed it back on the table, praising himself for the excellent catch. He continued to ramble the halls and followed the scent of coffee until he found the kitchen. There sat Brother Luke with a cup of brew and Danny's map inside a clear plastic bag.

"Are we feeling any better?"

"I don't know how I feel yet. Let's try a cup of that coffee."

Luke poured him a cup that steamed with an aroma even the stranger smiled at. "Let me know how it tastes."

Danny looked down at his hand and brought his lips to the cup, promptly burning his mouth. "Shit, that's hot," he huffed, setting the cup down. "I see you have my map. What do you think?"

"It has some merit. I have done a little research on it in the last few hours. The monastery has an extensive library."

"So, is it worth a bottle of wine? I told you this map is the shame of my family. I want no part of it no more."

"I think it's worth more than a bottle of wine, Danny. This is a map and the confession of a man who stole relics from the Church to make a living." Brother Luke stroked his furrowed brow. "The confession matches the records I found. I was lucky enough to discover the story of the man who seems to have been his partner, who also had an extremely rare item, but that man was never seen or heard from again after entering the hiding place of the relics." He looked up to see Danny standing above him. He needed a bath. It took all the monk's willpower not to cover his nose. "Please, try some of that coffee again. Just sip it."

Danny grunted and returned to the opposite end of the

table to take a sip from his steaming mug. With a crooked smile, he indicated that it was good.

"Our records tell of someone who was tasked with moving an exceedingly rare relic. The temptation to see what he was transporting got the better of 'em. So, he looked and then stole a piece of it. This map shows where he hid the portion of the relic and the relic stolen by his partner all those years ago." Luke gave a wistful smile as his heart beat a little faster.

Danny swayed, still slightly inebriated despite his nap. "It was a thorn removed from Christ's Crown of Thorns. It was taken while the crown was being transferred to its final home in the Cathedral of Notre-Dame de Paris. I don't know about the other one the confession is talking about."

"So, what shall we do about this?"

Having sobered up some, Danny's thoughts were all over the place. First, thinking of staying sober, then thinking about getting a drink to help him cope, then repeating the thought pattern until he thought he would go mad. Finally, he bowed his head in remorse for being a drunk. He began to shake. Tears erupted from within him. "I don't want anything for this information—just some peace of mind and possibly a small amount of forgiveness." The small confession of what he truly wanted was a step in the right direction and brought him some peace of mind.

"Please, my friend, stay with us for a while and let us help you get better. Give me a moment. I will be back. I am going to try and get my superiors on the phone, so we can make some arrangements for you and your map."

As Brother Luke walked away, Danny dried his eyes on his dirty sleeve, laid his head on the table, and tried to think. This proved difficult as it had been a long time since he had allowed himself to think about anything other than where his next drink would come from. His stomach growled, almost relieving his troubled thoughts, and he began rummaging through the kitchen for something to eat.

Meanwhile, Brother Luke finally got a hold of the Pope's secretary and explained what he had seen and heard from Danny. He arranged for the map and the confession to be taken to the Apostolic Palace and for Danny to receive help.

Cardinal Lintzinburg smiled, tucked the map into his cassock and replaced the boxes, erasing all trails leading to him.

Chapter Four

A TWELVE-FOOT, BLACK wrought iron fence enclosed an impressive villa. The guards were all strategically placed, each standing on high alert around beautifully manicured gardens and shrubs. You could hear the faint rustling of German Shepherds and Doberman Pinchers as they wandered the grounds.

The butler served a decanter of fifty-year-old Scotch to the terrace, where Kristoff and Cardinal Lintzinburg were seated, before swiftly retreating to his corner. On the opposite side of the deck stood Cersei, an exotic Brazilian women with stark black hair that set off a pair of laser green eyes. Kristoff's bodyguard and second in command, a demon of the first order, never leaving her master's side unless ordered.

Cardinal Lintzinburg looked out upon the grounds. "This is certainly a beautiful place you have here, and it has a certain Je ne said quoi." He faced Kristoff and raised his glass, "To success."

Kristoff nodded. To our success. Now, let's get down to

business."

"Yes. I don't have to tell you again that we must get rid of the old man."

"Not yet. We still need to be careful not to rock the political world." He gave the Cardinal a pointed look through eyes that couldn't make up their mind what color they were—blazing red or piercing black—as he took a sip of his Scotch.

Cardinal Lintzinburg stood and walked back into the study off the terrace, carrying his drink. "At least I have the map, and they won't get their hands on it.

Kristoff's left eyebrow raised. "The map you spoke to me about?"

"Yes."

Kristoff walked up behind the Cardinal. Cersei took a few steps closer to her master then noticed Kristoff wave her off. She returned to her corner as Cardinal Lintzinburg turned to face Kristoff. "I'll give you the map, if and when you kill the old man."

"Against my better judgment, give me the map and I'll send Cersei to visit the Pope."

Cardinal Lintzinburg smiled, reached into his suit breast pocket, and handed him an envelope. Kristoff reached up and grabbed his wrist and started to squeeze with the power only a demon would possess. Cardinal Lintzinburg's knees buckled. "PLEASE," he shouted in pain, "please."

Kristoff lowered his head and whispered, "never try to blackmail me again, Cardinal." He let go of the man's wrist just before he pulverized the bone. Kristoff helped him up and brushed him off. "Okay, now that the unpleasantries are over, let's finish our meeting."

Cardinal Lintzinburg grabbed his glass, poured a double, and took a deep drink. "What are you going to do with it?"

"I know of an archaeology student at Simon College who will be able to hunt down what's on the map. There's no need for you to worry about it any longer." He placed his arm around the Cardinal's massive shoulders as best he could. "Focus on the fact that you will see your dream come true and take your place on the seat of Peter. And don't forget that we expect your alliance with the cabal.

The Cardinal grunted, swallowing the rest of his drink, and set the empty glass down on a decorative end table. "I must be leaving."

They smiled and bowed to one another. Kristoff waved Cersei over. "Please escort Cardinal Lintzinburg out. And bring the car around; we have another appointment.

The Cardinal nodded and followed Cersei out.

Once his attendant had returned with the car, Kristoff slid into the backseat. "Cersei, did you do as I instructed?"

"Of course, boss. Jake was instructed to contact Joan and your surprise for the Cardinal is ready."

"Good, then let's teach this pious old shit a lesson. Hand me that detonator."

Kristoff smiled as he pushed the button, and the lead escort car of the Cardinal's security detail disintegrated right before his eyes. The Cardinal's car swerved to a stop, and Kristoff could hear the frightened man screaming at the top of his lungs, "Get us out of here!" The Cardinal turned and looked out the back window to see Cersei and Kristoff chuckling.

"Cersei, get this Jake on the phone."

She slid closer to her master. "Yes, sir," she purred.

The Senator's private phone rang. "Hello. May I speak with Senator Jake Howard, please?"

Howard's secretary passed the call through.

"Jake, please hold for Mr. Kristoff." Cersei handed the phone over.

"Jake, my dear boy, my assistant tells me she asked you to contact someone for me. Is that correct?"

"Why yes, she did. It shouldn't be a problem."

"I want to thank you for taking this matter on and speaking to her in person."

Jake smiled and unwrapped a cigar. *It'll be easy enough to get close to this guy.* "I hadn't thought of going personally. I was going to send one of my men."

"Jake, I can see you are a busy and powerful man, I also know that you are above most laws in this country. So, I would take it as a special favor if you handled it yourself."

Jake lit his cigar and took a long puff before responding. "Now, Kristoff you are correct about my status, so if I tell you that it will get done, you can rest assured that it will."

"Did I forget to mention, Jake, that like you, I am above the law. So high am I, you or your President could not touch me. So, let's get this done without conversation."

"Yes…yes, sir. I…I will get it done for you."

"Good and to show you how much I appreciate this favor, how would you like to become the next President of the United States?"

"I would love that, of course. Who wouldn't? Can it be done?"

"We will talk later when you have secured her. but remember I will be the one to welcome her to the team."

Cersei grabbed the phone and hung it up for her boss.

Damn, did that just happen? Jake hit the intercom button. "Helen get in here."

"Right away, sir."

The senator's large ribbed-glass office door swung open as Helen entered. She looked every bit the part that Jake thought she should be. Her pristine white blouse seemed a size too small for her ample breasts and her perfectly pleated red skirt matched her high heels. The look on Jake's face stopped her dead. She backed up a few steps. "What's up, boss? I've seen that look before. Like right before you make a kill."

"Helen, I need you to clear my schedule for the next few days and have my plane ready to fly out to Garfield Ledges, Ohio. By tomorrow mid-day."

"Yes, boss."

"Wait, I'll also need a full workup on a Joan Vitale."

"You got it, boss. Anything else?"

Stretching back in his chair, he took a deep draw of his cigar before exhaling, "If I think of anything, I'll call."

Chapter Five

JAKE FELL IN love with Joan Vitale the first time he met her. He took her like a bullet, first under the skin, then like an explosion in his heart and soul.

He had been walking across campus and just as he entered the administration building, he noticed a tall, slender woman. She wore a western shirt with a pair of cotton candy-colored blue jeans that hugged her every curve and showed a little skin through the rips in the jeans. The Texas hat and boots were a nice touch too. She reminded him of a country music star. The clicking of her heels echoed off the long hallway. Her silhouette glared off the old, tiled walls.

"Excuse me, miss? Excuse me."

Joan turned and looked up, her lips parted in a smile, revealing dazzlingly white teeth. "Are you talking to me?" she said, staring him up and down. A tad short of six feet, he wore a Savile Row tailored-made suit by Gieves & Hawkes.

"Yes, I am, young lady." His eyes mirrored her not-so-subtle gawking.

Finally, her eyes met his. "What can I do for you?"

His smile emphasized his cleft chin. "How about lunch, then showing me around the Archaeology Department?"

"Wow. It only took you a few seconds to ask me out on a date." She shifted her weight and gave him a tempting look at her profile. "The boys usually wait at least a couple of minutes."

"I'm not your average suitor, and I'm certainly not a boy." Jake moved in a little closer, giving her an admiring look and an inviting smile. "So, what's for lunch and where?"

She smiled back. "I'll play. Where's your car?"

"It's the limo over there"

He gazed at her longingly.

"Sorry, I doubt we'll have anything to accommodate your taste around here."

"Oh, you'd be surprised." He gazed at her longingly.

"Now, now, cool your jets. We haven't even been properly introduced yet."

"You're right. Hold that thought…please." Jake pulled out his phone and talked briefly to someone on the other end. Then he closed the phone and it disappeared back into his pocket.

"What was that all about?"

Jake just raised his hand in a wait-a-moment gesture.

She slipped into a flirting demeanor, pouting. "Come on, what was that all about?"

Once again, Jake gestured for her to wait, asking instead, "What do you do here at the school?"

"I'm an Archaeology major."

Just then, an intimidating man with a large frame and a fast gait stopped next to Jake.

"Yes, Al, what do you have?"

"Sir, I'd like you to meet Joan Vitale. Miss Vitale, I'm pleased to introduce you to Senator Jake Howard."

Joan stared at the man, speechless.

"Sir, Miss Vitale is studying for two degrees, one in Archaeology and the other in Ancient Artifacts," he added.

Jake nodded. "Thank you, that is all for now."

The chauffeur bowed and scurried back towards the limo. Before he reached the door, he whipped around. "Oh, I forgot to mention, boss, she just returned from Israel." Then he disappeared around the corner.

"Okay now, that was just plain creepy…but impressive. How did he do it?"

"My dear, you're the impressive one. I'll tell you how I did it, but first I want to know if you'll go on that date with me."

This guy is trouble. But what kind of trouble? He seems exhilarating. "Well, no lunch. Dinner only." Is it a deal?" She reached out her hand. "Deal?" she asked.

Jake took her hand and pulled her in close to him. "Deal," he said calmly, trying not to let her see the hypnotic effect her perfume was having on him. I'm looking forward to it. May I have your phone number? So that I can pick you up."

She dug into her purse and handed him her business card. "Don't worry about picking me up. I'll meet you wherever you choose."

The shadows of the night wafted into the Pope's bedroom as he tossed and turned in bed. His eyes fluttered open only to see the form of a demon dancing above his head. He sprang out of bed and began to pray the rosary.

Dressing quickly he made his way into the Apostolic Archive, a secret room in Vatican City where only the Pope could view the contents that lay within. He reached up and pulled down the scroll written by Mary Magdalene.

On this day of the crucifixion of our Lord Jesus Christ, I, Mary, The Magdalene, witnessed these events. The Tree that bound our Savior was hoisted up and driven into the ground on Golgotha. I watched all who participated in this momentous catastrophe and heard our sweet Lord and Savior say. "it is finished." The skies became black; thunder shook the ground, then lightning struck the tree and Golgotha. Creating an opening where the blood of Christ dripped down, I emptied my perfume from an alabaster tube and collected one drop of Our Lord's precious blood, for this will be the gift from God against the attack of Satan and his demons.

The Pope returned the document and went back to his quarters.

Joan and Howard met for dinner that night at the most prominent restaurant in town, The Garfield Ledges Tower. The view was breathtaking as the maître d' escorted them to their table against a back wall made entirely of windows. Outside, a paddle wheel on the river reminded Jake of a restaurant in Amsterdam. The sound of the water made him want to sway with the music inside. The harmony was remarkable.

Jake gently slid the small silver candelabra out of his line of vision of Joan, and the ambient light ceased to overshadow her face. Looking into her eyes, he could see a fierce determination, yet a certain emptiness accompanied it, pulling at him to fulfill a certain need.

"My name is Dominic, and I will be your waiter. You both look lovely this evening. What a fine couple. Is this your first time here? And if so, may I recommend a glass of our house vino?"

"Yes, it is our first time and please pour your house vino," Jake said.

This is too good to be true. What does he want, besides me in his bed? Does it matter? "I love this," Joan said as she took Jake's hand. "Thank you. This is so different from what I'm used to."

As the glasses of wine disappeared, so did the barriers between them. The chase and anticipation intensified to a new level.

"This wine has such a bouquet. Was it made in Italy?"

Jake lifted the glass to toast her. "This house wine was made in Tuscany by a private label, Antonio Pistone. Here's to this evening."

Feeling the wine, Joan waved her hand. Jake noticed her long, strong fingers—*on such a delicate hand,* he thought.

"Oh my God," she said, "I'd love to visit Italy. It's one of the places on my bucket list—Rome and the Vatican. What a dream trip."

"Speaking of Italy and Rome makes me think of a lovely dessert I would like to have prepared for us after dinner. Is that okay with you?"

She looked curiously into his eyes and smiled. "I love surprises."

Jake pulled out his phone and talked with someone for a few moments. Joan noticed the conversation took a little longer than his last one, though she tried not to pay attention.

She sipped her wine while he talked on the phone. "So, what is the real reason you're here?" she asked after he got off. I'm here to find a relic. Or the possible location of one."

"I didn't realize that senators were interested in such matters." She was resting her chin on the back of her hand. "Please, do tell me more."

"It's just a business deal with another organization. We have mutual interests."

Jake reached for his napkin as the waiter brought their

salads. He opened Joan's and let it gently drop in her lap. Joan raised her finger to pause the conversation and bowed her head to recite a small blessing.

Interesting, Jake thought. *Is she religious?* He wondered if he should ask, but feeling slightly uncomfortable, he decided to stick to small talk. "Have you always lived here in Garfield Ledges?"

"Yes. I had a pretty crazy childhood here. I come from a low-income family and did everything wrong until I realized I was living the hard way."

"Tell me more."

As he tried to look into her eyes, she adverted them. "Like any small town, we had plenty of things to get into trouble with." Before she could say more, the waiter replaced their salads with entrées. Joan had the Veal Scallopini, while Jake had Ossobuco alla Milanese. Pleased, they dug in.

Jake looked up from his plate long enough to notice that Joan had stopped eating. He followed her gaze out the window. "Is everything all right?"

"Everything is so lovely." Her eyes were watery with excitement and tears. They both paused to watch the moonlight reflect off the water flowing down the paddle wheel, creating a beautiful light show.

"Okay, so what are some of the exciting things that happen in Garfield Ledges?"

"Have you ever heard of the New Age movement? Where the belief is that people can and will channel unsuspecting minds into doing things they normally wouldn't do?"

Jake gave a slight chuckle. "Remember you're talking to a politician, but yes, I have heard of it. You're saying there was a movement up here in Garfield Ledges?"

"Professor Billy Campbell and I personally recruited the police to look into their dealings and we were able to eradicate the New Age group trying to channel our students and some others who seemed spiritually lost. There had been several strange deaths, and we found a torture chamber, which was unbelievable."

Jake's eyes widened as he listened.

"Oh, and Billy single-handedly brought to justice the man responsible for torturing several kids."

"This Billy Campbell must be some guy."

"Oh, he is. You can say he is out of this world and not be wrong," she said with a smirk.

When the waiter came over to recite the dessert list, Jake raised his hand signaling him to stop. "I've prepared a special dessert for Joan instead." The waiter nodded and disappeared. Joan's eyes danced with a sparkle, as her voice bubbled with excitement, "I love surprises."

"Are we done here?" he asked, nodding at the empty plates on the table.

"Yes, but don't worry, I won't turn into a pumpkin if I get home late."

"Good to know," he quipped, showing off that cleft chin and politician's bright smile."

Jake and Joan settled back into the limo, as the driver took off.

"Where are we going?"

"I told you I have something special planned for dessert."

Feeling tipsy and frisky, she moved closer and squeezed Jake's leg. He jumped a little as she whispered in his ear, "Come on, tell me what's for dessert."

Jake faced her as their knees knocked against one another, leaning in as if to kiss her, his lips brushed past hers and continued on to her ear instead. "Wait and you will see." Joan's eyes flashed open as he nibbled on her ear slightly.

"Damnnn," she howled.

Chapter Six

VITO PASSED SOME of the most beautiful paintings in the world by Raphael on his way to the Pope's quarters. They presented a stark contrast to the room in which the Pope's secretary had deposited him. The walls of the Pope's dining area were painted a dull gold, with few paintings on the walls and a large Crucifix. The table was long and covered with a white linen tablecloth with a gold hem and set with dinnerware bearing the crest of the keys of St. Peter.

Vito wondered why he had been summoned to the Pope's quarters. Perhaps someone had brought his past life to the Pope's attention. Just then, the Pope entered.

"Good evening, my son."

Vito knelt and kissed the Pope's ring. "Your Eminence."

The Pope thought Vito's mesmerizing ice-blue eyes were like his father's; some had called them steely, falcon-like, hard like flint, or wary—they were all of that. Nothing got past the man and his Benevolence had always found himself lost in those eyes. Vito even had his father's silver-black hair.

"You're wondering why you're here, yes?"

"As a matter of fact, I am." *The raw power of this man makes me want to do his bidding without question.*

"I feel your apprehension, but we will get to all that after dinner." The Pope walked through an archway, over to the table, and gestured for Vito to sit. "Please."

The Pope rang, and dinner was brought in. Vito watched as the Pope was served first. *This appetizer looks great,* Vito thought. After they served him, he looked around for the rest of their meal, but there were no more dishes of food brought in. Vito smiled when he realized that this was all that was coming.

"I hope you will enjoy dinner." His Eminence continued, "My meals are meager as an offering for the poor. Tonight is just a small dish of pasta and one meatball with olives and homemade bread. Please, my son, lead us in the prayer of thanksgiving."

They bowed their heads, and Vito began. "Heavenly Father, all glory and honor are yours. We ask you to bless this food so that it may nourish our bodies and that we may do your holy will. We thank and ask you to bless all those who have partaken in preparing this food. Also, the benefactor who has invited me here this evening."

They had eaten nearly half of their meals before the Pope spoke again.

"I have seen your name on the top of the graduation list and researched you. Does that surprise you?"

Vito placed his fork down, and picked up his napkin.

"No, Your Eminence. Rather I was surprised that no one had brought my name to your attention earlier."

Dabbing the corner of his mouth with his napkin, the Pope gave a sly grin. "Oh, why is that?"

"I was wondering how the church would accept a man like me into the ranks of the Priesthood."

"The Priesthood would always accept those that have made it past our vetting process. Also someone with your high I.Q. and eidetic memory would be highly desirable. I know of a few Cardinals who would love for you to become a Jesuit."

"Your Holiness, I don't understand why I am here tonight?"

"How is your pasta? I'm particularly fond of the meatballs."

"Almost like Mama's."

"Ah, tell me about your parents."

Vito broke eye contact and shrugged. "I don't remember much except that I always felt loved and cared for. And I loved my brother and sister; we were close."

"Those are good things to remember," the Pope remarked with a soft, wrinkled smile. They both dipped the last of their bread, and the Pope set his napkin down as he stood up, beckoning for Vito to follow suit. "I hope you found everything filling enough. My stomach won't handle a lot of food anymore. Let us help ourselves to a glass of vino in the next room and I will tell you why I have brought you here tonight."

The Pope poured two glasses of wine and handed one to Vito. The Pope raised his glass and gestured to Vito to take a seat. Vito sat, crossed his legs and looked up at the Pope as he took a healthy gulp of his wine.

"Vito, I knew your father, Stephano, well. He worked for me some years back as an intelligence agent."

Vito's eyes fixated on the Pope. "What?"

"Relax, my son…please. I will tell you about him, then answer any questions you have."

Vito drank slowly.

"But they shall never be repeated outside this room."

"So, you knew all this time about me and what happened to my family?" A hint of anger rose from deep within his breast.

The Pope nodded. "Unfortunately, I could do nothing to help you except allow the doctors to care for you."

"But why? You could have possibly kept me from that orphanage."

"Your father was guarding some relics, very precious to the Church. If I were to step in, the people that came after you and your family would have not only come after you again but would have come after your cousins and any other relations you or your father had."

"But still, after so many years, you couldn't have said or done something to honor them?"

The Pope moved his chair closer to Vito and laid his hand on his knee, looking sorrowfully into his eyes.

"My son, those who did this to your family have memories as long as the Church does."

Vito nodded. *I have already dealt with these animals.*

"Tell me, why did you think you were here for something

else? What could that be, my son?"

Vito looked at the Pope. "Maybe this should wait for another time."

"Nonsense, my son, please, go ahead and tell me."

Vito bowed his head, cleared his voice, and confessed everything to the Pope about his life—about how he saw his family murdered, about how he came out of the coma, and how Enzio Benetti adopted him. He also explained that Enzio sent him to the best of schools but also trained him daily for years in the gym and in martial arts with all types of lethal weapons. "It wasn't until later that I understood why he trained me to be so proficient in protection as well as killing. Enzio brought me into his business, contract-killing."

An exceptionally good listener, the Pope had not risked showing his emotions until he heard about the man's work as a freelancing executioner. To his credit, he maintained his composure and waved Vito on.

"An overwhelming rage consumed me over my parents being killed. I wanted to know who this person was who would bring such misery to a family. So, I went on a mission to find him, and when I did, something happened to me. I thought I could not be hurt any more than I already was." Vito squeezed his hands together and started to stand when the Pope placed his hand on his shoulder and, with a surprisingly powerful force, set him back down. "Relax, my son, just let it out."

"Father, this information crushed me even more because Enzio was responsible for their deaths. The man who took me in and taught me the trade of playing God had taken my own family from me. So, I went out to play God and find my revenge." He gave a heavy sigh and took another swig of his wine.

"Enzio had been diagnosed with brain cancer before he adopted me from the State facility. In the early years, the cancer took its toll slowly, but over time it progressed more rapidly and in the last year, he was going fast. Lumps the size of grapes appeared all over his head; a few were larger than golf balls. The morphine could not touch the pain. The disease was eating him up from the inside out."

Vito paused, seeming to recall a most unpleasant memory. His nose wrinkled. "The smell was putrefying, when I slipped into the room that night. Enzio could see the rage in my eyes. He tried to apologize as I and close the gap between us but I just shook my head and shouted at him, 'How could you do this to me?' I told him that he had robbed me twice in my life; first of my family that night long ago in Sicily, then again when he had made me love him unknowingly. That betrayal ripped me apart."

Vito's hands started to tremble, but he could not stop the flow of words.

"I put my hands around his neck and began to squeeze, when I suddenly felt a presence fill the room. I could hear Enzio gurgling, and I remember smiling… But I started to hear a familiar whisper. A voice that appeared to me every time I killed, like it was angry with me, though I could never understand what it was saying. This time, the voice got louder as I choked him, and I heard the words clearly, 'I did not give you this second chance in life to take life.'"

The Pope looked on thoughtfully. "God will speak to us in many ways. It seems you finally recognized his voice. What happened when you heard it clearly that time?"

"I bowed my head and released my grip immediately, but as soon as I did, my head exploded with gory images of the deaths of my family. I grabbed his neck again, this time to twist it and feel it snap in my hands. But the voice returned, even louder, 'I did not give you this second chance in life to take life.'" Vito hung his head in shame.

The Pope reached over and gave his shoulder a reassuring squeeze. "Go on, my son."

"I let go of him again, and Enzio started crying and begging me to kill him. It was hard for him to talk, but he just kept saying, 'Kill me and let me go,' over and over again. I told him it was no longer my job, and that the Lord would do a better job of justice than I…"

The Pope gave a quick smile in acknowledgement of this right choice.

"Then I walked out of that room, feeling like my soul had split in half." Vito took a deep breath, quieting the anger in his voice as he continued. "Shortly after, everything started to spiral downward in my mind, body, and soul. This life I had built, I needed to tear it down around me, and I had constant battles in my head that went on for what seemed like endless hours a day. It took me a while to realize that the spiritual battle had begun." Vito looked pointedly at the Pope, knowing he would understand.

"I wanted my life of easy money and to have whatever I desired. I loved playing God, but that inner voice kept tearing down those arguments with feelings of fear, remorse, and shame. Months went by with this torment going on inside me. And when I say torment, I mean my four horsemen of the Apocalypse: Terror, Bewilderment, Frustration, and Despair." Vito almost sounded like he wanted to laugh, though the bitterness in his voice snuffed out any humor.

"The tools of my trade felt like the answer to me, and I thought more and more about ending my own life. It seemed that my body had a mind of its own. I looked down and saw the cold blue steel reflection of my best pistol in my hand. I put it into my mouth without hesitating. I knew exactly how many pounds of pressure it would take, just a simple two pounds. I pulled the trigger, but I never heard the click. It never came. The gun jammed," he said, shaking his head in disbelief.

"So, I threw the gun on the table, and it went off, putting a bullet right into my stomach. The neighbors heard the shot and called the police. They got me to the hospital in time. It hurt like hell, but no permanent damage was done." Vito covered his face and began to weep.

"My son, my son," the Pope comforted him as he came to stand over Vito and pray the prayer of forgiveness. "With His unfathomable mercy, our Lord Jesus Christ brings you into His arms at this moment; feel His love and forgiveness. Be fresh as you were when baptized. In the name of the Father, and of the Son, and of the Holy Spirit. Amen." The Pope wrapped him in his arms and held him.

Vito sat there drying his tears as relief began to wash over him. The Pope helped him up and back into his private office. He paused and gave Vito a sober look. "Now, I know, my son, that you are the man the Lord has sent me for this most serious mission."

He went to his desk and sat down. "I have a specific job for you. It is to fulfill your father's mission with the Church. I will need you to help me foil the plans of what I believe to be an uprising of the most consequential magnitude. You will be the head intelligence agent for the RPCP.

"Your Eminence, what is the RPCP?"

"It is Retrieval & Procurement of Christ's Passion."

Vito stood there with a blank expression. Feeling torn, he lowered his head. *My God, why would you ask this of me? You know how weak I am. Is it not true that no man can worship two masters? Especially if it's oneself... won't the temptation of playing God come back to me? Or is this a test of my faith?*

"I don't believe I'm worthy. Your Eminence, or the one to help you in this matter."

The Pope nodded his head stood and turned to walk out. He turned back to Vito. "Take a few days, then come see me. I will have a standing order for your admittance to me."

Vito remained quiet, unsure of how to respond. When he

spurted out, "I may have acquired the IQ of a genius and eidetic memory, but I have a big problem with bouts of conscience and flashbacks that make me hesitate at the most inopportune times."

The Pope smiled. "Let us pray that God will send something or someone your way to strengthen you. Oh, by the way, you'll need to know that you will have enemies inside the church, as well as outside. Please, be very careful. Sometimes we must keep our family and friends closer than our enemies."

Vito grimaced. "I understand."

The Pope stood. "Good, one more thing before you go…"

The Pope called in his secretary. "You will be my witness to what is about to take place." Vito saw uncertainty and fear in the secretary's face.

Is he going to defrock me?

"Vito, kneel before me."

When His Eminence spoke these words, the room seemed to pulsate with divine energy, as if it were alive, breathing, and exuberant in glee. The marble floor shivered with power like an awakening beast, and a chill swept over Vito as he knelt. "May the Blessed Trinity fill you with all the gifts of the Holy Spirit. Receive this gift, and through your virtues, use it wisely, for few have received it, let alone someone of your age. Blessing, Vito," the Pope said. "Rise. You are now a Cardinal in Pectore."

Vito humbly rose as tears rolled down his face.

Cardinal Lintzinburg tore himself away from the secret wall within the Pope's quarters, his face twisted in anger and jealousy. He swore under his breath an oath to stand against anyone who spoiled his plans, even this meddling fool of a Pope.

Chapter Seven

JAKE FELT EXHILARATED. He didn't know why. He had done crazier things in his life, but he wanted everything to be perfect for this lady. She had made him forget about himself, which was not an easy task.

"Would you like a drink?" Jake asked.

She was still tingling from him nibbling on her ear, "Yes, I would. What do you have?

"You name it. We have it."

"Then I'd like a bourbon on the rocks."

"Knob Creek, is that all right?"

Smiling, she said, "Of course."

After much small talk and another drink, Joan felt the car stop. "Where are we?" She couldn't contain her excitement. "The tinted windows are so dark; I can't see outside."

Al opened the backdoor. "We're here, sir." Awaiting them was an ultra-modified golf cart with the body of a Rolls-Royce Silver Cloud, and a man standing beside it, ready to serve. "Best hurry up, sir, or we will lose our take-off position."

The Gulfstream G700 was warming up for take-off as they approached the plane's staircase.

"Jake, what are you doing?"

Jake shrugged like a schoolboy. "I thought we'd knock off one of those items on your bucket list—Rome, the Vatican?"

She stared at Jake for a moment in silence, then at her hands. They were shaking. *Who is this man?* Her voice trembled as she tried to sound sensible. "Jake, I can't just take off to Rome. I have responsibilities. I have no clothes."

"Are you sure?" Jake asked, motioning to the steward to hold off on the take-off.

"No, but I'm not sure what's happening right now. This is all so sudden. Please, wait." She lowered her head and realized she wanted this so badly, though a more rational part of her brain told her not to go. But like always, she never heeded the warnings. She always took what she shouldn't have. Her disappointment in herself made her feel inadequate, and a tear rolled down her cheek. Then she lifted her head in disbelief and shouted, "Let's go!"

Jake smiled.

Damn, this guy will feed my every need and want. But in the end, I'll still be left feeling empty, like always.

The sleek cabin seemed to speak to Joan, saying, *Please come in and enjoy your dream coming true.*

Yes, but at what cost? She wondered as she sat down and let the cream-colored leather envelop her body. The lush cushions felt like pillows, and she immediately felt less tense.

Sunlight peeked through the cabin windows as they prepared to land in Rome. Tying her robe tightly around her waist, Joan jumped up and lifted the window shade. Light poured into the cabin as Jake shielded his eyes. "My god, how beautiful the sunrise is on the horizon. The colors of the clouds and sky look so amazing from up here."

Jake put his robe on and slid beside her, giving her a playful shove. "Let's see these special colors you're talking about." Basking in the sunrise, they enjoyed their landing together. They were getting dressed when he felt her hot breath on the back of his neck.

"Why, Jake, you have goosebumps all over," Joan said, amused. "Are you cold?"

"No, that's what you do to me when you get that close."

She moved closer, placed her arms around him from behind, and ran her fingers through his chest hairs. "Now, what do I do to you?" she whispered and bit him lightly on the earlobe. Jake spun around and placed a wet, passionate kiss on her breast. She whimpered. "I can feel something else that I do to you," she whispered as she reached down to fondle him with those long, strong fingers of her delicate hand.

A knock on the cabin door momentarily distracted them. "Sir, we will be debarking soon," the steward reminded them. They both laughed and dove into their dirty little pleasures anyway.

Soon afterward, however, they really did need to get going. Tripping over one another, they retrieved their tangled clothes from around the cabin and dressed. Joan finally grabbed her purse and moved behind Jake once again. "Let's get a move on, big boy," she said, nuzzling his ear with her nose.

"I'm ready," he said, looking at his reflection in the mirror.

Reluctantly, she unwrapped herself from him. "In case I didn't tell you before, that was amazing."

"Honey, where will we be staying?"

"At my villa. I have a few things planned for us this week."

Indeed he had. Jake was a relentless tour guide. A week had passed, and Joan had become completely addicted to the adrenaline rush of Rome's never-ending beauty and wonders.

The two of them were leaving the Colosseum from their three-hour tour on the metro, barely able to make their two p.m. reservations for the Vatican tour.

The sun reflected off the café windows as they walked along, their shoes clicking on the cobblestone sidewalk with a pleasant rhythm. Through the windows of the café, Joan could see the red checkered tablecloths that reminded her of old Mama and Papa Italian restaurants. One café had large wheels of cheese sitting in mini wooden wheelbarrows, while bottles of vino with straw-like holders dangled from an almost invisible line across the archways. It was all she had always hoped it would be.

Joan felt an exciting relationship forming between herself and Jake. It struck deep, and she wasn't ready to stop feeling the excitement yet.

There was a hold-up as Jake escorted her into the Sistine Chapel. She leaned on him and stood on her tiptoes, "There seems to be a group of priests trying to get in."

"Lucky for us, this is our last tour for the day; the rest of the evening is ours." He squeezed her hand and kissed her neck.

They were admiring The Creation of Adam, the Sistine Chapel's central scene, when a fight broke out in the center of the room. A loud, rhythmic noise bounced off the marble floor and echoed around the chamber as everyone shuffled to the edges of the area.

A man with a knife started screaming. "Death to you, globalist priest!"

Roused by the noise, Vito stepped forward and began talking to the knife-wielding man, trying to quiet him down, but the wild-eyed man only grew more agitated.

Joan focused on the commotion, and the excitement in her mind seemed to slow time down as she watched the knife-wielder suddenly attack the priest.

The man lunged at him with both feet moving, leaving him off balance. She saw the priest strike the man's wrist, and she could hear the slap of skin. The attacker's arm went limp at his side. Like a matador, the priest sidestepped and applied a back fist to the man's mid-back, causing the assailant's head to snap backward, then forward, his momentum carrying him further off balance as he fell face-first onto the marble floor. The priest spun around, his cassock fanned out like a ballroom dancer's dress. He placed his knee in the center of the man's back for contact control, grabbed his knife hand and wrenched his arm back, past the bending point, till all that was heard was a crack and a scream.

Joan's eyes met the priest's. They locked into an eternal moment, something neither of them would ever forget.

Jake grabbed Joan's arm. "Let's get out of here."

Chapter Eight

LANDING IN D.C., Jake took Joan's hand, "I want you to stay with me here in Washington at my compound."

Al opened the back door of the limo.

She nodded. "That sounds like fun. But first, I need to reach out to the college."

"Okay, let me know."

"Of course."

"Can you pour?" Jake pointed to the bar, which was nearest to her seat.

She smirked. "What will you have?"

"Knob Creek, straight," he said, lifting three fingers.

"Knob Creek, it is. I remember from the last time. I'll have the same."

"I also remember you like Bourbon; I have a bottle of Last Drop Buffalo Trace Bourbon 1980 that I have waited to break open."

"My God, my father always wanted to taste that. I love bourbon because my father loved it. He'd sit and tell me all the ones he wanted to taste and would never be able to because of money. He even told me about a bottle that was $16,000 to $18,000. The Last Drop."

"Let's make sure you get to taste it."

Laughing, they clinked their glasses and watched the city go by. The shadows of people on street corners passed them up, and they couldn't hear the ghetto music inside the soundproof windows. Then came the shadows of the tightly knit houses in the suburban area. Row after row, till they had run out of silhouettes. Suddenly, the extensive outline of a mansion appeared through the window. They had hit the landscape of the ultra-rich: Jake's compound.

They rolled along the three-quarter-mile driveway, where the pink and white blossoms of the flowering dogwood and cherry trees danced in the breeze. Pulling up to the open portico, they were immediately consumed by the blooming fall fragrances. They walked through the massive double doors.

"Al, please take Joan's luggage to the second-floor guest quarters. She'll be occupying that wing."

Joan looked quite pleased despite herself. "Why, thank you, Jake."

"You, come with me," he said, wiggling his index finger and beckoning her to follow.

"Where are we going?"

"The sun is high in the sky. It's a warm, beautiful day, and I figured we could go to the pool."

"But I don't have my suit with me," Joan complained,

though she already knew where this was going.

They both undressed and jumped into the pool. After some fun and frolicking, they grabbed the plush bathrobes left for them by one of the many servants lingering about. Warm with laughter, Joan said, "I'll need to shower before dinner."

She left Jake at the pool and followed Al to the elevator to the second floor. As she went into her room, she couldn't help but smile. In the middle of the back wall was an Astoria grand Tuscan, four-poster canopy king-sized bed. On either side of the nine-foot bed were marble-topped gold inlaid nightstands.

Walking into the closet, she noticed that the special lighting system gave off the best light for dressing. The rows of shoe trays rotated, and the dress and pantsuit racks rotated on voice command.

I could get used to this. She noticed her clothes were already unpacked and freshly pressed. After showering and readying herself for dinner, she took the elevator to the first floor, where a servant met her and escorted her to an ostentatious dining area. There Jake met her, and arm and arm, they went to dinner.

"I took the liberty of ordering a dinner I thought you might like. Cheddar Bacon Chive Biscuits, Sauteed Asparagus with cherry tomatoes and glazed carrots. Prime rib with twice-baked potato."

She smiled. "I love prime rib; the menu sounds delicious."

He loved how her sensual lips showed off her perfect teeth, and her eyes expressed her deep feelings without a word.

"Tomorrow, I shall prepare dinner for you myself—my

specialty."

"And what is your specialty?"

Turning toward her, he arched his eyebrows. "I have many of those, but you will have to wait for dinner tomorrow."

"Oh my goodness, this is beautiful." They sipped their wine and watched their meal being served. They both ate eagerly after their busy day, bypassing dessert.

"I have a surprise." His staff cleared the table, and he came over to her chair, pulled it out for her, and said, "Follow me." She stood as he grabbed her, turned her toward him, hugged her, and gave her a tight squeeze on her derriere.

She snuggled up to him. "Stop that." He squeezed her again, and she teasingly hit his shoulder.

"You come with me, you naughty girl," he said, grinning. She followed him down a long, dark hallway, her lips turned up and her nose crinkled.

"Where are we going?"

"Shhh."

"Come on, tell me, please."

"Wait," Jake insisted, and he spanked her ass.

Her face flushed, and she bit her lip. "You know that turns me on."

He swung her around and stepped into her arms, reaching up to spiritedly grab a handful of her hair. He pulled her head back and planted a soft but forceful kiss on her lips. Her eyes closed, and she melted as her knees buckled. "Now, behave yourself till our meeting is over."

Joan's tumescence took over. "Okay, but you owe me."

At the end of the hall, they entered a chamber decorated with strange ornaments of satanic worship icons and tapestries. Joan immediately felt different the moment she walked in. Her skin rippled with goosebumps, while her body felt flush as her blood pounded through her veins causing her to become woozy. One of the most strikingly handsome men Joan had ever seen was directly in the middle of the room. She looked into the man's face, and she felt herself get wet immediately, nearly falling to the floor.

"Hello," was all he said, but his voice felt like it was caressing her entire body all at once. He smiled, and chill bumps suddenly danced over her skin. She had an orgasm right there and collapsed unceremoniously into the nearest chair.

"Joan, this is my partner, Kristoff," Jake said dully. "He and I have a favor to ask of you. An assignment."

Regaining her composure, Joan straightened herself in the chair, a questioning look on her face.

"We would like you to find something for us. Something extremely special and important."

Joan listened, without so much as a flinch.

"We'd like you to locate a particular relic for us."

Flustered, and exhausted, as if she'd been running, she could only reply with a pitiful, "Okay."

"I'm glad you are aboard our team," the man with the silken voice said. "Now, Jake will give you all the particulars. I hope to see you again soon." She had to look away as he rose and looked her in the eye.

My God, what just happened? His eyes were like red rubies.

The door closed after him.

"Jake, who the hell was that? And what just happened to me? I…I lost all control. I need to go home. Take me home."

"My dear, all women react to him that way, don't worry."

She started to whimper. "Please, just let me go to my room."

Jake grabbed her wrist and swung her around. "Get ahold of yourself," he snapped.

She gasped. "What are you talking about?" she yelled. "What the fuck is going on?"

"Go get yourself cleaned up."

Later, in the library, Jake handed Joan a folder. "This is the documentation and description of the job. Study it, and then tell me what you need to complete this."

Joan opened the folder. Staring back at her was a document that read: Journals of an Abbot. It was affixed with the official seal of the Vatican. She looked at Jake in disbelief. "Where did this come from? The document has the seal from the Vatican archives on it."

"Never mind that. Remember that whatever you need can and will be supplied to you. All we ask for is results. Do we understand each other?"

She slowly looked away from him and nodded. *What the hell did I get myself into?* Her thoughts raced as she started to read the Journals of an Abbot.

Chapter Nine

EXHAUSTED, VITO LAY down and felt all his muscles relax. Everything but his mind. His labored breathing and continuous sweating had kept him up all night. Not even his prayers or mantras helped. He got up, stumbled into the bathroom, grabbed a bath towel, and threw it on top of his sweat-soaked sheets. He tossed and turned as the minutes ticked by.

In distress, he spoke his fears aloud. "Lord, I know that I am unworthy of this task. For who knows me better than I, but You. I can't promise the restraint that is necessary for the job."

A voice came to him. "Vito, my son, why do you not have faith in yourself as I have in you? Most importantly, why do you not have faith in me? Throughout the ages, men have done what is necessary to do my will. They all lacked the strength and the courage to do the job, but they had faith and each saw to it that my will was done. You need not worry. Now sleep."

The next morning, Vito awoke energized, his mind clear. He called for an audience with the Pope. As he entered the Sala Regia state hall in the Apostolic palace, he couldn't help but fall in love with its many frescoes and marble floor.

The Pope walked toward Vito as briskly as he could with outstretched hands. "Good morning, my son. It is good to see you this early in the morning." His smile turning quickly to an expectant look. "Time is growing short. We must find out what Satan is up to. Sorry, but time calls for my bluntness, so I must ask your decision."

Vito angled his muscular body toward the Pope, then knelt and kissed his ring.

Standing up again, he said, "Your Eminence, after a gut-wrenching night of soul searching, God has answered my prayers and laid out for me my destiny. His spirit has invigorated me. Your Eminence, I now understand that I am the only one who can do this. So, what would you have me do?"

The Pope's smile returned.

Vito's face contorted when the Pope asked…what the…? Vito heard a wisp of air coming toward them and jumped on top of the Pope, bringing him to the ground as a dart flew past. Vito was up and charging the figure in the alcove when two other figures appeared from behind the columns. Vito took an offensive posture and without hesitation struck an open ridge hand at the would-be attacker's throat. The man went down quickly. Vito heard the sound of the other attacker coming from behind when he turned and squared off with him. They stood dead silent looking at one another measuring their next move. Vito caught sight of another dart flying towards him. His opponent also saw it and smiled when Vito went down on one knee and kicked out his other leg striking the attacker's supporting leg. The crack of the shin echoed in the chamber. Vito then quickly turned and took off after the first attacker who was dressed like a priest.

Farther along, the chamber was filled with priests in black cassocks, Cardinals in red and white, the Vatican Swiss Guard, and their iconic yellow, red, and blue uniforms, making it even more chaotic. Vito rounded a corner only to see his assailant running at full tilt toward an open window leading to an adjacent palace roof. As Vito continued the chase, the person slowed down and turned toward him. Her long black hair fell past her shoulders. Her green eyes glowed at him as she gave him a hideous demon smile, the disfigured mouth with black teeth spread across her whole face as her nose split to accommodate her mouth. "Till next time," Cersei said.

Vito stopped dead in his tracks unable to process what he had just seen. What type of animal or demon was that? He watched as she turned and plunged off the rooftop onto a wire waiting for her to sling downward and onto the next building.

Vito returned to the Pope while Francesco Pistone, captain of the Pontifical Swiss Guards, gave a booming command for everyone to relax. He walked around chest out, shoulders back, as he took an authoritative position in the center of the room. "Please be calm. I want the Carabinieri to double their guard around the Vatican, and, Sergeant Polo, I want the Swiss guard doubled here in the Apostolic Palace chambers. No one is allowed in or out without being vetted. I will have a new code given to all that need to know. If they do not have the code, they shall be detained and sent to me." He held a damaged, tipped dart.

"Is that what I saw coming at the Pope?" Vito asked.

Francesco held it up in a gloved hand. "Yes, please don't touch it. I suspect it is poisonous." Francesco called over one of his guards. "Get this to the lab. I want the analysis in my hands within the hour." The guard clicked his heels, bowed and left.

Vito knelt in front of the Pope. "Are you all right?"

"Please rise, my son. Thanks be to God and you, I'm just fine. This only confirms my belief that something of a dark spiritual nature is involved."

Vito nodded his head in agreement. As I saw firsthand only a moment ago, your attacker was not of this world, but from the dark spiritual world—Hell.

Vito yelled to the captain of the guard that there was a man with a broken leg in the other room and another with a broken hyoid and larynx. Also, there was another dart in there.

The echo of a loud foot stomping through the chambers came from Cardinal Lintzinburg from around the corner, asking, "Eminence, are you okay?" All heads turned to see a large out of breath, sweating man bent over, holding onto the nearest pillar for support.

Some of the priests and Swiss Guard could not contain their laughter.

Cardinal Lintzinburg waved them off, feigning laughter. *Damn that Vito, the old man is still alive. Kristoff and Cersei, I'll make you pay.*

Cardinal Lintzinburg stood bent over at his bar in his private quarters still wiping sweat off his large, flabby neck. After some thought of the morning's events, he pushed himself up, lumbered over to the bottle on the bar, and poured himself a double. He gulped it straight down and felt the burn. Exhaling the drink's heat, he filled two glasses with a hefty shot and walked back to his desk. He slammed one glass down on the desk as he held the other in a trembling grip before consuming the contents in one gulp. His quarters here were stark, not like his home in Germany with its thirty-foot-high ceilings and palace walls bright with golden inlay frescoes.

Once again, he cursed the old man for stationing him here. Now to fix that monster Kristoff and his bumbling idiot Cersei. He opened the middle drawer and grabbed a pen, a piece of plain paper, and an envelope. He slammed it on the desk and told the woman standing by the curtain to, "sit and write."

He stood behind her, bent over her shoulder. He knew Sister Genevie could hardly stand his presence, yet alone for him to be that close to her, but she had no choice. He was her superior and she was assigned to him.

"Dear Vito," he dictated. He could not bring himself to call him Father, let alone Cardinal. He raised his head and looked at his own stationery on the desk and chuckled to himself with contempt.

"I believe the one whom you seek may be at Simon College in Garfield Ledges Township, Ohio. One Joan Vitale. I think this information may be of some help to you on your journey."

"Sign it Sister G."

"Now address it to Vito Rosario and send it."

Chapter Ten

SENATOR JAKE HOWARD stood looking out the large, double-paned windows of his office in Washington, D.C., perspiration swelling out of his pores. He turned from the window as the more he thought, the more he paced. This next meeting was for him to answer for all the promises he had made. This was his reckoning with the cabal of the money men and women of the world.

The intercom buzzed, and the receptionist announced the arrival of his guests. He shook his hands to relieve the stress and pushed the button. "Send them into the boardroom."

Jake slid into the room to greet each of them. While Kristoff walked in with a broad smile and grabbed Jake's hand, shaking it heartily, Kristoff's new cabinet walked in with scornful looks.

"Let us get to the point," Kristoff said, as the team of men and women sat down. "Jake, where are we in retrieving our… merchandise?"

Jake rubbed his hands together and put his best face on. *Now let's wind his watch and send him home.* "I have my best man working on that as we speak."

Kristoff nodded, though a look of disappointment showed on his face. "You do realize that the election is in one week?"

Jake remained silent.

"We didn't back the wrong man, did we?"

Jake stood tall. "No, sir,"

Kristoff turned to one of the men at the table. "Van, stand up."

Smiling, a man with a greasy ponytail and a body like a fireplug in a suit two sizes too small stood and replied, "Yes, sir."

"Van, what happened to our forty million dollars in Russia last week?"

"As you know, we were attacked by a rival gang, and we are waiting on our interests to get it back."

Kristoff turned back to the senator. "Jake, what would you do if you were in charge?"

"I wouldn't wait a week for my results. I'd send our people in to get it and make an example of them."

"Very good." Kristoff nodded to his bodyguard, Cersei, who came up behind Van and snapped his neck. Van crumpled to the floor and the room fell as silent as the dead body itself. "There you have it, your example. Get me my merchandise. You have one week."

As the remaining cabal members left the room, Kristoff looked at Cersei and addressed her loudly enough for Jake to hear. "Stay here with Jake and keep an eye on him and his men.

I want daily reports. We only have seven days to accomplish my mission. Now go."

Jake looked over to see a Cersei with turbulent green eyes, almost phosphorescent in their appearance. She threw a coy smile his way, followed Kristoff out, and took up an offensive posture outside the door.

Jake fell into the closest chair, running his hands through his blond hair. *What in the hell am I going to do?* He needed information. Calming himself, he pressed the intercom. "Helen, I need Ron in here immediately."

Moments later, Ron appeared at his side. "What can I do for you, boss?" he asked, unable to keep his eyes off the dead body in the conference room.

"How are we doing in Jerusalem? And how damn close are we to achieving our mission?"

"I haven't heard from Joan in a few days, so I am leaving for Jerusalem in two hours."

"You see that body, right? That will be us if we don't complete our side of the bargain. We have just one week."

Ron gave a single nod of understanding.

"Before you leave, get rid of that damn body."

Ron reached for the phone, dialed a number, and barked an order. "I want Samir at our location within a day." He hung up, resigned to a restless trip, before shuffling over to haul the dead man from the room.

Jake had second thoughts about working with this cabal, mostly Kristoff. That son-of-a-bitch was sick and scary to deal with. He felt he was dealing with two people in one, and you never knew who was coming to the damn party. Was the Presidency worth all that he was giving? The only good thing to come out of this arrangement so far was when Kristoff ordered him to visit Garfield Ledges Township, and he had met her. Joan. She was the one.

Helen bounced in and tried to get Jake's attention. She needed Jake's help to move up in this town and she was willing to do anything. Helen was just about on top of him when he noticed her. "Someone just reported that one of Kristoff's people is loitering around outside the building."

Jake shook off his melancholy feelings about Joan and returned to his present problems. "Don't worry. That's probably just Cersei. She's supposed to be spying on us."

Helen nodded as she turned to leave, then paused. "You know, you need to get your head in the game. You can't always be thinking about Joan."

"Get the hell out of here, Helen."

Cersei made her way down to the private garage and into the senator's parking area, where she watched a black SUV take off down the ramp.

The private security guard at the gate asked, "Can I help you, miss?"

As she looked at him, her eyes began to glow. Her gaze locked on his, and he couldn't look away. He lost all control of his thought processes. "Who was that, and did they file any report?"

Grabbing his clipboard from the counter in the guard shack, he read, "That was the senator's man, Ron Wolneski. He's headed to the airport, and we'll pick up his car in an hour."

Cersei moved closer as he talked. The guard could not back up nor protect himself from those eyes, and he barely noticed when she pushed a dagger into his chest. She stepped back as her gaze followed the guard stumbling forward and crumbling to the ground, still looking into her eyes. "Thank you," she said with a smile.

Chapter Eleven

In his private chambers at the Apostolic Palace sat the Pope, Francesco Pistone, captain of the Swiss guard, Vito Rosario, Cardinal Lintzinburg, and four members of the Order of Mysteries.

When the Pope nodded, Francesco stood to address the gathering. First, he bowed to the Pope, then began: Your Eminence, trusted colleagues, what I'm about to reveal to you should not leave this room until we have further concrete proof. I had the contents of the dart examined by the best scientist in Rome. Francesco frowned. "The elements in that dart did not come from this earth."

Only the Pope could calm the assembly. Once quiet was restored, Francesco went on. "The liquid in which it was dipped was not from anything on the periodic table." Once again, the men in the room protested in disbelief.

"How could that be?" was the operative question. No one wanted to believe the alternative, that this was something of a dark spiritual, other-worldly nature. The Pope stood and looked sternly around the room, his tone commanding. "Voi siete uomini di fede non abbiate paura della verità." *You are men of faith, do not be afraid of the truth.*

Francesco spoke. "I'm having a small sample sent to the Swiss academy of medical science for confirmation. Please remember, if touched or ingested in any manner, it will kill you within moments."

He walked around the room, looked into each man's eyes, and said, "One more piece of information: "the man with the broken hyoid and larynx was dead on site, and the other man crawled to the other dart and injected himself. These killers are resolute and loyal to their boss."

The Pope watched as Cardinal Lintzinburg lowered his head and sat silently. *Who could have done this? And why? Was Vito the target?* After hours of discussion and no resolution, the Pope broke up the meeting. Vito nodded at the Pope to get his attention. As everyone filed out, the Pope called for Vito. Again, Cardinal Lintzinburg's rutted jowls turned red, burning with anger, and he expeditiously left.

The Pope waved Vito over. "What is it, my son?" Vito opened his sport coat, grabbed the letter he had been hiding, and gave it to the Pope. The Pope's eyebrows furrowed. He shook his head. Then he turned the paper over again and looked at both sides. "Where did this come from?"

"I received it this morning. I googled this Simon College in Ohio. They turn out some of the most exemplary Archaeology students and professors. There is a graduate student there by the name of Joan Vitale.

"Joan? Please, step into my quarters." Mia's quarters were one of the older classrooms complete with cloak room.

The door creaked closed as she entered. "Sure, what's up?"

"My, you look tired."

Mia grabbed Joan's hands and pulled her close, her eyebrows arched. "Is everything okay?"

"Yes, I came in on the red eye from D. C. this morning, but everything is fine." Joan stepped out of Mia's grasp, rubbing her eyes. "Just a rough night reading about a new assignment. Thanks for asking."

Mia held out an object covered with an old dust cloth and tied in the center with an even older strip of material. "I'm leaving tomorrow for Jerusalem again, and I wanted to give you this."

Joan smiled and accepted the gift.

"I wanted to thank you for all your help over the past months on the dig in Jerusalem. Please, do not open it till later." Mia hugged Joan and kissed her cheek. "Thank you again. Now get out of here."

Joan gave Mia a curious look, hugged her, and put the gift in her purse.

She had almost forgotten the magical and mysterious feeling she got when walking the grounds of Simon College. The college sat in the center of a small town surrounded by tree farms and quaint, eighty-year-old houses with gingerbread architecture, many of them turned into offices. She looked up to find herself in front of one that housed Simon College's administration office. The rustic outer office radiated a comfortable feeling. Quite the opposite of the dean's office.

While some friends and ex-professors walked in and out with a smile or a "hello," time moved slowly. Finally, Dean Alexandria appeared. "Joan, come on in," she said.

Brushing down the wrinkles in her pants, Joan responded, "Thank you for seeing me."

The dean shook Joan's hand. "How are you? And how is Mia?"

"Mia is such a treasure. She is doing fine, and I'm also doing well. Thanks for asking."

"Please sit," Dean Alexandria said, gesturing toward a chair.

"I know you carry a full schedule," Joan said, crossing her legs, "so I'll get to the point. I have taken a position as the head curator for an excavation in the Middle East."

Interested, Alexandria stood and walked around to the front of her desk and propped herself against her desk with one butt cheek. "My, this is a surprise."

"I will be leaving immediately and wanted to thank you for all your support over the years."

"I'm sorry to hear this. I wanted to offer you a position here at the college.

Joan shifted in her chair. "Oh, I had no idea."

"I always knew you'd one day be a valuable resource. You

have much to offer."

"What kind of position did you have in mind?"

"The second chair in Archaeology."

Joan's eyes went wide. "What an opportunity! I'm sorry I have accepted this other job. I'm afraid there's no way out of my commitment."

"Are you sure it's not too late to take the job? Just say the word." The dean gave a little pout, knowing how hard it would be to fill this position.

Joan shook her head. "No, I'm sorry but I really can't."

Chapter Twelve

THEY APPROACHED THE cave opening to the dig site. Joan noticed how their long shadows covered the red dirt. There was an overwhelming smell of dank mustiness on top of the powerful scent of decay. As Joan stepped through the archway first, her foot slid on a moist rock, causing her to trip. Samir's quick grab kept her from hitting the ground.

"Thanks," she said as she felt the beautiful necklace that Mia had given her. Every time she touched it, she felt grace and comfort come over her. She stood upright and squinted at the path ahead. Joan cursed under her breath about being shanghaied into this job. She looked over and smiled at Samir in his cream-colored Bastian shirt, which had become part of his self-imposed uniform. He rather liked strutting about as second in command.

She moved more carefully inward as they entered a large opening. "Okay, Samir, let's get this generator turned on." Soon, they had the cave lit up with strings of portable lights.

Joan turned to Samir. "According to my research, this is the lair where the relic should be." She looked at her notes one last time, then confidently pointed to a section of the room farther back. "We should strike that wall over there."

Samir hit the indicated spot with his pickaxe; dirt particles dancing in the beam of light. His first strike had left a star-shaped hole in the wall. He grabbed his handkerchief and brought it to his nose to block the stale, horrendous smell.

Joan sneezed and covered her face. There had been a death in this room at some point.

"Careful now," she said. "According to the map, this wall is where the main archway should be."

Samir grabbed the pick with both hands and looked for a strategic spot to strike. He hit the sweet spot and brought down a decent chunk of wall exposing the archway. As part of the wall came down, Samir backed up, grabbed Joan, and moved her back. The resulting rubble covered their boots, up to their pant legs. When the dust settled, they peered in, then they looked at one another.

"What the hell?" Joan said in disappointment. They could only see more rock and emptiness: "I don't understand. This was supposed to be the level and room of the relic. She picked up another pickaxe and they both started hammering on the wall at a grueling pace. The sweat fell off their bodies like they were in a steam bath. Samir waved and got Joan's attention. "Stop," he said, as he wiped the sweat off his face, "rest a moment." He got them a canteen of water. With their backs to the wall, they slid down and sat looking at one another. Samir shrugged, and they drank greedily.

Joan looked at the hole they had carefully made in the wall. "I know this is the main tunnel to get in. Once we're in the next room, I will recalculate the area."

After a rest, they cleared the archway enough to walk through. Joan entered first. Without warning, the earth crumbled beneath her feet. She tumbled downward through a shaft, until she hit solid ground, bouncing with a loud thump. Her eyes closed tightly, only to see dots of different colors. She gasped for air, and the foulness of it made her gag. All she could hear was Samir yelling, "Joan? Joan, are you all right?"

She tried to clear the dancing-colored specks in her head as she coughed out, "Please hurry, and get me out of here."

"Can you move?"

"Yes."

"Okay, move to one side, as far as you can. I'm going to lower down this lantern." The lantern's light created eerie shadows as it moved down the shaft.

Hearing Samir run off to get the ropes and the winch, Joan looked up to see the shaft cut into the cave and built with a trapdoor. "Damn it. I should have remembered trapdoors were standard for this time period." She slammed her hand on the ground, cursing herself.

Joan pulled herself up the wall and brushed the dirt and rubble off her clothes when she noticed it was not just dirt. It had a significant contaminant of bone mixed with it. Examining the soil on the floor confirmed her suspicions. There were more bones as she gently moved the dirt around, then her finger hit something solid. She gingerly inhaled and noticed that a particularly sweet odor had begun to seep up through the soil and bone.

Her pulse quickened when her fingers got tangled in some torn cloth. Slowly moving the fabric and soil, she noticed that the material's decay was at least half-a-century old or more. Then she felt the ribs of a man or woman protruding out of the ground and she snatched her hand back. Shining her lantern over the body, she noted that the corpse had barely decayed, though it had a gaping hole in its chest.

Sitting inside the body's chest cavity was a box. *What the hell is this? This body must be that of one of the thieves from the journals. She would study the clothing to find out what era they came from. But why hasn't the body decomposed at the same rate as the clothing? Did this box have something to do with that?* Again, she smelled something sweet.

As she cleaned the box, she examined it. It was about an inch deep, two-and-a-half inches wide, and three-and-a-quarter inches long and made entirely out of bone. She marveled at its preciseness—how perfectly flat each surface was. It was sealed shut, without apparent seams and no obvious way to open it on any side. The symbol on the top translated to "the Alpha and the Omega." She turned it over in her hands and felt a sensation of pure energy rush through her body—tingling, warm, and healing. Giving it one last look, she confirmed her hypothesis. *This must be the stolen treasure from the thief that never made it out.* She placed the box in the extra pocket in her vest that was designed to carry valuables.

She forced her eyes to look at the light above. "Samir? Samir?"

Joan tilted her ear upward. She thought she heard someone shouting. Just as she was ready to yell for Samir again, she heard it. The familiar voice of Jake's lackey, Ron, barking out orders. "Get those men out of here and put Samir in the car with us. And you, go check the inside of that cave."

Trembling, Joan quickly turned the lantern off and hid out of sight at the bottom of the shaft. She could hear someone shuffling around the entrance she and Samir had made.

Ron yelled from outside, "What did you find?"

Unable to see anything noteworthy through the archway, the man called back, "Nothing in here, boss."

"Then get your ass out here and let's go."

Joan listened until she heard two vehicles take off, spitting gravel everywhere, leaving her in total silence. She shrunk down to the ground and started quivering. Shit, shit, shit. Jake, why? She pulled her phone out. No bars. "Fuck."

She felt her fear turn into adrenaline. She needed out. Placing her back on one side of the shaft and her legs on the other, Joan arduously inched her way up the twenty-foot drop. Six feet into her journey, she panicked as the wall began to crumble. Using all her strength, she was able to bridge herself a foot above the deteriorating wall. *Thank God,* she thought, feeling a headache forging its way through her brain. She closed her eyes and pushed upwards.

Three-quarters of the way up the shaft, just as Joan paused to catch her breath and rest her quaking legs, the shaft wall collapsed beneath her feet. Her stomach did flip-flops as she somersaulted downward. The sudden crash sucked her stomach into her back, and simultaneously, depressed her lungs, forcing all the air out of them. It felt as though the blood had drained entirely from her brain. She stretched her arm out and dug her fingernails into the dirt as she tried to pull herself across the floor. She whimpered and everything went black.

Joan's eyes flickered open. She didn't know how long she'd been lying there, but she tried to piece together everything that had happened. She tried to sit up and lost her breath from the pain. "Damn," she whispered in a short, controlled breath. Bringing herself up into a leaning position against the wall, tears wet her cheeks.

Forcing herself upright, she checked for broken bones. None, thankfully. She moved into a slow shuffle, then into a wobbly walk. When she stepped on her pickaxe, a smile spread slowly across her face. She reached into the depths of her anger to fuel her adrenaline, grabbed the pickaxe, and started to cut footholds into the wall to climb out. Light from the moon at dusk came shining through the shaft as she made her way up. Eventually, she reached the top.

There was no one around. Samir was gone. The temperature

had dropped dramatically, and her cold sweats were starting to burn her cuts. Her face and lips trembled. All the while, she kept wondering: *What the hell is Jake up to?* She sat down under a homemade lean-to to take stock of her injuries and the day's events. She took the bone box from her vest pocket and looked it over more carefully. She knew it was unique. Again, she felt a rush of energy pulse through her hands. She needed answers, but who could she trust?

Shaking, Joan reached for her phone. When she could not find it attached to her hip, her mind answered her question, her eyes went wide, her adrenaline spiked, she felt nauseous and kicked the dirt. *Shit, it can't be*. She let out a short, piercing scream before wobbling back to the opening on the floor. She shone her light down, and there it was. At the bottom of the shaft, her phone lay glimmering back up as if smiling. *Oh God, please.*

After a short tirade of abusive language, Joan looked around and made some quick assessments. She grabbed the equipment Samir had gathered. She drove in an anchor, tied her rope off, hooked herself to the flip-line and descended. She reached the bottom and grabbed the phone. She had begun to pull herself back up, when suddenly her rope came untied from one of the safety knots. She felt weightless as her body plummeted downward. She let out a scream, but at that instant the second knot caught, and her body bounced on the rope. She started another tirade, only this time it was of prayers, as she quickly pulled herself out onto solid ground.

Frustrated and exhausted, she dialed a number.

"Hello, this is Billy Campbell."

"Oh my God, Billy, it's so good to hear your voice right now. Thank God."

"Joan, is that you?"

"Y-Yes." A thickness in her throat betrayed her as a tear slid down her face. Her body started to heave. She couldn't choke out any words, just tears.

"Joan, are you hurt? Are you all right? Joan? Talk to me."

It took her a minute or two to control her sobbing enough to be able to talk. "In trouble," was all she could spit out.

"Breathe, Joan, breathe. I'm right here. Just take a few deep breaths and talk to me."

She did as Billy told her to and in a few minutes she was able to stammer out his name, " Billy…"

"Yeah, I'm right here, Joan."

"I need help."

"I got that part," he said, hoping a little levity would calm her. "Where are you?"

"I'm at a dig site, looking for an old relic stolen many years ago. I fell through a trapdoor covering a shaft about twenty feet deep and I found a box. It's made of bone that seems to be entirely sealed by the precision of its construction."

"Are you in Jerusalem? And does that box symbolize the Alpha and the Omega?"

His tone cut her like a knife. "How did you know that?"

"Rumors about a specific relic in a bone box surfaced

recently."

Do I have something that special? Is this why I feel a wave of energy every time I hold the box? "Wait a second, are you saying I have that box?"

"That's what it sounds like. I won't know for sure till I examine it. But you need to be careful. Some nasty people are looking for that box and will stop at nothing to get it."

"What can you tell me about the relic?"

"Joan, did you hear what I said?" Billy sounded exasperated.

"Of course, I did, but you need to trust me. Tell me what you know. Please."

"I'll explain everything that I know when we see each other. How soon can we meet?"

"First, there is another relic I must retrieve. I should be finding it soon, if all goes well."

"Joan, you must be smart about this. You are playing with a powerful tool that will cause a spiritual war if you are not extremely careful. What do you plan on doing with it?"

Startled by a shuffling noise behind her, Joan turned to find one of her crew stumbling towards her, bleeding and battered. She dropped the phone. "Olaf! What happened to you?"

"I escaped those men and saw them cram everyone else into a van. What's happening?"

Before she could answer, the man fell forward into her arms. She struggled against his weight to gently lay him down. Then she scooped up the phone, frantic. "Listen, Billy, I have to go. I'll call you later to set up a meeting. I appreciate the info."

"Joan, please be careful. Let me know where I can meet you."

"I'll call you soon."

Joan looked down at Olaf and patted him on the cheek. "Olaf? Olaf, wake up; everything is going to be okay."

Olaf blinked through bleary eyes.

"I'm going to try to get help."

"No, please, no," Olaf said. "Call my brother. He will know what to do."

She called Olaf's brother from his phone and explained that Olaf was hurt and needed to be picked up immediately at the dig site. After she hung up, she turned back to Olaf. "Okay, he is on his way. I'll wait with you till he gets here."

"Please, no, you must get out of here."

Joan hesitated, but fear made her accept his advice to flee.

She ripped the cover off her phone off, and broke open the back. Then she removed the SIM card, and hurled it off into the rocks, before hurrying away.

Chapter Thirteen

Everyone's attention turned to Ron as he hustled in, impeccably dressed in a three-piece suit, his tie bound so tightly to the tie bar and straight pin that it didn't move an inch. A 24-carat-gold timepiece hung across the vast front of his vest.

Samir struggled against his restraints as he tried to turn to see who had just entered the room.

Ron snapped his fingers and stretched out his arms as his men put a white lab coat on him. He asked simply, "Samir, where is Joan?"

Trying to turn, Samir asked, "Who are you?"

"Wrong answer."

Samir was terrified when he saw the blade. Before he realized what was happening, he felt a hot liquid trickle down his neck and threw his head back from the unspeakable pain. His scream echoed in the walls and in his very bones. His body jolted. Then he slumped in his bindings, barely able to feel the blood running down the side of his neck and arm. Barely comprehending that his ear had been sliced off.

"Here, take this," Ron said to one of his men. "You know what to do with it." He returned his attention to Samir. "Has she found the relic?"

"Please, I don't know."

"Find a towel for that bloody hole," Ron snapped at someone Samir couldn't see.

Another instrument of torture had appeared in the man's hand, The cattle prod crackled with electricity. Samir's body trembled uncontrollably.

Ron waved the prod back and forth. "Now, I know you know what this is." Spittle sprayed into his captive's eyes as he continued, "but let me tell you that I will be using it quite differently than what it is intended for."

Tears fell from Samir's eyes. "I don't know the answer to your questions. You kidnapped me before I could see if she found anything," he wailed.

Placing the cattle prod on his genitals, Ron squeezed the trigger that sent the voltage through Samir's testicles. The jolt lifted Samir and the chair off the ground, and his head tilted forward as he passed out from the pain.

"Get some water," Ron yelled.

After dousing Samir, he slapped him awake.

"Now, once more. Has Joan found the relic? My time is growing short." He grabbed Samir by the hair and pulled him forward. Next time I pull the trigger, this prod will be well inside of you."

Chapter Fourteen

"DAMN YOU, JAKE. Why couldn't you just trust me?" Joan muttered to herself. Her anger had returned. She was having difficulty containing her fears as anxiety rushed through her. She felt like a freight train that had jumped the tracks.

When she got to her car, a quarter mile from the dig site, she stopped to take three deep breaths to calm herself, but her mind continued to race. *I'm sure he had spies in my crew.*

The mid-evening moonlight shone on her Volkswagen Thing, a nifty vehicle initially manufactured for the German Army. She zipped through the hills and streets of Jerusalem until she felt something akin to a physical slap on the back of her head. Her adrenaline spiked, and chills overcame her. Realizing that Jake could be waiting for her at her house, she felt overwhelmed by impending danger. She stopped her car and tried to take some deep yoga breaths to calm herself. Breathing still hurt. Glancing in the rearview mirror revealed no vehicles on the street. Maybe, just maybe, she could make it home. She drove slowly past her house and parked behind it.

White clouds swirled past the black backdrop of the sky, as the wind showed its temper. She crept up to the back door looking everywhere for any possible danger. The refrigerator's hum could be heard through the door but all seemed quiet inside. She grabbed the screen door and opened it carefully until the wind took it and nearly ripped it off the hinges. She managed to let herself in the entry door just as the fear reached her throat and she screamed as she slammed it behind her and locked it.

Joan scanned the house quickly and then crawled up to the front windows and looked out, but saw no one. Opening the front door, she looked both ways before scooping up her mail, and quickly retreating into the house. Two letters fell from the pile when she tossed the mail onto her desk: a colorful, handwritten invitation and a bulky, plain envelope. Her night light threw ominous shadows against the walls.

The rubble lodged in her shoes crushed on the tile floor as she grabbed a decanter of her favorite whiskey and poured herself half a glass of the amber liquid. She refocused on the colorful envelope and retrieved it from the floor.

Taking a knife, she slid it across the gold-laden envelope and pulled out an embossed invitation to the Golden Pyramid Awards, celebrating yearly achievements in Archaeological Anthropology. She allowed herself a smile, thinking, *Wait till they see my find this year. Everyone else's will pale in comparison.*

Joan picked up the other envelope, turning it over and back. She examined it; this one was different. It had no postage or address on it. She dug her knife in and across the envelope and Joan jumped back as a dried bloody lump fell onto the table. It looked like an ear.

"Jake, you sick bastard. What have you done?"

She reached for her phone and realized she had gotten rid of it. Something froze in her brain. *Where is Samir? Has he told Jake about the progress we made? Please, no…*

It was then that she heard the pounding on the front door. She ducked down and turned the night light out. The door burst inward. Joan recoiled and watched as a body fell through the doorway. She made ready to run out the back door when she heard men talking.

"Sonny, are we going in?"

"Nah, no one's here. Let's just leave him and go."

"You sure you don't want to check it out?"

Joan belly crawled into her bedroom as she heard someone in the living room. The footsteps felt like they were getting closer. She closed her eyes and held her breath, waiting for the worst to happen. Another creak in the floor, followed by more footsteps.

"Hey, let's get the hell out of here."

"Wait, she must have been here and left already. She found the ear."

Standing in the doorway between her bedroom and the hall, she heard one of them say, "Okay, boss, I don't see anything anyway."

She heard the squeal of tires spinning on the pavement,

smelled the iron of blood, mixed with the humidity in the air, and started back into the living room. As she approached, she saw that the body was that of Samir staring up at her through bulging eyes and a swollen, bloodied face. Joan fell to her knees as she choked back the tears. "Samir," she sobbed, cradling his head and rubbing his cheek. "Hold on. I'm getting you help. Just hold on."

When the ambulance drove away, Joan decided. Jake would never get his hands on that relic; the relic would be hers in a day. Her assignment was at its end, and she would call for her money before its time.

Dialing the banker's private number, she told him, "Rex, I'm going to need my next advance, and I need to move my crew and our equipment."

"No can do, Joan; you must produce something of value before we can extend any more credit."

"Rex, I'm right there. I can feel it. But I need to move everything to get to the relic. I wouldn't ask if it wasn't essential," she said as she held the bone box at eye level and marveled at it. She smiled to herself.

"Joan, I'm sorry, I can't do it. Even if I wanted to, it would have to go through the committee, and you know who sits on it."

She slammed the phone down. "Jake," she seethed as she plopped down at the bar, grabbed the decanter, and emptied it into her tumbler. She had started to tip her head back when she saw her reflection in the mirror at the back of the bar shelves; staring back at her was a woman at her wit's end, her face bleak and colorless.

You know you need this money. Yes, I know, but where else can I find that kind of money? Joan just stared at herself and shook her head. You know that there will be some rich fish at the ceremonies. She gulped down the rest of her drink and picked up the phone again.

"Hey, Rex. It's me again. I'm sorry about hanging up on you, but I've found someone to co-sign the loan. I will be there first thing in the morning. Please have everything ready." She listened for a response, then said, "Thank you."

She tried to concentrate on her plan, but her thoughts grew foggier by the minute and her mind began to wander. *Jake, I loved you once; I don't know how I fell for your bullshit though.* She went to the bar and grabbed another bottle. Ignoring the empty decanter, she broke the seal and drank greedily. Annoyance started to bubble up from deep within her as she realized how her wantonness collided with his self-centeredness.

Joan was still under the influence, when she was awakened by a knocking on the front door. Peeking from behind the curtain, she saw that it was a limo driver. She pulled open the door so suddenly she lost her balance and almost flung herself into the man standing there. She straightened up, giggling. “Oops. What can I do for you?”

“I’m here to take you to the Ramat Aviv in Tel Aviv.”

“I vaguely remember leasing you for the day?” Her mind was racing as she pieced together her plan for the money.

“Yes, ma’am, you rented the limo for the day.”

“Oh good, let’s have some fun. Come on in, take a seat while I put myself together,” she told the driver, leaving him at the threshold without showing him inside. She returned a few minutes later, dressed and concealing her bloodshot eyes with a large pair of sunglasses. Teetering, she caught her balance. “I need to find a special outfit for my event that says I’m classy, rich, and don’t need anyone, but I’m available for the right guy.” She smiled and grabbed the driver’s arm, her balance still a little impaired from her overindulgence the night before.

Chapter Fifteen

RON SAT AT the bar in an upscale club in the Waldorf of Jerusalem enjoying his favorite drink, a Moscow Mule: two ounces vodka, two ounces fresh lime juice, four ounces ginger beer, and chilled champagne, served with lime wedges and mint. He noticed a young man checking him out and waved the bartender over. "Bartender, get that young man at the end of the bar another of whatever he's drinking and put it on my tab."

The young man smiled as he sipped the fresh drink, and Ron walked over and sat next to him. When Joan came into the bar, Ron sighed. "Damn," he whispered to the guy, "I guess this'll have to wait till later. Some business just walked into the room needing my attention, and I've got a special surprise for her." He nodded towards Joan. "I can't let her see me before tomorrow night though." Ron bent down and kissed the young man on the back of the neck. "My room number is 1201. Until later." The young man smiled and thanked him for the drink, looking longingly after Ron as he left.

Cersei sat down at the other end of the bar, texting on her phone and drinking her favorite drink, The Devil's Tongue: three parts Spirytus vodka, three-quarters olive brine, a dash of Tabasco, and two Mediterranean olives. Her choice was shaken not stirred. She blended in with the opulence of the nightclub atmosphere, but kept grabbing at her silk stockings because she was not yet used to being in human form. She sent out her message to Kristoff, "I just arrived." She decided to play with some human entertainment. As she stood to find her prey, the phone rang. "Hello?"

"I want you to stop bringing undue attention to yourself," Kristoff snapped at her from the other end of the line. "I told you we must stay under the radar with our mission."

"Everything is fine, boss. I'm here in Jerusalem, waiting on Ron to make his move, and I will make her talk."

"No, Cersei, you will work with Ron and his plan. I don't want what happened in Washington, D. C.. Do you understand, Cersei?"

"Yes, boss, without a mark on her." She rolled her eyes, and hung up.

Vito was driven to the lavish venue for the Golden Pyramid Awards late the following afternoon. He looked up and around the building, imagining that the Waldorf of Jerusalem was the most opulent and extraordinary hotel in the world, especially with its personal butler service and the fleet of Rolls-Royces it maintained for private transportation.

Checking in, he received a 24-karat-gold iPad that kept him in the loop of all the amenities and scheduled events. Most important to him was attending the ceremony for the Golden Pyramid Awards.

His room was furnished with the deepest and richest purples, and blues. The whites were as white as snow. The wall and ceilings are combined with gold-plated mirror frames. Truly a paradise.

Cardinal Vito Rosario checked out the clothes his butler had laid out for him. He had only two changes with him for the ceremonies and he picked the wrong one. He chose to go with a black tuxedo instead.

"Please replace this uniform with my black tux, Sajid." Checking one last time in the mirror, he nodded at his image. *You'll do.* He patted the picture of Joan Vitale in his inner breast pocket as he entered his floor's elevator. *She's a looker, for sure,* he thought, pushing the button to the mezzanine floor.

Vito walked into the bar and ordered a drink. He started to chat up a large, boisterous man dressed sloppily in a tux and bought him a couple of drinks. After the second one, the man said, "My name is Gerald," and, with a hiccup, added, "Thank you."

"Mine is Vito. Would you like another?" Gerald looked at the bartender and tapped his glass for a refill.

The man drank them as fast as Vito would buy them. *He*

will make quite the commotion. Three doubles later, and in the middle of a woeful tale on why the man should have won an award, Vito thought he saw Joan at the entrance and excused himself, saying, "I have to go. I'm due at the ceremonies."

The other man slurred and said, "So am I. I'm just going to finish this last drink you graciously bought me." He nodded as Vito left the bar with a wave.

As Joan left the elevator onto the mezzanine ballroom floor, every head turned to look at the stunning young lady in red.

Vito was stunned by the beauty of this woman. She was even prettier in person than her picture. Just then, an inebriated Gerald came into the room. Vito gave him a smile and a nod. Gerald yelled "hello again," and nearly tripped over a couple in front of him. While everyone's attention was drawn to the commotion, Vito came up behind Joan and stood next to her.

It looked perfect like they had both arrived simultaneously at the entrance of the ceremonies.

Joan looked up at Vito in surprise, and they smiled at one another. She felt a little déjà vu, though she let it go.

"My, don't you look like James Bond? Have we met before?" she said.

"I don't believe we were ever formally introduced."

"So, we have met?"

"No," came a slurred voice from behind them. "I'm Gerald." The voice was that of a tall, rough-looking man in a tuxedo that looked like someone washed it in a machine, hung it up to dry, and forgot to iron it.

Vito stepped in closer to Joan, blocking Gerald's path to her. Her perfume consumed his senses. His muscular body seemed to burst at the seams of his tux as he reached for Joan's hand. "My name is Vito Rosario. And yours?"

"Joan Vitale. Nice to meet you."

"And you, also."

"Are you here by yourself, Vito?"

"Hey," Gerald's voice spoke from behind her again. "I'm here by myself. Why don't you come with me?"

They turned briefly to see Gerald, the man Vito befriended at the bar, who was quite inebriated and maintaining his balance by a thread. Vito turned back to Joan, took her long, gloved arm, and placed it in his. "Let's go, all questions to be answered later," he said as they stepped into the ceremony's ballroom.

"This is a nice change of pace. Saved by a gentleman."

"Would you care to share my table with me this evening?"

"I believe I'd better; that man is still staring.

Vito nodded in agreement. The music wafted by their ears, and the bright-hot Hollywood lights sparkled around them. The smell of perfume, mixed with cologne and cigar smoke, assaulted their senses as they made their way to Vito's table.

Taken their sits she slid off her black evening gloves.

A loud thump vibrated the room as the MC hit his mic and cleared his voice, welcoming everyone to the ceremonies. "I hope that everyone is enjoying themselves and this fine meal. Our program will start shortly."

Dinner was served, and they had both settled on the roast duck. "This is cooked to perfection," Joan said, cutting into her meal. As they ate in silence, listening to the live band, they both felt a sense of ease.

Once again, the MC thumped his mic. "I can see some of you still finishing up. Don't worry, we won't disturb you." The room chuckled at the slight joke. "We will now start with our keynote speaker, followed by the awards."

As the program proceeded, Vito and Joan continued to enjoy both the meal and the company. After what seemed an appropriate period of time, Vito slowly began to steer the conversation towards his own ulterior motives. "What brings you here tonight?" he asked casually.

Looking pensive, Joan placed her utensils down. "I belong to the Archaeology Guild. One of the sponsors of this event. By the way, do you know this woman who just won the award for the oldest find?"

"No, I don't."

"That is Anne. We attended the same college—Simon College in Garfield Ledges Township, Ohio."

Vito pretended to shutter. "All I know about Ohio is it's cold there in the winter and I hate cold weather."

She smiled and reached out to pat the back of Vito's hand. "Big baby, it's not that bad. The fall weather is quite beautiful." She let her long, graceful fingers linger on his hand and Vito could feel his body temperature rising.

Joan pretended not to notice. "She has quite a story from

multiple injuries and a near death experience to becoming an award-winning archeologist." I'll tell you her story sometime."

Vito smiled. "It all sounds so interesting and mysterious."

A server approached their table. "Excuse me, would either of you like an after dinner drink?" Vito withdrew his hand from under Joan's and let her order first.

"And are you an archaeologist?" Vito asked once the waiter was gone.

"Yes, I am. I'm presently working on an excavation not far from here, Rabbi Pinchas Street. How about you? Are you on an excavation yourself?"

"No, not this year."

Joan scanned the room, then turned back to Vito.

"What are you are looking for?"

Just as Joan was about to answer, the awards announcer keyed the mic and announced, "Vito Rosario."

"Vito, is that you?" was Joan's knee jerk reaction.

Shaken from his thoughts, Vito stood and walked to the front of the room to receive the night's last award. He steadied himself and started to thank all the proper people and institutions that had helped him. Vito then thanked the Catholic Church for the introduction to Israel's Antiquities Authority.

The Israeli Antiquities Authority had given special permission to enter the Qumran caves. The only access to the cave was to repel 200 feet, which was said to be the distance between heaven and earth. He was applauded for enduring thick and suffocating dust and returning with what might be a missing piece of the Dead Sea Scrolls. The value to humanity was immeasurable.

"Why didn't you tell me you were here to receive an award?" Joan asked the second he returned to their table. "Congratulations."

"I got wrapped up in listening to you."

She slid her chair closer threaded her arm through his. That is very sweet of you to say, but it goes both ways. I don't know why I feel so comfortable talking to you. I just know that I don't want to stop."

"We don't have to. I know a place that serves the best coffee. Interested?"

"Yes, if I'm not being too forward."

"Let's go."

She pointed down the stairs. "I'll meet you right down there at the bottom. I need to use the powder room."

"I'll walk you," he offered.

"No need. I'm a big girl." He stood and held her chair. "Thank you."

"Okay, I'll meet you downstairs."

As Vito walked toward the steps, he caught himself not paying attention to his surroundings. *Damn. That woman is something else. Lord, help me, or I will be in confession tomorrow.*

He heard a scream, and people started to scatter, pushing and tripping over each other. Someone shouted his name.

"Joan?" he called out. He turned and dashed up the

staircase, two or three stairs at a time. At the top, he looked left toward where he had last seen Joan, and he caught a glimpse of her dress as someone pushed her around the corner.

Vito's training kicked in. His brain fixed into a grid. In seconds, he navigated his way past all the other guests and staff until he stood at the corner where Joan had disappeared. His other senses took over, and he smelled the intoxicating perfume she had been wearing and followed.

Dragged by the kidnapper, Joan fell to her knees to defy the man. "Who are you?" she yelled. "Why are you doing this to me?"

"Shut up," the man spat, as he grabbed a handful of hair and pulled her back up into a standing position. Her evening gown tore, the rip stopping just below her waist. "Jake wants his relic. You're going to take me to it right now."

Vito could hear their voices and pinpointed where they were. Taking the next stairwell down, he managed to outflank the man. Joan's captor tried to shove her around the next corner, but Vito maneuvered in between them and stepped into her captor's face. "I'm going to ask only once. Who are you?"

The man seemed to consider answering, but thought better of it and reached for his weapon. Vito reached out, quick as a viper's strike, and shoved the man's elbow deeper into his suit pocket. With his right fist, he hammered the bridge of the attacker's nose, which erupted like a shaken soda can. He went limp and cracked his head on the floor as he landed.

"Vito, Vito," Joan said as she tugged at his arm. "We need to get out of here," she pleaded.

"Okay, wait," Vito said as he turned and frisked the guy, taking his wallet. "Now," he yelled.

She paused, took off her pumps, hiked her skirt, and bolted down the corridor.

They rushed down the stairs and out the back emergency door, sounding more alarms and creating more panic. "Stay here," Vito said to Joan at the curb, then he turned to face the crowd surging before them. Vito snaked his way through the pandemonium to the valet's kiosk and grabbed his car keys. He was turning to leave when he was stopped short by the sight of police officers rushing past him to get inside the building.

He hurried back to Joan and grabbed her hand, leading her quickly toward the private valet parking area. They jumped into the car simultaneously, then looked at one another. Joan's dress was no longer around her waist; it had ridden up, now showing her panties. "Damn, don't look." The more she wiggled to pull her dress down, the more her hair fell into her face. Vito looked away and snickered saying, "What was that all about?"

"I don't know. How did you know how to knock that guy out like that?"

Again, Vito repeated his question, "What was that all about?"

"Please, not now, get me out of here."

She held her dress together as they walked to one of the

outside tables and sat down, waiting to be served. Vito could feel Joan shaking beside him. “Turn around,” he said, letting Joan get into position before putting pressure on the occipitalis muscles at the back of her skull. She slowly raised her head, and her eyes became clear of the pain of stress.

“What did you just do? I feel so much better. The weight on my shoulders is gone.”

“I just applied a little pressure in the right place. Here, take my coat and cover your legs,” Vito said as he handed over his tuxedo jacket.

“Look at you, James Bond showing modesty, fixing my tension, and making me feel comfortable. Who the hell are you?”

“Well, ain’t that sweet?” came a voice from around the corner. Joan turned to Vito with horror in her eyes; then they both turned and stared at their worst nightmare.

Chapter Sixteen

TURNING THE CORNER into the café, Ron looked at them with a sarcastic grin. "Don't bother to get up." Vito saw the com-link in Ron's ear and complied.

"I've seen what you do to people you go after," Ron said to Vito.

"I bet he didn't tell you that he was an assassin or that he is now a Cardinal in the Catholic Church." This tidbit of information was addressed to Joan.

Vito looked him in the eye. Ron seemed to squirm beneath Vito's hardened stare. *I wonder how he knows I am a Cardinal of the Church. Lintzinburg! Has to be!*

Joan turned quickly to look at Vito. "Is that true?"

Vito bowed his head, wrinkling his forehead as he sunk back into the chair. "Yes, but there is a lot he's not telling you."

"So, Vito, did she tell you anything about herself?"

"We were just getting to that before you interrupted us."

"I'll save you both some time."

"No," Joan pleaded. "Don't do this."

"Shut up." Ron glared at her before looking at Vito again. "You sit still and don't even think about moving. I have a sniper trained on you." Ron muttered something into his com and then said, louder, "Show him your sight."

A red dot appeared on Vito's heart, lingered for an ominous moment, then disappeared.

"Joan, you have been a naughty girl. You've not been answering your calls. Not checking in, you have everyone nervous."

Joan bit her lip. She looked at Vito and then back at Ron. "I was going to contact you tomorrow."

Ron ignored her. "Hey," he said, focusing on Vito. "Let me tell you about this cheap, two-toned blond you're falling for. *Tsk, tsk,* a Cardinal yet." Vito started to rise and go on the offensive when the red dot appeared again. He sat back down, and Ron laughed. "She was born in a slum. You know, where poverty and drug addictions are the norm. You could even set your clock to the crime. The sun would go down, and she and her kind would always come out. Like cockroaches."

Joan seethed under Ron's pompous smirk.

He continued, "She grew up with the case of the wants, you see. She went on the prowl when she wanted something and found someone to pay the bill.

He ran his fingers through her hair, taking a deep whiff of her perfume. "Now I know why you want a shot at this. She does clean up good. Why do you think she is here tonight? She's looking for some money."

Vito turned toward Joan as she bowed her head to hide the tears. He went to hug her when Ron said, "sit still."

They all heard the whine of a large motor closing in on them.

"Ha, that should be our ride," Ron said.

Some fool had just drifted into the far lane and was heading directly into the café. Vito grabbed Joan and dove for the ground. A flying table upended and hit Ron. When the large van stopped in front of their table, the side door pulled open, and all they heard was, "Joan! Jump in!"

As Vito and Joan scrambled inside, multiple pings sounded as bullets hit the vehicle.

They clung to the backseats while the driver tried to run Ron over, screaming, "You bastard, this is for my ear!"

"Samir?" Joan shouted in surprise. He was covered in bandages, but the adrenaline made him as lively as ever. "How did you know where to find me?"

He put the van in reverse and left rubber on the street as he backed up and turned around.

"I went back to your home and found my ear and the invitation to the ceremonies," he explained. "I watched you come in, I waited a few hours, and then all hell broke loose.

"Let's get back to the dig," Joan said.

"Please, let me out at my car. I have to leave you for now," said Vito.

"But why? I could use your expertise. Is it because of what that bastard said?"

"No, not at all. But I have another appointment."

"Will I see you again?"

"Bet on it," Vito replied. As if on cue, he felt his phone vibrate. Checking his text, it read:

> *Be aware, Cardinal Lintzinburg has given your location away.*

Vito sneered. Too late.

Chapter Seventeen

AFTER DROPPING VITO off, Joan and Samir headed to the dig site before Ron and his men could follow. The tension in the vehicle was palpable; Joan felt nauseated from all the adrenaline pumping through her. She noticed Samir shaking, his eyes never leaving the road. Oblivious to the full moon and the sky full of stars, her thoughts crossed between Vito and the problems she had caused Samir. Finally, she turned to Samir. "I know you didn't hire on to get into the middle of Jake and me. I'm so sorry for almost getting you killed. I had no idea what he was up to—still don't—but it's no good."

After a long moment, Samir glanced at her. "It's late. Let's just get the relic."

She continued to stare at him, her make-up smeared, dress torn, and arms crossed.

"That was a close call, Samir. Thank you."

"All they wanted was the damn relic. Do you have it?"

"No, not yet, but I know where it is. We'll have to get it the hard way. Pull up to the area where I fell through the floor."

"All right." Samir continued slowly, then stopped the Jeep. "Is this the spot you want?"

"Yes, get the generator and let's get some lights on. Only in this area though," Joan said as she pointed to the archway.

Joan lowered her head and slid out of the Jeep, trying not to rip her dress any more than it already was. She carried her high heels and slowly plotted a course through the gravel to her tent. She changed into a pair of khaki shorts and a vest that barely covered her bosom. Tying up her boots, she smacked her legs, walked outside her tent, and said to Samir, "Let's go. Grab those lanterns for us, and I'll bring the climbing gear." She strapped on her tool belt.

They met back at the entrance, where the tunnel was. Samir noted the climbing gear and returned to retrieve the Jeep's winch cable. He held the hook in one hand and turned the power on, leading the hook to the archway they had uncovered, and carefully secured their climbing gear to the winch.

"It will be daylight in a few hours," Joan said. "Let's take advantage of this time and get in and out before Jake and his men get here."

Samir visibly shuddered at her mention of Jake.

"I'm sorry, Samir," Joan said softly.

"Let's just get it and get out," Samir replied.

"Good. Let me drop in first, then you follow."

They dropped onto the softer dirt and bone mixture and Joan released herself from the gear. She recalculated the map and paced off sixteen feet. She turned right and paced another eight steps that put her directly in front of a wall. There seemed to be an engraving under the dirt. Wiping off the debris, a short poem with an asterisk at the end appeared:

I TRAVELED THE SHADOWS OF MY MIND
SEARCHING FOR BOUNDARIES THAT NEVER CAME
SO, I STOLE WHAT I THOUGHT SHOULD BE MINE
AT LAST, I COULD NOT LEAVE
SO, MY TREASURE STAYED BEHIND.

The asterisk was different from the writing on the wall, and it was a brass insert. Smiling, Joan gently put her center punch in the middle of the asterisk and gave it a tap. The whole asterisk popped out. There behind it was a golden box the size of a small matchbox. She carefully pulled it out and cleaned it off. The top of the box was made of glass. Inside lay a royal red cloth. Laying on that cloth was a thorn from the crown that had once been forced upon the head of Jesus Christ. The sudden range of feelings that overcame her was all encompassing—from fear to awe. She held on to the feeling of reverence and bowed her head.

Before she could turn to show Samir, she felt something cold on the back of her neck. “Don’t move.”

Joan froze. Goosebumps traveled faster than the speed

of light. The gun barrel slid on the sweat on her neck. All she heard was the pounding of her heart, which seemed to block out all thought; even her fight-or-flight instincts stalled.

After what seemed to be endless terror, she cried, "Samir, what are you doing? We found the relic."

"Please, Joan, this is hard enough. Just give me the damn relic."

Joan's stress levels spiked as she heard fear and resignation in his voice. His resolve was shaky.

"Don't think of doing anything stupid," he said when she hesitated to hand him the relic.

"I won't, but listen…"

"No, you listen, Joan," Samir said sharply. "They took my ear, put a cattle prod up my ass and pulled the damn trigger. Now they have my family. What else can I do? I'm sorry."

Joan started to turn to her right with her left hand holding the matchbox while Samir brought his right hand up, the gun now pointing upward. Taking advantage of the fact that he didn't want to hurt her, Joan smacked Samir where his ear used to be. He screamed and reached for his ear using his free hand. He pulled the gun down and squeezed the trigger, missing her by mere inches. Trying to refocus through the pain, as the gunshot noise loudly reverberated off the cave walls, Samir screamed, "You bitch!"

Joan pulled out her pickaxe and buried the point into Samir's head. His eyes popped wide open as if he were unable to believe what had happened. He crumpled to his knees.

Looking up at her, he tried to speak, but nothing came out. His head bounced off one of the protruding rocks but it didn't matter. Life had escaped him.

Trembling, Joan looked down through her sweat-matted hair, her eyes bloodshot and rimmed with tears. She noticed the box was gone, and her throat and mouth suddenly tasted sour. She looked around and didn't see it. Shit. It had to be under Samir. Squatting next to the body, she lifted and rolled it over.

She saw a glint of light as if the box winked at her. With a sigh, she grabbed it and ran for the climbing gear before sliding to a sudden halt. She ran back to Samir's body and frisked him for the keys to the van. She looked at him one last time—he had been her friend.

Back at her tent, she shoved her journal, dress, and heels into a duffle bag. She knew she couldn't go home. *Where can I go? I was lucky the first time to avoid Jake.* Frantically, she grabbed her wallet and counted her cash. Three hundred and seventy-six dollars and some odd change.

She drove to the nearest gas station. The chimes on the front door announced her entrance. The woman behind the counter eyed her as she walked straight to the ladies' room. Staring at herself in the mirror, she thought she looked like a cartoon character with her dry matted hair and dirt from the dig site smeared into her make-up. She looked deeper in the mirror to find herself and let out a sob as the trauma of the night's events hit her. Trembling, she turned the water on, grabbed a few paper towels, and cleaned herself up. She reshaped her hair, put it in a ponytail, and brushed the dirt from her vest and shorts. Giving herself one last look, she marched out of the bathroom. She gave the attendant a wink and a nod as she brought her finger to her lips.

The attendant's eyes followed Joan to the door as she came out from behind the counter. She hesitated, turned around, grabbed something from behind the counter, and ran out after Joan. She caught up to her just as Joan was opening her car door. Joan swung around, ready to punch the woman with her keys protruding from each knuckle. "Wait," said the attendant, "I have something for you." She opened her lunch bag and crammed something in it. "Here, please take it. My boyfriend used to beat me all the time. Get far away from him. Good luck!"

Joan looked at the woman with surprise and gratitude. "Thank you, and God bless you." She gave the woman a half smile, got into her car, and drove off. Looking into the bag, Joan found a pre-paid phone and a peanut butter and jelly sandwich. She grabbed the food and gulped it down. Turning off the main street, she pulled over, set up the pre-paid, and looked up the nearest hotel to her home.

Joan parked two blocks away from the hotel. Still out from the night before, she felt like she was doing the walk of shame as dawn broke. As she walked up to the hotel, she was impressed by the wrought iron gates that separated the premises from traffic. To the right side were the entrance to the hotel and a view of Jaffe Gate, the main entrance to the Old City. To the left was a beautiful view of the western wall and the Church of the Holy Sepulchre. She had never seen such a vast, lush green lawn. The stark contrast to the sand-colored building was jarring, but the sight of gnarly, thirty-foot olive trees was striking.

The new morning light exploded into the lobby through the skylight and windows. The floor and walls looked like a kaleidoscope with dancing, colored figures. She dropped her bag on the floor and graced the clerk with a 24-karat-gold smile. "Good morning," he stuttered.

"Hello, Uzziah," Joan said, addressing him by the name on his tag. "I'm going to need to check in a little early." She reached up, placed her hand on his, and repeated the knock-out smile. "My friends won't be here till late this afternoon."

"Do you have a reservation?"

"No, not yet. I was hoping you could help me with that."

"How can I help you then?" the clerk asked as he tried to match her smile.

"I have my company credit card," she said, pulling out of her back pocket, "Can this hold my room till this afternoon? My luggage will be here with my friends later."

He looked her over, enjoying what he saw but he knew she was trouble. "I'm sorry, but this is highly irregular. Your name is not on the credit card, so I can't do that."

She took his hand between hers and puckered her lips in a pout. "I'm sure you can help a lady in distress."

"Let me see your identification, please."

She leaned in closer and whispered, "I have been separated from my purse and wallet. But I have enough money for the down payment on the room, and I will come down and give you all the info you need when my friends arrive."

Once more, Uzziah smiled. "I'm going to set this up as a reservation and allow you in the room early. Come back down and look for me when your friends arrive." He winked at her. "We'll arrange the paperwork to match."

Joan reached over the counter and kissed him square on the lips. "You are a real gentleman." She hefted up her bag and grabbed her company card and room key. With a wave and a smile, she looked for Room 315. Feeling pretty good about herself, she got off the elevator and read the sign that indicated her door was to the left, halfway down the hall.

As she headed to her room, a scrawny, half-dressed gentleman popped out of his room into the hallway, his fedora sitting crooked on top of his head. He was hanging up his suit for the dry-cleaning attendant to pick up when he noticed Joan standing there with her mouth wide open, laughing. "I take it those are your only clothes."

Stunned, the man wearing only his boxers and t-shirt said, "Oh, I'm sorry," and rushed back inside. His hat flew off and hit the floor.

Still laughing, Joan stopped dead in front of her room. A plan had just popped into her head. The sight of small-flowered print wallpaper and the scent of fresh deodorizer greeted her as she entered her room. She dropped her bag next to the solid oak dresser, then opened the door again and stuck her head out. The hallway was empty. She propped the door open with the latch and ran down to grab the clothes the gentleman had hung out for the dry cleaners, picked up the hat, and placed it on her head. She ran back to her room giggling, locked the door behind her, and tossed the stolen suit onto one of the queen-sized beds. She stripped down and took a hot shower, then flopped on the other bed spread eagle, not even bothering to dry off, and slept for a few hours.

She woke chilled and sauntered to the spacious kitchen and made herself a cup of hot coffee. Now it was time to see if she had what it took to put her plan into effect. She dressed in the gentlemen's clothes and looked in the mirror. Not a bad fit, except that her bosom pushed the shirt to its limits. Joan tucked her hair under the hat and tilted it slightly to the right. She shrugged. *Time to test it out.* She grabbed her bag, and took the stairs to the lobby this time

She went right up to the front desk in the lobby, cleared her throat and in a deep gruff voice, asked Uzziah, "Any messages for Room 313?"

Uzziah checked his computer without even looking up and replied, "No, sir."

"Thank you," she said and left.

The afternoon air had a brisk summery breeze that wafted in with the aroma of coming rain. It was time for part two of her plan. She got on her phone and looked up houses for sale in her neighborhood. Securing three addresses, she drove over to the nearest car rental agency. In a rented mid-size sedan heading towards her home, she rubbed her nose. The deodorizer in the car was losing the battle against the smell of stale cigarette smoke. She noticed two women sitting and talking on a porch in one yard as dogs barked behind the chain link fences down the street.

In contrast, children played on the driveways. The first and second addresses did not have what she was looking for. As she approached the third address, she saw what she needed: a "For Sale" sign. A large tree shadowed the front yard, and it was quiet, except for the children's laughter coming out of one of the houses down the road.

Joan scoped out the house to make sure no one was home before she pulled up in front and hopped out of her car. She popped the trunk, walked up to the "For Sale" sign, and wrenched it from the ground. She quickly placed it in her trunk, slammed it shut, and took off.

She drove closer to her home and looked for any cars out of the ordinary. In her block, she spotted the vehicle she had anticipated. There was a loud thunderclap, and the golden sun was swept away by ominous clouds. The trees looked like those advertising balloons that dance in the wind and wave about. The rain started to streak the windshield. She pulled her hat down tight over her ears and jumped out of the car, popping the trunk as she came along the side of the vehicle that could not be seen by the unwanted guest watching her house. She pulled out the sign with her bag and placed it in the spot she needed, pushing it into the ground with both hands.

Stepping back to appraise her work, she rubbed her hands together, pleased at what she had done. House For Sale. Joan grabbed her bag, walked to the front door and unlocked it. She closed the door and locked it behind her, never even looking up.

When she did, she raised her hands to her face and let out a whimper, followed by a muffled scream.

They had torn her house apart, looking for the relic. She ran to the window and peeked out to see if she could get a good look at her tail. Joan knew she needed to leave this house and the country quickly.

Running to the bar, she rolled out the keg, unscrewed the tap, poked inside with a hanger and scooped out a plastic bag. She wiped the bag down and retrieved the boxed artifacts and tried again to open the bone box. But it wouldn't budge. Pissed off, Joan tossed the bone box and the gold matchbox onto the bar.

She needed to pack. Rummaging through her bag, she dug out her torn red dress and pumps and threw them onto her bed to make room for essentials.

Packed and ready, Joan returned to the boxes on the bar and grabbed an old brown paper bag and a pair of scissors. She wrapped both boxes in brown paper and dropped them into another container, which she also wrapped. Her phone produced a name and address, which she wrote on the package.

Then, package and bag in tow, she ran back out the front door, not even bothering to lock it, and headed for the closest 24-hour post office.

At the post office, she gathered a few envelopes and a pad of paper and wrote three letters—no small task. Half an hour later, she finished mailing the package and the letters. One letter was addressed to Vito, and another to Billy Campbell. The last letter was to Jake. As she went to drop the envelopes into the outgoing slot, she decided not to mail one of them and tossed it into the trash can.

As Joan was running to her car, a young woman tried to wave her down with the letter addressed to Jake in her hand. The girl gave up, shrugged her shoulders, saw the stamp on it, and mailed it.

Chapter Eighteen

Vito sent a text message to the Pope:

> *Believe Lintzinburg has given me up. Heading to site. Relic close; ours soon.*

Vito came upon the dig site and stopped about a mile out. He could see the lights on and hear equipment running. As he approached the area, shadows seemed to be moving. Focusing on the apparition, he recognized Ron but didn't know the man with him. Vito ducked down and watched as a group of Ron's men reported while two other men brought up a dead body from the pit. Ron affirmatively nodded his head. Dropping the body, they all marched away.

Vito crept up to the body and found Samir with a pickaxe buried in his head. *Shit, how did that happen?* He raced back to his car and followed the caravan of cars behind Ron. When they stopped in front of a house, Vito drove past it.

The dark crimson and purple sky looked like the point of the crescent moon had just relieved them of their duty leaving the area in a dull grey light. Vito took up a position behind the house waiting for them to leave.

Ron shouted, "Be careful. That "For Sale" sign wasn't there earlier." Ron and the crew cautiously approached the front of the house as the lights were on, and the door was ajar. Ron sent two men in with weapons drawn. "Check it out and do it quickly."

Ron got the all-clear sign after a few minutes. Everyone stood motionless inside the front door as Jake checked everywhere. Nothing. Disgusted, Jake did an about-face and marched back out the front door. "Ron, get me back to the hotel. I want a lead on that woman within hours, not days."

Ron yelled at two of his men. "Relieve those morons in the car. I want you two on the roof of that garage to make sure she doesn't come back. If she does, call me immediately. Tell the other two to meet me at the hotel where I will deal with them."

"Yes, sir," the two gunmen replied. Once Ron was out of earshot they argued over who would do the telling and who would do the shooting.

Meanwhile, Vito stole up the back steps, slipped his knife between the door jam and found the space he needed. With a click, he slid the backdoor open and snuck in. The amber light cast his shadow upon the wall and through the doorway. Slowly, he looked around, categorizing what he saw in order to get a sense of who Joan Vitale really was. First was the food in the fridge: carrots, celery, lettuce—all organic. He guffawed. *No wonder she looked good in that dress.* Next were the cheeses and nuts. Piled up next to the refrigerator were cases of bottled water. The walls were devoid of personal pictures. The paintings would have come with the house when she rented it. He noticed the turntable and bar.

The floorboards groaned underfoot as he moved into the bedroom. The dress she'd worn just that evening lay on the bed. He picked up the dress or what was left of it, and brought it to his face, inhaling deeply. The fragrance seeped deep into his brain, overloading his olfactory senses. Feelings of concern, loss, nostalgia, kinship, and melancholy flushed over him in a way he had never felt. He keyed in on an emotion that hurt, even more, loneliness, and he tossed the dress back onto the bed. With urgency, Vito looked for any clue she might have left him. He knew she would not take off without letting him know where.

Vito stopped at the turntable and stared at it. Something was off but he couldn't tell what. He reached over, turned it on, and the album dropped. Music started playing, and the tune sounded familiar to him, but no name came to mind. He knew she had left this album cued for him to find, so he continued to listen. Then he heard Four Dead in Ohio by Crosby, Stills, Nash, and Young.

Ohio! That's where she went to school—Simon College.

"I knew you would find my clue."

Vito swung around. Joan stood in the doorway. She ran to him and wrapped her arms around him, sobbing. "I killed Samir. He was my friend! But he gave me no choice," she cried as she held tighter to Vito, her tears washing his face. "I couldn't leave without seeing you one more time."

He pulled himself away from her and looked into her eyes. What he saw scared him; it was pure terror. He stroked her hair and comforted her. "Coming back here was a mistake. We need to get you out of here."

"I need to tell you a few things first," she said, drying her eyes. "I don't know if you are an assassin or a priest. I think you're closer to a priest than an assassin, but you have the moves."

"It's "yes" to both, but those are longer stories than we have time for." He went to the window and scanned the street. "I don't see anyone yet, but we can't stay here."

Laying in the mud on the roof across the street, the gunman sighted Joan and rolled his chin a little. "Hey, Sonny, we should take them out before they decide to run."

"No, let this play out. I'll call for confirmation.

He felt a tap on the shoulder, and there was a phfft.

"What the hell did you do?" Sonny yelled. "The boss wanted her alive."

"Why in the hell did you tap my shoulder then? That means to kill."

"You jackass, you're not in the army anymore. Let's get the fuck out of here."

Joan suddenly flew backward onto the floor.

"Oh, my God, Joan…Joan!"

"Shit," he had seen these types of wounds before, and they were never good; the dark blood usually meant a liver shot. *She had five to ten minutes tops.* He took her hand, placed it on the wound, and told her to "keep pressure on this." He hurried to get something to prop her head up, saw the dress, rolled it up, and placed it on the wound.

"Vito, I need to tell you something."

"Hold on, Joan." He pulled his phone out and called 911. "They'll be here soon. Talk to me, girl."

She coughed and a small amount of blood came out of the corners of her mouth. Vito brushed her forehead and removed the hair out of her eyes. Joan's eyes started to close, and Vito patted her face. "Joan, stay with me."

"Vito, I, I can't let you love me. You are a priest, and I started this journey with you for all the wrong reasons."

"You misunderstand, Joan. Like you, it's not sexual."

Joan continued, "I'm not worthy of being a friend. You don't understand. All I wanted to do is use you." She reached up to rub his face but coughed in pain and her eyelids started to flutter.

As he bent down, his tears fell onto her face. "Everything will be all right," he whispered, "Stay with me." He looked into her eyes. "Joan, it doesn't matter to me what your motives were to start with; it's what they are now. If no one had shown mercy and forgiveness to me, I certainly would not be here."

"I do have such peacefulness with you. I feel saved and certainly forgiven. You know, this feels good," she nodded her head, and tears blurred her sight. "Vito?" She could barely see him.

"Stay still and quiet," Vito said, holding pressure on her wound.

"Vito, I don't have… time." Slurring, she bowed her head towards him, "remember two relics…"

She closed her eyes and exhaled the last of her life. "No, stay with me." He shook her. "Joan, stay with me." He bowed his head, and then a searing pain stopped time.

Chapter Nineteen

HE EXPANDED HIS lungs, his massive chest pulling at the buttons of his shirt, but he could not get enough air to breathe. He felt dizzy.

Vito's brain commanded him to do multiple things at once, but all he knew was that he wanted revenge. He felt all this was his fault, like his family. His straining muscles and protruding veins wanted to tear something apart. His body reacted without forethought, and he stood and carried Joan to the bed. Vito bowed and prayed for the dead: ***Eternal rest grant unto them, O Lord, and let your perpetual light shine upon them. May her soul and the souls of all the faithful departed, through the mercy of God, rest in peace. Forgive whatever sins she committed through human weakness and in your goodness grant her mercy and eternal rest. Amen***

A brilliant, blinding light brought on such a deep headache that Vito thought he might pass out. Thoughts exploded with long-forgotten memories of a demoralizing orphaned childhood and an even worse adult life. The flashback hit with no warning; he saw the man he used to be, a cold-blooded killer.

The son of a bitch who adopted him and taught him, Enzio Benetti, formed an image in his mind of him training him with all kinds of handguns and sniper rifles. Then martial arts, which covered knives, swords, and the sai. And last was his survival training in all climates, as well as in the most challenging situations. Then came Enzio's final betrayal.

Vito remembered when he removed the blindfold and stepped out of the rented vehicle. He felt the cold blue sky hide the sun's heat. Enzio packed a couple of bags with the minimum number of items required to survive and took him to a secret location in Virginia. Vito caught the bag tossed to him as Enzio said, "This is where I was trained."

"So, where are we?"

"In due time, my son."

After the first mile, Enzio bent over, trying to catch his breath as Vito glided up the mountain effortlessly. A smirk appeared on Enzio's face as Vito's eyes landed on his.

"We will be there in another seven miles; keep going."

"Old man, will you be able to make it?"

"I'm old and sick, but I'm not dead. I hope you can still do what I can do at my age, if you make it that long without getting yourself killed."

With a laugh, Vito tossed him half the apple he was eating. "Just keep moving, old man."

Inside a thousand yards of their destination, Vito heard

cracking twigs and motioned for Enzio to be quiet, but it was too late. Men in full combat gear encircled the two. Vito glanced at Enzio, then keyed in on who might be the leader and advanced toward him. Within seconds, Enzio and Vito lay on the ground tied up like steers for branding.

These guys are good. Vito raised his head high enough to see Enzio kicked square in the jaw before feeling the jab of a syringe in his neck. The trees seemed to split down the center before him, and Enzio looked like he was melting into the ground as everything went dark.

Vito awoke to the sounds of Enzio screaming in pain. "Enzio?" he shouted.

A musty copper odor made him nauseous as he tried to jump up. The chains around his wrist snapped him back onto the concrete cot. The drab olive walls were solid, and the bloodstained floor was either grey or silver. Sweat poured off his body as he was reminded of his childhood home, the orphanage. He couldn't tell what time of day it was or how long he had been in this hole.

Silence engulfed him until he heard footsteps moving toward his cell. Vito laid perfectly still when the door swung open. The first one got a kick straight to the jaw as the next two held him down. He got his knee up high enough to connect with the closest attacker. At the same time, a third man pulled out a semi-automatic Glock 45 and put it to his head.

"Enough, or we kill you and torture the old man until we get what we want."

Relaxing his muscles and keeping his mind on high alert, he allowed them to drag him down the hallway towards a grimy army-green door with half the windows out and the other half scratched and painted over. Splintered paint from the knife marks in the doorway looked ominous.

A soldier yanked the door open as it fought with a groan. Thick cobwebs blocked all light coming into the room. The hanging interrogation lights scantly lit the place. The decomposed rodent in the corner was dried and brittle; the smell of vomit, urine, and alcohol pierced his nose. The broken and cracked concrete floor started to shred his knees as they dragged him to the chair, then chained him down.

"Leave us," one of the soldiers said. The rest of them backed out of the room.

Without warning, the man delivered a vicious blow; Vito's head snapped back as the man walked back and forth in front of him.

"Now that I have your full attention…I do have your attention, don't I?"

Vito spit out some blood, shook his head, and said, "I'm going to kill you."

With a deep growl came another brutal blow. When Vito picked up his head again, he saw the man pick up a syringe on the table. Sneering, he jabbed it into Vito's neck and pushed the plunger down with a maniacal laugh. "Now listen up; where are you from, and who sent you here?"

"I don't know what you are talking about."

He felt the breeze of wind before the blow arrived. Nauseated and dizzy, darkness came over him.

Over the intercom came a command, "Enough for now."

Vito awoke lying on a board that seemed to stink of vomit.

"Look, Sleeping Beauty is awake. Let's start with an easy question. What is your name?"

"Where is the old man?" Vito asked instead of answering, choosing his words carefully as he did not want them to know of family ties.

They tilted him so that his head was lower than his lungs. Another man threw a cloth over his face and held his nose as someone poured water over his mouth. When he began choking, they dumped more water. The feeling of drowning took over. He tried to inhale, only to take water into his lungs. His legs shook, and his body went into tremors. The panic was overwhelming. He fought to stay awake.

"Raise him," someone commanded. Vito coughed and spat up water as they turned him upright. "Now, what's your name?"

Vito silently talked himself down from his panicked state. His best weapon kicked in—his mind. Fighting the drugs, Vito slowed his heart to a mere fifty beats per minute. He slowly exhaled, then inhaled and said, "Vito."

"See, that wasn't so bad, was it?"

Two more times, and then I have them.

"Now, where are you from, and who sent you here?"

"I want to know where the old man is."

They rocked him backward and he felt the rag and cold

water hit his mouth while they held his nose. Fear flooded his mind and body. The fight-or-flight instinct kicked in, and adrenaline amped his body to such a state that he passed out when he could do neither.

His captor yelled, "Stop!" He bent over Vito and slapped him awake. "Okay, who sent you here? I can do this all night, but I doubt you can."

"Fuck you…I'm going…to kill you."

The man snapped his fingers, and they proceeded again. Vito brought his heartbeat down to twenty beats per minute and passed out.

"All right, stop. Check his pulse."

"Boss, there's no pulse."

"Don't just stand there; go get help." One of the men ran out of the room, and the captor started CPR. Vito's eyes flew open, and he slammed his head into his captor. The man passed out and fell on top of Vito. Vito grabbed his gun, shot the other man, then secured the keys to his chains, unhooked himself, and pushed the unconscious man off him. He slid off the board, which he held onto to steady himself, and dropped to the ground but when he tried to walk, he saw two of everything and could only wobble out the door.

High above, in the observation room, the men laughed. "Wait till he tries to get out through the obstacle course. Let's go."

Vito had turned right and started down the hall when he heard one of the other men yell, "Get him!"

His feet would not listen when he told them to run; his body was slow in coming back online with his brain. He tripped through the first door in sight. The room was dark with sirens that blared, and red lights strobed so fast he couldn't get his bearings. It felt like an epileptic seizure had taken hold of him. Going down on one knee, he bowed his head. Blackness and pinholes of lights danced through his head, and he fought to regain control of himself.

Somewhere a door slammed shut.

Someone was nearby. All he could make out ahead was what looked to be thirty office cubicles. He crawled to the end of the row and lifted his head only to see two soldiers closing in on him. Diving into the cubicle across the aisle and shaking his head to try and clear his blurred vision, he inhaled sharply before jumping up to take the two soldiers out. The closest one was straight ahead. As the soldier turned towards Vito and aimed his weapon for the kill, Vito said, "Mother, what are you doing here?"

The confused soldier turned to look for someone. Vito shook his head, but all he could see and hear was his mother standing before him with a gun in her hand. She was pointing it at him, and she had a large hole in her face. "Vito, why did you do this to me? Come to me like a good boy and take your punishment." He heard a gun go off as he moved toward her and fell to his knees.

"Momma, is that you?" Vito stuttered.

"It's me, Vito. Don't shoot."

Then he heard his father, Stefano, call him. "Vito, vieni qui, help me."

As Vito jumped up and whipped around to look for his father, a bullet grazed his upper arm. His body spun around, and he went to his knees again. "Papa, Momma's here. She's shooting at me," Vito moaned.

"Vito, why did you shoot me and your brother and sister? Vito, stop! You're killing us."

Vito closed his eyes and saw the brutal murders of his family before him. Stefano lay there with one arm blown off and a hole in his stomach. Both his sister and brother had identical wounds: shotgun blasts to the midsection of their tiny bodies. He lowered his head and started to weep. "This can't be. I'm sorry, I'll never do it again. Help me."

The movement of the soldiers woke him. He quickly checked himself for any injuries, finding the wound on his upper arm, and he pushed hard on the shirt to slow the bleeding. The pain jolted his mind. *That can't be my family. They are dead.*

Vito jumped up and fired twice, once to the left, dropping the soldier there, and one in front of him, killing the second soldier. Three more soldiers came looking for him, outflanking him on either side while one pushed him forward through the office of cubicles.

Now at the last cubicle with nowhere to go, he crawled up under the desk. All three soldiers walked by him, yet found nothing. They yelled at one another, "Where is he?" Vito started to drip sweat onto the floor as he pushed himself tighter against the underside of the middle desk drawer, like a spring-loaded tension rod.

"Boss, I don't know where he went. We cleared the room. He must have gotten out before all the doors were closed."

"Get out there and check the grounds."

"Yes, boss."

Vito waited a few moments before silently letting himself down, then duck-walked to the door. He looked around and opened it slowly, choosing to run to his right when voices started to float towards him. One voice among them was quite familiar to him. He stopped at the doorway and peered in. There was Enzio sitting at the desk in front of mic. His knees buckled as he felt a jolt to his heart.

"Enzio, how could you? You bastard." Vito brought his pistol up. "Give me a good reason I shouldn't pull this trigger."

You could see the spittle fly from Enzio's mouth as he yelled, "Listen to me, boy. This was the only way to see if you had what it takes to do this work."

"Bullshit." Vito raised the gun and pulled the trigger. Enzio cringed in anticipation of what was to come, but nothing happened except the sound of a click. The gun was empty.

Chapter Twenty

THE BRILLIANT, BLINDING light started to change colors in his mind. The flashback ended abruptly. Vito raised his head, knelt by Joan's body, and whispered a promise. "I swear I will not let this go unavenged like my family did all those years ago. I will find these men and make them pay."

He noticed the rare looking necklace around her neck, removed it, and placed it around his own. He kissed the top of her head good-bye.

Vito felt an uncontrollable surge of adrenaline as his anger spiked upwards. "God have mercy on their souls, for I will not. Forgive me, Lord." A self-righteousness seemed to generate from him. Terror in one eye and destruction in the other. His training flooded back to him along with all the hurt, betrayal, and lies.

A noise from outside brought him back to the present. Vito had picked up on the sound coming from outside the window.

"Let's get out of here." Two men started to take off when one gunman dropped part of the firearm he was disassembling.

Blurred by Joan's blood, he looked out the window, left then right. His eyes squinted to fine laser points as he took in everything in a grid-like form. What would he have done if this were his mission? He'd look for the quickest way out of the immediate area—that's how he would have planned it. It only took a moment or two for him to find the movement he was looking for his escape.

With the speed and agility of a young warrior, Vito was gone. He grabbed a knife off the kitchen counter and ran through the open back door. Ahead of him, he spotted the second shooter. The man carried himself like he had military training. Vito headed toward the first man. The military man had reassembled his weapon and lined up his shot, finger on the trigger. Vito did a quick 180-degree turn and angled himself at the second shooter. He dove into the shadows to allow the cover to obtain a clean strike, dropped to one knee and steadied himself. With the intent to kill, Vito let the knife fly.

Not waiting to see if he had hit his target, Vito was up and chasing first man. He must keep this one alive. He needed to know who ordered this kill. Angling across the alley and street, he closed the distance. Smiling, he heard a broken, throaty sound as the military man fell dead.

Closing in on the remaining henchman, Vito noticed shadows coming from behind him. He looked ahead for some reflection, but dust and dirt don't reflect much. The stone walls only gathered shadows. The wall in front of him seemed to spit pieces of stone as he got close to the building, and he knew someone had opened fire. Vito stopped his pursuit of the first man to deal with the men chasing him. *They must have called for backup.*

"All right," he said, walking towards them with his arms in the air, keeping a calculated distance.

"Stop shooting," one of the men called out. "Jake wants him alive."

"That's more than I want from you," Vito yelled.

He knew that there was no room for error in his calculations as he paced off five steps into the hub of his imaginary wheel and slowed time down in his head. In his mind's eye, he saw his younger self in the same situation. Four attackers surrounding him, and the moon making their shadows seem to dance off the dirt-strewn walls of the building.

Vito was close enough that he could smell their collective breaths. The smell of sweat, fear, and cologne, blended with the horrible spice they'd had on their recent meals. Their last meals.

These men were incompetent and used to preying on the weak and innocent, and Vito Rosario was neither.

The closest man charged, swinging a club downward to strike Vito in the head. Vito took a quick step forward, raised both arms, and used his forearms to block the attacker's arms below the bat and hands. Then he stepped into a neutral position stance where he could control the attacker's arm with his left hand while he used his right hand to grab the club, disarm his attacker, and feed the butt end of the club into the man's face.

Vito took the bat and pushed the first attacker into an oncoming attacker who wielded a knife. He took one step to the left and quickly reversed himself, holding the bat up as if he were prepared to hit a home run. The man with the gun appeared shocked as he looked into Vito's eyes.

The gunman's head erupted like a melon as the bat connected with its target. The man hit the ground before his gun did. Vito threw the bat down and faced the oncoming knife-wielder. Vito sidestepped the man just as he lunged and grabbed his attacker's knife hand, cracking the bones. He grabbed the knife and with one more turn the blade flew true, plunging deep into the chest of the last man standing.

Vito looked around and watched them squirm. He dragged the man with the broken wrist and threw him down beside the man who had once held the bat. "I have one question for you; your answer will keep one of you alive. Who ordered the hit on Joan and the attack on me?"

"I don't know what you're are talking about," said one of them.

Vito snapped his neck.

"Jake Howard!"

No sooner did he get the words out than a bullet passed through his brain. Vito rolled away and was up in an instant, running a zig-zag pattern.

"Boss, do we pursue?"

Cersei shook her head. *Who is this guy? He is no ordinary*

assassin or priest. Kristoff, you've got competition. "No, let him go." Cersei pulled out her phone and hit speed dial. "Boss, good thing you sent me to check up on these imbeciles. I just cleaned up their mess over here at Joan's place. As for the morons that killed her, you can visit them in hell right now if you like."

"Good. And Cersei… no more fuck ups. I'm holding you personally accountable."

She bowed her head in anger and blinked as her phosphorescent eyes seemed to dim. "Yes, boss. I let Vito go so he can lead us to the relic."

The driver stopped the Rolls Royce outside St Peter's Square and opened the back door for the dignitary inside. Kristoff stepped out of the Rolls and looked around. The sky took on a bitterly ominous look with each step he took. You could hear the cobblestone bricks crack. "Surround the area."

A legion of demons flew up to position themselves next to the statue of the angels and saints. Kristoff returned to his limo and had the driver take him into the square, where Cardinal Lintzinburg met him, escorted him into the Apostolic Palace, and into the cardinal's private quarters.

Kristoff helped himself to a drink. "We have a problem. I want my relic but no one knows where it is."

Cardinal Lintzinburg squirmed. "I'm working on it."

Wind swirled through the room ripping the curtains closed. Lintzinburg started to choke on what looked like black particles of a substance. "I want that relic. Do we understand each other?"

Lintzinburg grabbed at his throat and nodded.

"Good. You have three days." Kristoff turned and marched out the door. He paused on the steps of the palace and looked to the heavens. I'll return soon to drop these walls around their feet. None will be saved, for your words will eat dust when I am through.

Kristoff entered his limo and yelled to the driver, to get him out of there; "This place makes me sick."

"Yes, sir."

"Get Jake on the phone.

"Here you are, sir."

Kristoff growled, "Jake, if you want to make it through the week to the election, you had better have that relic in three days." He hung up without listening for Jake's reply.

Chapter Twenty-One

LOCKING HIS DOOR behind him, the keys made a loud noise as they hit the bowl on the table, and Vito got out of the tux he had just ruined. He whipped around when he heard a banging on the door.

"Who is it?" He hustled to the door. Peeking through the peephole, Vito's mind went from agitation to curiosity. *How did they get past hotel security?* His fingers fumbled on the door as he unlocked and swung it open. "Let me see that badge again."

The man before him looked like he had just stepped out of a men's health and fitness magazine. His straight white teeth gave him an innocent smile, while his hair seemed to be a little long for a government agent. He pulled out his wallet again, showing an intimidating badge with the letters *FEU* on it.

Vito's swollen, bloodied hand reached up and grabbed the badge to examine it. "What does that mean, FEU?"

"Federal Espionage Unit, a special unit of the U.S. government. Would you like to clean up and put some fresh clothes on, sir?"

"Come in. What is this about?"

"Have you heard of the Crown of Thorns, the relic that's in Notre Dame cathedral?"

Vito swung around with a suspicious look, and his body tensed. "Of course I have. What about it?"

"There has been a lot of chatter about a left-wing organization trying to get their hands on this relic."

Vito exhaled, not realizing he had been holding his breath. "What left-wing organization? "And why is that? That piece is under lock and guard 24/7."

"Dear Cardinal, I'm sorry I didn't introduce myself. My name is Glen. May I call you Vito?"

Reaching for the dish towel, he wrapped up some ice, banged it on the counter, and wound it around his hand. "If I said no, would that stop you?"

With a disarming smile, Glen said, "yes, it would. I'm not your enemy."

"Time will tell, won't it?"

"But it would be better if you let me ask the questions."

"This is a two-way street, my friend. If not, you can leave now."

"Cardinal, please. This is of great importance to us."

Vito pulled out the kitchen chair and sat down. "If something is wrong, then I, as the head intelligence agent of the RPCP, should know."

"Okay, I'm not at liberty to give out the information you are asking for, but…" He paused, looking Vito up and down before saying, "if you put on some clothes and come with me, I'll take you to meet my boss."

"And why should I go with you?"

"Come on now. It's precisely who you are that demands that you go with me."

"Fine," Vito said with a smirk.

As they entered the slum area of Tel Aviv, they stopped in front of an abandoned church. Walking briskly to the side door, one of them pulled up on the annulus, twisted it, and the door popped open.

Showing his badge at every level, Glen and Vito finally entered what looked like a war room.

"Please, have a seat."

"How about some explanation?" Vito said as he grabbed a chair.

The sounding *swoosh* of the door gave away that someone had entered the room. Glen acknowledged the person and started his introduction. "Vito, this is Russell Carter, head of the FEU, and quite possibly the most highly trained special ops soldier in the world today."

"Hello, Cardinal." Russell strolled over with his hand outstretched; they each tested their grip power and nodded to each other. "I'm grateful that you accepted our invitation. Please, disregard the compliment from Glen, for we know titles like that are transient at best," Russell said.

"It seems you have a small problem that you need my help with."

"Cardinal," Russell continued, "I've done nothing but read files about you for some time now. And I must say I'm impressed. I know your training level. You could have disabled my man if you wanted to."

Glen turned and looked at Vito in a different light. Vito smiled at him and shrugged.

"What you shall hear tonight must stay within this room, and you will sign documentation to that effect."

"Sorry, but my boss will find out if I'm asked," Vito retorted.

"I assumed that. I welcome the Pope's voice in this."

Russell laid down a folder in front of Vito. "Please notice the dig site and what was found there."

As Vito leaned in to read what was in the folder, he found it more challenging to believe. He finally looked up and said, "Is this true?"

"That is why you are here."

"Where did this information come from?"

"We have been watching Joan's dig site ever since she hired on with Jake. Joan wore an old and rare object around her neck—the one you now wear around yours." Vito shot Glen a glance and smiled as both he and Russell stared at Vito's neck.

"How does it feel when you wear it?" Russell asked. *Does it truly have powers?*

"I never thought about it," Vito said. *It gives me comfort, and the flashbacks are reoccurring more, yet it gives me strength.* "Why would your government want it or keep tabs on it."

"We have had agents watching Joan for sometime. It's not the necklace we are after but the other relic she was hired to retrieve and possibly any other items she may have collected at that site. Also, the company she keeps is dangerous."

"What company are you talking about?"

"What Joan did not know was that Samir worked for us. She also didn't realize that we were tapping her phone and listening to her conversations."

"By the way, your man Samir is dead. Killed by Joan. So go on," Vito said.

Glen and Russell looked at one another, and with a nod from Russell, Glen left.

"I see you didn't get the memo about Samir."

"She worked for Jake Howard, a senator, who employs Ron Wolneski. Both work for a perilous man called Kristoff, who runs the largest cabal in the world."

"What did Joan have to do with any of that? She was an archaeologist."

"Kristoff and his group make kings, queens, dictators, and in this case, the President of the United States."

"So what does that have to do with Joan?"

"The cabal needed a powerful relic to pull this off. They learned of a piece of the crown of thorns and where it was hidden. They believe, and some say it's true, that this relic holds the power over life, death and the ability to bless anyone who has it."

"So, they what? Hire Joan to find its location and unearth it for them?"

"Pretty much."

"And again, what does the FEU do?"

"POTUS has tasked us to look into the cabal. They are accused of espionage and treasonous acts for rigging elections."

"So, once again, I ask, what do you want from me?"

"We need to know what you know about the relic, especially since Joan is dead, and now Samir, as well."

"There are a lot of things I know."

"Come now, let's not be coy." Russell grabbed a chair with its back facing Vito and sat with his arms resting on the top.

"I don't know you yet. First, you show me I can trust you, and then maybe we'll talk."

Chapter Twenty-Two

RETURNING HOME, VITO was walking between the complexes to his side door when a familiar sight stopped him. *The boy reminded him of himself many years ago.* A young boy dressed in grey wool pants that were too short for him with a baggy jacket over his off-colored shirt came running up to him, waving a letter. He came to a stop in front of Vito. "Hey, my momma says this belongs to you; it was delivered today to our house."

He took the letter, then reached into his pocket for some change for the boy. "Thank you," he said as the boy took off.

Vito trudged up the three flights of stairs and found his bilocale. He sat down in a kitchen chair and laid the letter down on the table in front of him. He looked at it for a long while—thinking about the past few days.

Finally, Vito opened it, and a 10,000- lire note fell out. His heart skipped a beat. The letter was from Joan.

Dear Vito,

I have written this letter for you to retrieve the relics, and yes, I mean plural. It is time for you to put that Genius I Q and that Eidetic memory to the test. Okay, here we go. I have left you 10,000 lire to start you on your journey. Be safe; when you arrive, go to the local watering hole and buy yourself a drink. Make sure to use the lire to pay. I wish I were with you.

Love,

Joan

Vito looked at the 10,000-lire note, picked it up, and repeatedly examined it. *What the hell?* He thought. *This is only worth about $5.09 U.S. dollars. Do the colors mean anything? Or could it have been the person inscribed on the note? Through the years, the look and the people have changed.* He looked up the lire note on the internet and found the one he was holding was different in one way. It had two sets of six digit numbers on it. 413107 and 811440. His mind raced, *How? What? Where? When? and Why? How, where, and when didn't matter. Why the numbers and what were they?*

Why the numbers? It's easier to give a code. What kind of code, Ah, latitude and longitude? He quickly compared the serial numbers on the note to coordinates on a map—latitude

41o 31' 07" N, longitude 81o 14' 40" W—would be Simon College in Ohio. Vito pulled his phone out and made travel arrangements to Simon College.

At Kristoff's compound, Cardinal Lintzinburg removed his biretta and ferraiolo and tossed them down on the nearest lounge chair before pouring himself a Scotch. "It seems to me we killed that girl too early."

"Believe me, those responsible have started their punishment in hell already," Kristoff replied. "Now let me remind you that I have returned to claim my rightful place in heaven. Earth is in chaos; the United States is completely reversing all its moral values that the founding fathers instilled into the pathetic little documents like the Declaration of Independence and the Constitution." Looking upward, he mocked God. "Ha, and you thought that you'd bless these people. It didn't take me long to show them that lust, greed, power, and money, were better."

The temperature of the room rose sharply as Kristoff's eyes glazed over and turned a different color. The demon looked out the window as the wind shook the trees and the harbingering clouds rolled in. "Soon now, the name of God will be removed from the face of the Earth."

Cardinal Lintzinburg backed away as Kristoff turned back toward him with an eerie, satanic countenance, continuing to boast of his plan. "Russia is at war, and I will have biological weapons released when I'm ready. Meanwhile, China is buying up land in the United States with the permission of my President."

He grabbed Lintzinburg and yelled, "But I seem to be at an impasse because of the incompetent people around me. I want that relic. NOW! Our time is short." With a feverish snarl, he released the Cardinal.

Lintzinburg shook off the assault. "Good thing I'm on this team. I intercepted the text between Vito and the Pope. Vito has some clues about the whereabouts of the relic. He's on his way to Simon College."

"Do we have anyone we can send over there?"

With swagger, Cardinal Lintzinburg finished the rest of his drink. "Yes, I have prepared for this contingency. When I heard that the old man had made Vito the head of all church relics, I sent Sister Genevive to work in the administration building at Simon College. I remembered you mentioned a relic at that school."

"What makes you feel you can trust her to accomplish what we need?"

"She came to the church in Rome later in her wayward life. Genevie decided to enroll in the religious life as a novitiate, and I became her benefactor. Her qualities are remarkable. She's been run down by men and by growing up in the foster care system. Not to mention that she has severe resentments towards her last boyfriend. I believe she would do anything to get some payback."

Kristoff poured himself a drink. "You still haven't told me

her qualifications."

"This exotic little redhead borders on obsessiveness, and sometimes her streetside still comes out. She is capable of showing her people-pleasing side and then exacting judgment on her prey. A work of art to watch."

As his face flushed crimson, Kristoff placed his drink down. "This better work."

Cardinal Lintzinburg followed suit and placed his empty on the table. He faced off with Kristoff. "It will. Did I mention that I have her daughter, and the father, Vito, doesn't know? She blames him for messing up her life. Did I mention that that man is Vito Rosario?"

Stepping back, with a deep grunt of new appreciation for Lintzinburg, Kristoff said, "Oh my, how Machiavellian."

Cardinal Lintzinburg chuckled. "Hell hath no fury like a woman scorned."

"There is another player on the field now. They're called the FEU"

"Who are they?"

Chapter Twenty-Three

BOARDING THE PLANE, Vito noticed that he had picked up a tail from the FEU. He did not mind, as he figured he could use it to his advantage later. The night lights illuminated the small portal windows as the aircraft traveled down the runway, starting its forty-five-degree turn to head north/northwest. The city lights mesmerized him, Vito felt he could reach through the windows and run his fingertips across the peaks of the city's skyscrapers. He felt the necklace around his neck vibrate and silently thanked Joan for showing him what loneliness was all about. *May you rest in peace and may God's perpetual light shine upon you.*

He laid his head back, closed his eyes, and fell into a deep sleep. When he awoke, the plane was in its final descent. Shaking his head, he realized he had slept the whole ten hours.

According to his calculations, he had another couple hours

before he arrived at the college.

Vito shut the taxi door and looked around at the storybook setting with its century-old gingerbread houses nestled amid a lush, wooded landscape. Here and there, open fields and fenced courts suggested the focus on sports for which the school was well known.

Vito stopped one of the students passing by. "Hello, is there was a place where someone might get something to drink?"

The young man tilted his head and smiled. "You've come a long way, haven't you? By the way, love the accent. Ain't you some sort of priest or something?

"Why yes, I am. The collar must have given it away."

The kid snorted. "You allowed to drink?"

Vito couldn't help but laugh. "I believe I am old enough."

The kid shook his head and winked. "Okay, man." He turned and pointed to the other side of the campus. "If traditional beverages are what you want, coffee or soda, there's Cal's up the road. If you're looking for libations, you can go to the Derby and Sash around the corner and across the street, and you should have some fun there."

"How about a place to stay?"

"You're in luck. The Derby and Sash is right across the street from the Garfield Ledges Inn.

Hours later, after checking in, Vito stood in the evening

dusk; he saw the driveway leading to the Derby and Sash Tavern. The gray stones looked like a carpeted landscape with old, blackened, oil-soaked railroad ties, creating T-shaped parking spots. Large white pine trees surrounded the tavern. The largest old pine grew so close that it looked like it was touching the building by the side door. The Derby and Sash Tavern was lit up by old fashion incandescent lamplights that threw a soft, warm, yellow glow on the doorways and drive.

The whitewash that covered the outside of the building was cracked and peeling and reflected light in off-beaten shapes. Years worth of paint had sealed the windows shut.

This should be interesting.

Once inside, a gentle, warm feeling came over him. The bar area seemed friendly with laughter and soft music. He was waiting there when the bartender asked what he was drinking. "I'll have one of your namesakes."

"That will be a Derby and Sash. $4.25."

Vito gave him the 10000 lire and smiled.

The bartender turned the bill over in his hand. "What the hell is this?"

Vito's smile faded. "It's a 10,000-lire note, Italian money." A few customers laughed. "You ain't in Italy, dumb fuck. You're in the good ole United States." The bartender picked up on this, crumpled up the note, and threw it back in Vito's face. Vito smiled, picked up the bill, unwrinkled it, slapped it back down on the bar, and slid it forward.

The bartender took back the drink, picked up the lire,

and shoved it back into Vito's chest. Vito didn't budge. A man standing behind him pushed him and said, "Hey asshole, we don't take that cartoon money here."

Two things happened simultaneously. The man next to him went to punch him. At the same time, the man behind the bar raised the whiskey bottle to hit him in the back of the head. Vito moved sideways, used an outside-to-inside parry to get behind the man, and pushed him toward the bartender, who came down with the bottle and knocked the man out.

Vito turned and was getting ready to put the bartender down when a loud explosive voice yelled, "Enough." They all turned except Vito, who stayed ready.

"What's going on here?"

The bartender trembled, his adrenaline having amped him up. "Pete," he yelled, "this joker tried to pay for his drink with this cartoon money."

Walking over to Vito, the man called Pete smiled, grabbed the lire, looked at it, and then looked at Vito. "Where did you get this? I'd better hear the truth from you, my friend, or you'll wish you'd got thirsty somewhere else. Capeesh?"

Vito looked the man in the eye. "A friend of mine, Joan Vitale, gave it to me."

Pete turned to the bartender. "Lex, you're fired. Get out of here. I don't want to see you again. Take these two idiots with you. Empty your pockets first. Now go. What? You didn't know, I knew you were stealing from me. Get out. I'll be keeping your last check."

Pete turned and smiled. "How is Joan?"

Vito's strong Sicilian face went slack. "I'm sorry to tell you she's dead."

Pete poured himself a shot, lifted it to Joan, and drank. Almost an hour later, Vito had filled Pete in, and Pete gave him the strange message Joan had given him to tell Vito. It had three parts: 1) Good things come in threes, 2) Find the seat that is across from the time, and 3) find what your third item is. Vito picked up his drink and looked around the bar.

The lower area of the bar was made of hand-peeled, wooden log walls. Some of the logs still had bark on them. It seemed the more he walked around it, the more Vito felt like someone was watching him. The knots in the logs looked like eyes.

Knick-knacks and all types of paraphernalia filled the shelves. The corner shelves had old books and manuscripts on them.

Some tables were round and sat four people, while others were larger and sat six to eight. The four-person tables have lamps that doubled for antique candlestick phones and connected to other four-person tables.

Vito looked around until he found a table that felt right. He sat down, took a drink from his glass, and nodded. *This ain't half bad.* His eyes wandered through the crowd and over every table. Next, he checked the walls for a clock but found none. *Sitting across from the time,* he mused. There was no clock, he wore no watch, and he didn't see anyone with one. Everyone had cell phones. He took another sip of his drink and asked himself what is in threes? Of course. He was in the Derby and Sash drinking a Derby and Sash; he needed to find another Derby and Sash. His eyes roamed the room again, taking in every article of clothing, poster, painting, and decoration that could be a Derby or construed as one. Nothing. So…no Derby…what about a Sash? Again he looked the crowd over to see if anyone could be wearing a sash, but nothing. He lifted his head and scanned the room until he finally found what he was looking for.

He got up and wandered over to the window, a place to tell time—day from night. He looked at the window sash. *That's the third Sash.* On a shelve below it, sat an oddball item that had nothing to do with the magic motif of the place. He picked up the cylinder, slipped it into his pocket, finished his drink, silently thanked Joan, and left with a nod to the new bartender for the night, Pete.

Back inside his room at the inn, Vito looked at the cylinder. It reminded him of an old fashion music roll. Looking end to end down the center of the roll, he could see something inside. He opened the desk drawer and found a pen that he used to push out a rolled-up paper. Unrolling it, he found nothing on either side of the parchment. He knew what this was. He needed a trip to the store. He called a taxi, whose driver recommended the all-night Walmart Supercenter in Streetsboro and was willing to wait for him. Vito picked up his items and was back at the inn within the hour. The taxi driver drove off with a grin, compliments of the generous tip Vito gave him.

Mixing half a cup of rubbing alcohol with one teaspoon of turmeric, he patted down the paper roll, and instantly something began to show. Fifteen minutes later, the invisible ink produced the following document in. He read.

Αναμειγνύοντας μισό φλιτζάνι αλκοόλ τρίψιμο με ένα κουταλάκι του γλυκού κουρκουμά, χτύπησε το ρολό χαρτιού και αμέσως κάτι άρχισε να φαίνεται. Δεκαπέντε λεπτά αργότερα, διάβασε, Vito, αυτό που κρατάτε είναι ένα μουσικό ρολό τροποποιημένο για να περιέχει έναν κώδικα αποκρυπτογράφησης.

Πρέπει να πάτε στο κτίριο διοίκησης και να πάρετε έναν χάρτη εδάφους. Αυτός ο χάρτης θα αντιστοιχεί με τις πλευρές που είναι αναρτημένες σε όλους τους διαδρόμους από τούβλα και ψαροκόκαλο. Βρείτε ένα μέρος για διαλογισμό. εδώ θα υπάρχει ένα όργανο του χρόνου. Πρέπει να ενεργοποιήσετε τον κύλινδρο για να ξεκινήσετε την Ώρα του Ελέους.

Για να προετοιμάσετε το ρολόι, πρέπει να πιέσετε προς τα κάτω το κεντρικό κομμάτι και να το γυρίσετε αντίστροφα και να τραβήξετε προς τα πάνω το κεντρικό κομμάτι, βγάζοντάς το από το στέλεχος που γλιστράει στον κύλινδρο στο στέλεχος. Μπορεί να πάει μόνο με έναν τρόπο. Αντικαταστήστε το κεντρικό κομμάτι και πιέστε προς τα κάτω μέχρι να κουμπώσει και, στη συνέχεια, περιστρέψτε δεξιόστροφα σε μία πλήρη περιστροφή. Τώρα έχει οριστεί για την Ώρα του Ελέους

"Vito, you are holding a music roll modified to contain a decipher code. You must go to the administration building at the college and get a grounds map. This map will correspond with the signposts on all the brick and herringbone walkways. Find a place for meditation; there will be an instrument of time there. You must activate the cylinder to start at the Hour of Mercy."

"To prepare the timepiece, you must push down on the centerpiece, turn it counter clockwise, and pull up on the centerpiece, taking it out of the stem. Slid the cylinder into the stem; it can only go one way. Replace the centerpiece and push down until it clicks, then turn it clockwise in one full rotation. It will then be set for the Hour of Mercy."

A bell rang as Vito entered the administration building. The person behind the counter said, "I'll be with you in a moment." As Sister Genevie rounded the corner, her mouth fell open. There stood the man that shredded her heart. He never knew that he had affected her in that way. She now stood emotionally naked in front of him.

"Genevie, is that you? Oh my God, it is," Vito roared.

She swallowed her pride. "Vito? That is you, isn't it? Oh my." She came around the counter and hugged him. He grabbed her and spun her around. She felt a flood of mixed emotions pierce her heart. The office space was so tight that Vito knocked Genevie into some chairs and the people sitting in them as they watched the pleasant reunion. Some laughed with their excitement while the others got out of the way.

"What are you doing here?"

Vito laughed. "What are you doing as a nun?"

"Well, it's one heck of a story."

"You'll have to tell me sometime. Right now, I could use your help."

"What is it that you need?"

Vito grabbed her hand and nodded toward the door.

"Sure. Beth, can you please help up front? Thank you. I'll be outside for a moment."

Vito led her into the hallway. "So, how long have you been here?" he asked.

"For a little while."

"Would you happen to know a student named Joan Vitale?"

"Oh my, I was just talking about her. Why do you ask?"

"I'm down here on a mission."

"A mission for who?"

Vito's face turned red. He faced her, reached into his back pocket, and pulled out a letter from the Pope. As Genevie read it aloud, her face broke into a disbelieving grin.

> Cardinal Vito Rosario, in Pectore. In charge of the RPCP: Retrieval and Procurement of Christ Passion. This extends to acquisition and preservation.

She laughed nervously. *Oh boy, God does have a sense of humor. Cardinal Lintzinburg never told me Vito was a cardinal in the church.*

"What time do you get off work?"

"I can get off about anytime I want. Is now a good time?"

"Yes, please."

"Let's go back in. I'll need to tell Beth I'm leaving."

"Okay, do you have a meditation garden on the grounds? If you do, can you take me there?"

"Of course." Sister Genevie excused herself and collected her things.

They walked in silence as Genevie led the way. Vito clutched his letter between his hands as they walked. Finally, she broke the silence. "How do you know about our meditation gardens, and what are you looking for?"

"I have so much to tell you, Genevie."

"That would be Sister Genevie."

"Yes, of course, I'm sorry."

"I have something to tell you, if this is about Joan…" They both broke into silence not knowing who should go first.

Vito watched the caretakers robotically move along the lawn, cutting and manicuring the beautiful grounds. As he and Genevie shuffled through the grass, the squirrels dropped their nuts and scampered away. Inside the gardens were overhead swings hanging from the adjacent building. Straight ahead was a water fountain. A tunnel made of flowers ran the entire length of the garden and colorful rose bushes—pink, yellow, and red—grew everywhere. The two sat on one of the hanging swings in awkward silence, neither of them not knowing what to say. Vito finally broke the silence.

Chapter Twenty-Four

"WELL, LET ME see if I can catch you up on what's been happening."

"With whom?"

"Joan and I. I met her at an awards ceremony in Israel, and we shared a table and dinner that night, and we got interested in one another."

Sister Genevie started to feel flush. She squirmed and turned away from him.

Vito went on, not noticing Genevie's discomfort. "I saved her from being kidnapped by her employer that night. He had hired her to find a relic. One of her employees was kidnapped and tortured when she tried to get the relic. She did not know that her employee worked for the FEU, the Federal Espionage Unit of the United States government. His name was Samir.

"Did Joan ever find out who her employee worked for?"

"I don't know, but he betrayed Joan and found himself dead. These people that hired her run the largest cabal in the world. I also believe that a faction of the church is involved with them."

Genevie shrunk in the swing as Vito cast blame on the church.

"It seems the cabal has plans for getting one of their own elected to the presidency of the United States and with that will come a spiritual war. But to accomplish this, they will first need an exceedingly extraordinary relic, and that's why they hired Joan—to find and dig up this relic. She worked for a man named Jake; the only other person's name that I know is Ron. Since we're dealing in the spiritual realm, I expect a spiritual equivalent of some sort will take place. I also have a letter from Joan that I must decipher before finding out where she hid the relics. This needs to be done before Jake finds them first."

"Maybe I can help you."

"I was counting on that." He pulled the folded letter out of his pocket. "I've got the first three clues:

> "1) The 10,000-lire note whose serial numbers got me to Simon College.
>
> "2) It bought me a drink and another clue to find a strange object. My reward was this cylinder." Vito shook the cylinder he was holding.
>
> "3) Inside the cylinder was a roll of parchment with nothing on it, until I figured out that she had used

> invisible ink and written it in a foreign language and backward. She also told me how to prepare the cylinder for the decipher code to be read."

"You must be pretty good at this stuff," Sister Genevie told him with begrudging admiration. "Now let's look at the parchment scroll and see what else there is to find."

Vito read out loud from the parchment scroll. "You must find a place to meditate and find a timepiece."

"That's an easy one. We're sitting on it. We have a sundial across from the fountain."

Of course, he thought, *a sundial.* He looked at Genevie's face and got lost in his thoughts. *My God, she is beautiful with the sun sparkling on the tips of her red hair and reflecting off her green eyes.* He shook his head and said, "it's a sundial, a timepiece. A time to meditate."

They both looked at the letter again and Vito said, "We have the meditation gardens and the sundial."

An unexpected strong gust of wind stormed through the gardens and blew the scroll out of Genevie's hand. She screamed, "Vito! The parchment!" She gave chase as the paper darted this way and that, followed by another burst that shot it upward. It wafted and floated to the ground right in front of Vito, and he stepped on the corner of the scroll. Genevie ran to pick it up, but she could not stop herself in time, and as she collided with Vito, the wind hefted the paper up again and tossed it straight into a passing lawnmower. All they heard was the ripping sound of the mower grinding the parchment to bits.

They looked at one another and Sister Genevie began to cry. He grabbed her and hugged her to calm her down as she rolled her eyes and gave a sly smile, tinted with only a tiny bit of remorse.

He broke off the hug and started to pace back and forth. There was something else he needed to do. As he tried to put his memories in order, a sense of failure was seeping into his mind; he felt he was losing control. He had to calm himself.

Concerned that she would not see her daughter again if she failed at her mission for the cardinal, Genevie grabbed him and shook him gently. "Vito," she whispered, we can figure this out. Come on, relax. Get that memory of yours working."

Vito's head started to tingle as he touched Joan's necklace around his neck. He began a silent prayer for God's help not to go into a flashback, but it was too late. His mind felt that familiar pain and saw the blinding light.

His hands hit his temples, and he fell to his knees, wailing "Papa, Mama." There they stood. His father with one arm missing and a hole in his chest, his mother with a hole in her face, walking toward him. "Why, Vito. How could you do this to us?" she pleaded.

She reached for him. Vito grabbed his mother, bringing her close and squeezing her. "I didn't do this, please. I love you."

Vito felt a set of strong hands grab him from behind and yank him up and away from Sister Genevie, whom he was strangling.

Billy could feel the presence of God all around him. He said a silent prayer as he placed his hands on Vito's head. Vito's eyes sprung wide open, and he no longer saw the bright light. He felt calm as he looked around. Sister Genevie was holding her throat. Billy was helping her up, saying a prayer for her healing.

"What happened? Oh my God, what have I done?" he said, noticing his outstretched hands.

Genevie screamed at Vito. "You could have killed me. What happened to you? If it weren't for Billy, I might be dead." She looked at Billy. "Thank you for your help. You probably saved my life."

"Since Joan's death, I have been getting flashbacks and I don't know why. They are always about my family's deaths. I see their mutilated bodies. I'm so sorry, Genevie. Can you please forgive me?"

"Are you going to be okay"

"I, I think so." Vito looked around to see Billy staring at him. "Thank you so much." He grabbed Billy's hand to shake it and felt a strong current run through his own body. He looked into Billy's eyes and saw all the peace in the world looking back at him. He dropped Billy's hand, took a step backward, and felt the answers to everything and nothing run through his exasperated brain.

Billy smiled. "Are you all right?"

"I am now."

"Good. My name is Billy. I just learned your name from Sister yelling it out."

"Billy, how are you?" Genevie said as she bowed her head, a little embarrassed.

"You guys sure know how to greet someone."

"Let's try this again," said Genevie. "Billy, I'd like you to meet an old friend of mine. His name is Vito."

Turning to shake Vito's hand, Billy said, "You don't look well. Is everything okay?"

"I just got some bad news, that's all," Vito replied, shaking Billy's hand. "Thank you for intervening."

"You're welcome. Always glad to help. I'm sorry about your bad news. Is there anything I can help you with?"

"No, I'll be all right." Vito walked to the circle of bricks surrounding the sundial and studied it.

"Do you like old sundials?" Billy asked.

"I like all old treasures of mankind. They tell us stories about our civilization."

"You're in luck. You'll like that one. If you look down, you'll see all types of symbols on the corner of each brick. I always wanted to know what they meant. If you ever find out, please, tell me."

Vito looked down and saw what Billy was talking about. There was a crazy-looking symbol on one corner of every brick. As he was studying them, the sun came out from behind the clouds, reflecting off the sundial and onto one of the bricks, and it lit up the symbol on it. Vito smiled.

Billy looked up at the bell tower. "Doggone it. The weathervane isn't moving, and the fraternity students probably dared their pledges to tie it down again. Please excuse me."

When Billy had walked out of earshot, Vito turned to Genevie. "Sister, look at this," he said, pointing to the bricks. They followed the symbols around the sundial, and each brick had a small mark in the upper corner.

"Now which symbols and in what order are we to put them?"

He smiled at her waving the cylinder and I remembered what the paper said. He walked to the sundial and pushed down on the dial in the center. When he heard a click, he turned it counterclockwise and lifted the dial out of the unit's stem. Then he lined up the cylinder and dropped it in, replaced the dial and turned it one whole rotation clockwise. The unit was now set.

Vito looked at his watch. It was 2:56 p.m. and he remembered the Hour of Mercy. "Sister? Do you have any paper with you?"

Genevie nodded and dug through her purse.

"Get ready to write what you see. You will see symbols lighting up on those bricks if I am right. Are you ready?"

"Just a second…okay, I'm ready."

They stepped back and waited to see what would happen next. The more sunlight hit the dial, the more they heard a hum. The bells chimed the three o'clock hour, the hour of mercy, the time of Christ's death.

Vito crowded around Sister Genevie to see what she was writing. She wrote each symbol down carefully, making sure not to tear the paper as she wrote.

Billy returned and paused to observe them. Both were holding their breath. "Looks like you guys are deep into something. I must be going. It was nice to meet you, Vito."

"You too," said Vito as he looked deep into Billy's eyes.

A deep comfort come over him.

Without looking up, Genevie said, "Have a good afternoon, Billy. I'll see you soon."

Vito paced the gardens in prayer. Sometime later, he could wait no longer. He ran up to Sister. "Did you get them all?" he asked.

Waving the paper in his face, she jumped with glee. "Yes!"

As Billy hurried to get back to his students, he turned to look at Vito once more and nodded with a smile. Vito tilted his head and smiled back.

"There's something about that guy. He has such an angelic way about him," Genevie whispered.

Vito watched the young man walk away. "Yeah, I noticed that too."

Chapter Twenty-Five

Sister Genevie handed Vito the paper with the symbols on. "Now, what do we do?"

יש לך כל כך הרבה מצוין. ידעתי שתבין את זה. אחרי הכל, מצאת את
הרשומה ביחידת ההי-פיי. אם הייתי אתה, הייתי קונה חבילה של מקלות זוהרים
לקחת איתי. אתה תצטרך אור כדי לעזור למצוא את מתגי האור. ובכן, תצטרך
להיכנס למנהרות מתחת למכללת היירם. לך לקדמת האודיטוריום. משמאל
למדרגות המובילות לדלתות הכפולות, תוכלו לראות מעלית. פתח את הדלת
אבל אל תתוו לא. תצטרך להשתמש בידית נסתרת מתחת לרצפת הפלדה. רצפת
הפלדה מתאימה לתחתית בחוזקה. ישנן שתי דרכים לפתוח אותו. אחד משתמש
מגנט כבד כי יהיה להרים את הדלת גבוה מספיק כדי שאתה מקבל את הידיים
שלך מתחת ולהרים. השני הוא להחליק משהו חזק וצר בין הרצפה לקירות ולחטט
כלפי מעלה. ברגע שזה נעשה, תראה גרם מדרגות מעגלי יורד. קח את המדרגות
בתחתית; תיזהר שיהיה חשוך. השתמש בידיים שלך כדי להרגיש במורד המנהרה
על חמישה מטרים ולהרגיש סביב עד שאתה מרגיש מתג אור. תלחץ על זה.
זה ייתן לך אור עמום. אבל אתה תראה דלת פלדה בתוך קיר המנהרה. יש רק
דרך אחת לפתוח את הדלת הזאת; תסתכל בתחתית הדלת, תראה איך זה קובע
לתוך מסלול שקבור עמוק לתוך הרצפה. עכשיו יש ידית שצריכה להיות מדוכאת,
והדלת תשוחרר. ברגע שאתה מושך אותו פתוח, תצטרך להחזיק אותו פתוח.
ברגע שתעזוב את הדלת, היא תיסגר, אז תהיה מאוד זהיר. עכשיו שאתה בצד
השני של הדלת, תצטרך למצוא מתג אור אחר. תפתח את אחד מקלות הזוהר
האלה, תמצא את המתג ותדליק את המנהרה. תעקוב אחרי המנהרה עד שתגיע
להסתה. הימין ייקח אותך דרך לתא. זה שימש לרכבת התחתית בשנות ה-1800.
ללכת שמאלה יביא אותך לחדר עינויים בשימוש על ידי אדם שעבד פעם במכללה.
תפסנו אותו במהלך הפשיטה שלנו על המנהרות בחיפוש אחר העידנים החדשים.
תמשיך לעבור דרך התא הזה, ואתה תלך כמה צעדים שמובילים לחדר המגדלים.
הנה השרתים המשמשים לשידור ההודעות הנסתרות שלהם באתר אינטרנט חינם
של משחקים לילדים. עבור סט המגדלים האחרון ופתח את מארז השרתים,
ותראה חבילות. תוציא אותם, ויהיו לך את שני השרידים. אחד מהם הוא הקוץ
שנגנב מכתר הקוצים של ישו. השנייה היא קופסת עצמות שלא היה לי זמן להביא
איך לפתוח. אז אני לא יודע מה יש בתוכו. בהצלחה ויטו.

He took the symbols, "all right, Sister, let me recap my journey for you. First I received a 10000-lire note which got me to the Derby and Sash. Next was the cylinder I found at the bar. Inside that was the parchment that brought us to these symbols."

"Joan like to use a lot of secrecy."

"Yes, she did." He started to read, then paused. "They have one more instruction: Remember Exodus 24:4. She said it would send me in a new direction to find the cipher."

"What does Exodus 24:4 say?"

"Google gives this interpretation."

> *And Moses wrote the words of the Lord. And he rose early in the morning and built an altar at the mountain, and twelve pillars, according to the Twelve Tribes of Israel.*

"Where is the campus library? I want to check this translation out."

"Funny, you should ask. It's right behind you."

"Let's go."

A breathtaking expanse of grass, flowers, and trees flanked the herringbone walkway leading to the library steps. Once inside, Sister Genevie walked straight to the religious section and removed the first bible she saw. At the same time, Vito looked for his favorite bible, the Ignatius Bible. They compared the wording of the translations, and agreed on the Exodus 24:4 verse from his favorite:

> *And Moses wrote all the words of the Lord. And he rose early in the morning and built an altar at the foot of the mountain, and twelve pillars, according to the Twelve Tribes of Israel.*

"So, we know that Moses has the ten commandments and that he went and built an altar, at the foot of the mountain. Twelve pillars, according to Israel's Twelve Tribes. This was to be a peace offering to the Lord."

"What does that have to do with the cipher?" Genevie asked.

"I don't know…I don't know if it's the altar that we need to look at, or if there's something in the Twelve Tribes that tell us about codes. It could even be that the Lord spoke in a way only Moses could understand. We need to look at some of the original transcripts of the Bible, and the only place I know where we can get those is at the Vatican."

She gave him a curious look. "Is it possible for us to do that?"

"Of course, it's possible. I'm the curator of all ancient relics belonging to the Vatican. I will book a flight to Rome for this afternoon. What does your work situation look like?"

"I'd have to talk to my mother superior to see if I can get off work for this."

"Do you want me to talk to the Pope for you? Or would a letter from a cardinal help?"

"How long do you think it will take?"

"We must get this done ASAP. I don't know how long it will

take to get all the answers."

"Ok, let me find out if my mother superior will allow me a quick vacation." She picked up her phone and went around the corner. She hit speed dial number one.

"This is Cardinal Lintzinburg."

"Listen, I need to travel with Vito to help him decipher the clues. We'll be in Rome by tonight or tomorrow morning. I'll call when we land." She came back around the corner only to bump into Vito. *Shit, did he hear me?* She flashed him a smile. "All is good on my end."

"I believe I heard Jake say there was only one week to get this done, so if we don't come up with the answer in a few days, all hell will break loose. And I'm afraid I mean that quite literally."

Chapter Twenty-Six

Billy's hundred- and thirty-five-pound German Shepherd barked before the doorbell rang. Billy peeked out the window and saw the U.S. Postal Service at the door. "All right, HD, sit, I'll get it." No one knew exactly what HD stood for or why Billy called his dog that. Actually, HD didn't really belong to Billy. He was more a companion to the professor. HD was a force unto himself.

Billy opened the door for the mail carrier, who smiled and said, "Good afternoon." She looked down at her clipboard. "Are you Billy Campbell?"

"Yes, ma'am."

"I have a certified package for you. Please sign here."

Billy signed the delivery form and took the package. "Thank you, Have a good day," he said absently, closing the door behind him. He opened the attached envelope and removed a letter. His whole body went on high alert, as did HD's, even before he read it. He recognized the handwriting.

Dear Billy,

I hope this letter finds you well. As for me, I'm not so well. I am sorry that I couldn't call you back. I have found myself in a similar situation that you found me in all those years ago with the New Agers, and I know now that this is a spiritual war. On top of that, a rigged presidential election is clearly underway. I have no time to get into it, but I could use your help again. You will find two exceedingly rare relics in the package I have sent you. One is a thorn from the crown of thorns Christ was forced to wear at his crucifixion; the other is a bone box that you believe to contain the one drop of Christ's blood.

Remember the towers of servers inside the tunnels that we found while investigating the New Agers. Would you please locate the package there? My new friend Vito will come looking for them through a set of clues I have arranged for him to receive. Vito is a good, Godly man, and a cardinal in the Church. I believe he can and will take care of himself.

Please be careful. My ex-boss will be looking for these relics too. I have tried to throw him off the trail, to give Vito time.

Now, for the bad news, if you are reading this, I am dead.

Please watch over Vito without interference.

Good luck and thank you for all you have done for me in the past and will do in the future. I imagine I could really use some prayers.

Love,

Joan

Chapter Twenty-Seven

JAKE ENTERED HIS study panic-stricken, looking to the crackling fire to calm him. To no avail. The fire did light a path to his tan, worn leather and mahogany chair behind a desk of rich hand crafted mahogany. As he sat down and tried to open his desk drawer but he was terrified and his hands were quivering. *This Kristoff has lost his mind.* Jake grabbed for his pistol when something tickled his brain; in his drawer was an envelope with Joan's handwriting on it. He glared at it, studied the letter, turned it over and back again, smiled, and opened it.

Jake,

You are a bastard. How can you make a person fall in love with you by pushing all the right buttons, then turn around and lie to them, and finally put them in grave danger? To say nothing of the way you set me up with that Kristoff madman.

I did fall for you and the whirlwind relationship—the trips, shopping sprees, first-class travel, and accommodations wherever we went. Yes, I did see that love you had for me, and how it would pop up and shine through that facade of yours that you wore like cheap armor.

You sent me on a fool's errand, not telling me how important and dangerous the dig was. This mission forced me to lie, cheat, steal, and even kill, and I will never forgive you for that. And, if I have anything to do with it, you will never see those relics. They are safely hidden outside the country.

~Joan.

Jake lowered his head. He couldn't shake off the loneliness of missing her. He noticed something odd. He placed the letter under the dim lamplight and saw the impression of another letter written on top of his letter from Joan. He reached inside his top middle desk drawer, moved the paper clips and staples out of the way, pulled out a pencil, and shaded the letter.

Underneath Joan's letter to him was a letter from her to Billy Campbell and the answer to all his problems. With a smile, he calmly put his gun away, pulled out his cell phone, and hit number one. Ron answered in two rings. "Ron, get up here to my study. We have a breakthrough and I have a mission for you."

Chapter Twenty-Eight

The lettering on the door read: *Literature 101.* The new semester had started, and college students clamored into the lecture hall as rain poured outside. A whiff of dampened compost circulated the room. The professor's feet dangled from the front of his desk, and he nodded to his students.

This was going to be one hell of a storm.

The professor yelled just above the noise, "Welcome, students. My name is Professor Billy Campbell; let's take a seat. I realize this is the beginning of a new semester and today is Friday, and we can't wait for the weekend, but I promise to make this exciting, especially since we will meet only on Fridays.

The chatter had settled to a whisper when the glint of light off a nose ring got Billy's attention. One student dressed in all black yelled out, "What are we going to study this semester?"

Billy shook his head. "We'll look at the mysterious, bizarre, and unexplainable."

Some students looked at one another and smiled; another said, "Cool, this should be different." Lightning cracked outside the windows, and the lights flickered out. The eighty-year-old building was showing its wear and tear. A loud groan turned to a deafening silence. He pulled out his cell phone and turned the flashlight on. His shadow took on the appearance of Quasimodo.

Billy started to tell a story to pass the time when the lights suddenly flickered back on, and the classroom door was kicked open. Three men marched in and trained their guns on the professor. Some of the students jumped, while others screamed and wrap their arms around themselves to give protection to themselves. The man who seemed to be in charge, the one dressed in sport coat, dress shirt, and khaki pants yelled, "Are you Billy Campbell?"

The flash of guns, the screams from the students, and the fake bravado all sounded and looked like a cheap movie playing. The professor waved his hands for quiet and got it immediately. "Students, stay still." He turned to the intruders and said, "What can I do for you?"

"Ben collect all the cell phones now," the sport coat guy said, as he walked to the front of the class. "If I see anyone trying anything stupid, trying to be a hero, I will have my man Sam, the nervous one over there, shoot you. Do we all understand the consequences?"

They all shook their heads and pulled out their phones.

The headman put his gun away. "Professor, we've been employed by a mutual friend's employer. We know that you have our relic, and we want it. This can go easy, or it can go badly, especially for your students."

"Leave the students out of this. They know nothing."

"Where is the relic?" Sam, the tall skinny man shouted.

Billy looked at the third man, the nervous type waving a gun around at no one in particular. "Let's go. I'll show you. Just leave the students out of this."

"I'm leaving one of my men here," the head henchman said. "Ben, just in case we're not back within..." He looked at the professor, "How long?"

"An hour," Billy replied.

"You heard him. In one hour, start looking for us and take one of the students just in case," the man with the gun said. "All right, Billy, let's go get a relic," he said as he shoved Billy forward.

Chapter Twenty-Nine

"JUST FOLLOW ME," Billy said, as they stepped into the harsh rain of the late afternoon storm. Howling winds and fog were beginning to descend on campus. "It's not that far."

"Make sure you stay within arm's length of us," one of the men yelled.

Billy guided the two shooters around the lecture hall and down the side of the auditorium; the strong winds puffed out their sport coats as they fought to stay calm. Their pant legs got soaked as they trudged through the bushes and flowers.

"Don't try anything heroic," the leader said.

"See the front of the building by the stairs? There is an elevator next to them. We'll have to get to that booth, open the door and pull up on the false floor. A set of circular stairs will run into the underground tunnel system. I'll go first, then you guys follow."

"No. Sam here will go first, then you, then me. Got it?"

Billy nodded.

Once inside the tunnels, Sam nodded to Joe, looking around, "Let's get in and out of this place. I don't like it in here."

The maze of tunnel walls was made up of old stone and clay with metal inserts here and there. The floor had some brick in it; most areas had trampled down rock and stone with cement, covered with a layer of dirt. The pungent odor made him nauseous. There was old conduit from the late 1800s hanging everywhere.

The walls were wet from the humidity. There were separate rooms with beds built into some of the walls, while other rooms had plain old wooden bunks. Rotted Burlap dresses and sacks lay about the floors. Twine rope, 40 inches in length to a half-inch in width laid about. It could have been used for men's belts or to tie someone up.

There had been an attempt to add electricity throughout the tunnels, and in some areas, it had succeeded. Where the lights worked, there gave off only a soft glow of light, dulled by the dingy, dirty bulbs.

The cold breeze whistled as it blew by the mold and dank water. When it came through, it gave them goosebumps. In some areas, the tunnel width was about three feet, wider in others. Some of the rooms were large with areas sunken down to give the room a more significant ceiling height. Some sort of nets hung from the ceiling.

The tunnels and rooms mirrored what was above.

"I need to find us some light," Billy said as they got further into the tunnels.

Two of the men were sweating in their sport coats from the dank humidity. "Hurry up, let's get the package."

Billy felt along the wall until he came upon the light switch and flipped it on. A dim light flickered overhead.

He trudged across the tunnel and found the hidden metal door. "I need to slide this door open.

"What door?"

"Look closer."

A door hidden in the wall was in front of him on the side of the tunnel. Be careful and stand back." As they did so, Billy stepped on the latch, unleashing the door with his foot. He scampered through the doorway, which sprung closed behind him, leaving the other two guys on the opposite side of the door, yelling, "Shit. Get back here!"

Sam's face with his pug nose and caterpillar eyebrows was so full of fear it almost looked comical. They pulled out their cell phones to call Ben, but there was no signal. As they looked around trying to find a way out they both could not shake the feeling they were being watched. They gave off an odor of fear from their sweat-drenched shirts. When they tried to speak to one another, their tongues stuck to the roofs of their mouths. Joe walked intrepidly until his labored breathing took its toll; then he had to rest. The longer they were in this damn tunnel the more claustrophobic they felt.

"Stay here and try to open this door," Sam said to his partner.

"I'll follow the tunnel to see if I can get in or out another way."

Meanwhile, Billy sped through the tunnels, opening and closing certain areas, sealing the relics from the two men. As Billy passed close to the relics, his entire body started to vibrate subtly; he knew he was in the presence of the divine.

Chapter Thirty

BEN STEPPED AROUND the front desk and held the pistol so all the students could see it. He heard his phone vibrate. Clawing for it in his side coat pocket, he hit the receive button and yelled, "Hello."

"I need an update now," Ron hammered.

"I'm here in the classroom waiting for Joe and Sam to come back with the relic."

"How long have you been in that room?"

"We got here and grabbed Billy. I assume Joe and Sam have him somewhere in the tunnels trying to get the relic. It's been about hour."

"Damn, it's too risky for you to be in that room. I want you out of there, Get back to the Garfield Ledges Inn, and wait till you hear from us."

"But Joe told me to grab a student and look for them. It's been over an hour."

"Listen, numb nuts, do you remember what happened to the two shooters who killed Joan? Now do what I tell you and get the hell out of there."

Ron made a phone call to Jake; Jake and Kristoff sat and listened to Ron tell his story, "Hey boss, one of the morons was holding a whole classroom hostage while the other two went with this Billy Campbell guy to get the relics."

Kristoff heard Billy Campbell's name and slammed his hand down on the table. His eyes flashed red with satanic lust. "Ron, leave that man to me. I'll take care of him. Gather your men, send them back to the hotel, and wait for our call."

"Ron, you get on with your mission," Jake said. as he turned to Kristoff. "Do you know this, Billy Campbell?"

"Yes, I do. We went head-to-head on another matter some years ago, and I owe him some extraordinary attention. Wait here." Kristoff retired into his room alone.

All Jake could see was a red and purplish light from under the door. He could smell the sulfur, and it made him gag. He thought he was going to throw up.

"Yes, master?" The demon retribution said.

"Do you remember your predecessor and how he died at the hands of a man named Billy Campbell?"

"If I remember correctly, sir, he is no man. He's an angel."

"I have a job for you. You cannot kill him, but I want you to put the hurt on this Angel of God. He has been hiding amongst men for too long and interfering with my plans over time. Go to Garfield Ledges Township, You will feel his presence as you get closer. Take a dozen of your best warriors with you. I need you to hold him till I summon you. Remember, you cannot kill him, or you will tip my hand before I am ready."

As Billy walked back to his classroom, some students were milling around outside the door to his classroom. Others took off. "Are you all right?" asked a couple of his students. "The man they called Ben got a phone call and just left."

Billy waved his hands. "Please. Is anyone hurt?"

They all said "No," but that didn't stop the questions. "What's going on?" "Who were those guys?" "Where did they take you?" "Why did they take you?"

Waving his hands again, Billy yelled above the noise. "Listen. They thought I had something of theirs."

A few of them yelled out the same question, "Did you?" and "Where are they now?"

"No, I don't have anything of theirs, and I lost them on the other side off campus by the sports complex. Now get out of here and go home. I'll need to get the campus office to report this."

They wander off, saying their "Good-byes."

Billy's whole body started to tingle, and not in a good way. The last time he had felt like this he had been under attack by demons. The sky grew darker and the smell of sulfur fouled the air.

The last student had just turned the corner when a bolt of light hit Billy from behind. He hit the ground, tumbling forward and then sideways as more bolts hit all around him. Billy slid behind some bushes and knelt, stretching his palms up. He started to pray, gathering more and more strength from his prayers. Finally ready, he stood in the center of the attack and let the power of his angelic prayer fly. A ripple in the atmosphere and the bending of light was all that human sight could perceive.

Billy looked around with a smile until he heard a whisper too late that four demons had descended upon him. They encircled him and each demon clenched one of his extremities and stretched his body out spread-eagle. The more Billy struggled, the more demons took shots at him. His energy and prayers almost exhausted, the ordeal had become unbearable. With every blow, he got weaker. They did not stop until Billy bowed his head and looked like he was dying.

"Stop," came a hideous voice above all other sounds. "Do not kill him. Take him into the tunnels now."

As though out of nowhere, one last attack struck Billy in the heart; the only sound heard was a warrior's cry. Billy's head flopped one way and then another before he bowed and slumped over. The last demon Quietus shook with fear, for his bolt had flown before the lord demon called for a halt. Turning to fly away, he flew right into the lord demon himself.

"Master, that bolt flew before your command reached my ears," he said.

"No worries, you will never live to see the results." The master demon buried his hand deep into the lower demon's chest and ripped out its essence.

Chapter Thirty-One

VITO PLACED SISTER Genevie's bags above her seat and put his luggage case next to hers. Closing the hatch, he noticed his travel FEU companions from the first trip, plus two more. He recognized them as Ron's men. Waiting until take off, Vito went to the back restroom, ignoring all four agents. Before reaching the bathroom door handle, a woman flashed an FEU badge at Vito. Utilizing a stage whisper, she said, "There are two of us aboard with you." She smiled and started to walk past him to use the bathroom on the other side of the plane.

"Be careful," Vito said. "There are two others on board. From Jake, I'm sure."

The flight attendant walked up and down the aisle. Over the intercom system, they heard the announcement: "Would you please take your seats for take-off to Rome? This international flight will be ten hours and thirty-six minutes. Please place your trays in an upright position, seats forward, and fasten your seatbelts. Thank you."

Jake's limo pulled into the Garfield Ledges Inn. He was booked into Room 100 and had the chauffeur take his bags inside. "Al, get hold of the men and meet me at the Township Tower."

About half an hour later, the men ordered their dinners, and Jake started the meeting. "Sam, can you get us back into those tunnels?"

"Yes, I can."

"Good. Tonight, we'll get in there and have a look around. What will we need?"

"Flashlights and some jimmying tools should do it."

"All right. Get it done. We'll meet back at my room at midnight."

Jake and his men made their way through the grounds of Simon College as the stark white clouds against the sky's black curtain played a game of hide-and-seek with the moonlight. Ben turned on his flashlight, and Jake slapped him on the back of the head. "Turn that light off. We'll be seen a mile away."

"Jake, there's the elevator," Sam said. "I'll raise the false floor and get us down there."

Sam went first, followed by Jake, Ben, and Joe. "Now, turn your lights on," Jake said. The men shone their lights around the tunnels, looking for the switch that Billy had used.

"Here it is." Sam flipped the switch. Nothing happened. Jake and Ben kept looking around, while Sam and Joe started to argue.

"Is that the right switch?" Joe yelled.

"Of course, it is. It's the only one on the wall."

"This Billy is smarter than you give him credit for," Jake said. "He came back and killed the electricity. You better pray that he didn't remove the box with the relics in it, or you'll both be removed."

"All right," Joe said. "Shine those lights on that wall; there's supposed to be a hidden door inside it."

"I don't see anything on this wall," Ben said.

"Come on, it was there, right, Joe?" Sam said.

"Yes, that's how he got away."

"Let me see." Jake got down on his knees and examined the floor and wall. Brushing away the loose dirt that lay around the wall, Jake found a track. Following the track, Jake came upon a footswitch. He stood up. "Get back," he said before he hit the switch. A door appeared and shot to the right.

Joe started through the door.

"No," Sam yelled, but it was too late.

Jake took his foot off the pedal and the door sprung back. Joe screamed as it crushed his foot, tearing it halfway off the bone. Jake stepped back on the switch, and the door sprang open again. Sam grabbed Joe and pulled him back.

"Get him out of the way," Jake shouted over Joe's agonized

moans. "Let's get that damn door open!"

Ben wrapped Joe's foot and whispered, "We'll get you out of here as soon as we can. Hang in there."

Meanwhile, Jake opened the door again, but this time he kept his foot on the pedal, and sent Sam in to find out if there was a lock on the other side of the door. Sam scoured the chamber and found nothing but another tunnel. He followed it twenty feet in and found more of nothing except for a broken conduit tube running along the wall. Fearful, he grabbed it anyway and ripped it off the wall. Yelling, "I got something," he brought it back, wires and all, and placed it into the channel that held the door open.

"Back up," Jake said as he took his foot off the pedal. The door stayed open. "Sam, Ben, get in there and search that tunnel."

"Yes, boss."

Jake went back to check on Joe. "How are you holding up?"

"It hurts like hell, but I'll make it."

"Good. I'll send Sam to get you when we find the relics. Sit tight." Jake turned to go through the door but paused. "Better yet, I'll just help you now." Turning back to face Joe, Jake pulled his gun, and put one bullet in Joe's head, another in his heart. "Sorry, you know I can't have any loose ends."

Coming up behind Sam and Ben, Jake saw a fork in the tunnels. "Each of you take a tunnel and find those relics."

As they walked through the tunnel, they scrutinized the tunnel walls, floor, and ceiling for other traps.

Billy summoned what strength he had left and prayed for help from above. Michael had watched Billy being tortured and knew he had to do something immediately. He sent a healing prayer arrow.

Michael stood before a host of angels, one hand on the scabbard of his sword and the other on the hilt. The host of angels bowed in prayer. "Billy, we cannot use a frontal assault to free you yet. But we will help you survive for now."

The prayer was invisible to all except angels, and the only thing the lessor demons would see is the result of the prayer. Only Lucifer would have been able to see it, being an angel himself, although a fallen one.

Billy shook violently and raised his head, whispering a prayer of thanksgiving and then addressed the demons. "You'll need more than that to kill me."

Incensed, the enormous demon Retribution stomped around and yelled with a hideous laugh, "Take him inside the tunnels to the room with the wire net hanging above some baskets. "The net is on a pulley. Crank the net down low enough to place this creature in it. Be careful not to grab the net. The wire is as sharp as a scalpel.

"What do we do then?" a lower demon asked.

"You crank the net back up and set the brake on the pulley. From below you can see that the wires of the net make diamond-shaped patterns. See those baskets? They are precisely cut into diamond-shaped pieces meant to catch body parts as they fall.

The weight of the person or angel's body in the net will slowly be cut as gravity pulls him through this net. It will take longer for the bone to sift through, but it still gets the job done."

"Lord, we're not supposed to kill him."

"Oh, he won't die. His wings will keep him afloat for about an hour before he becomes too exhausted to hold himself up. So, we will take him out every hour, on the hour. If he gets cut up a little, oh well."

Chapter Thirty-Two

SETTLED IN ON the plane with drinks ordered, Vito turned to look at Genevie. The sunlight that shone through the window accentuated her beauty. He had never forgotten how lovely she was. She was one of those rare gems blessed with exotic beauty and the personality of a saint.

"Okay, Genevie, tell me what made you decide to become a nun."

She gave him a sneer, then grinned. "You know I was pretty much a mess after we broke up and you set out to do your thing. Becoming a nun helped me put myself together. By the way, it wasn't your fault that I broke up with you. It was me. I had no self-esteem. You gave me all the materialistic things in life and more, but I just couldn't respond to that type of love. I didn't feel I deserved it."

Vito's stroked her arm, as his eyes stole her smile. "All I

wanted was for you to see yourself through my eyes. You were and still are a wonderful person inside and out."

"That's not quite true, but thank you, even if I could never see myself that way."

"I always felt bad for you in that sense."

"I guess I just had to learn the hard way. Let's leave it at that."

Vito reached over, put his arms around her, and squeezed her tight; she could feel his genuine love pour into her. She returned the hug with watery eyes. *I can't keep deceiving him but now is not the time to tell him the truth.*

She turned away and looked out the window, her tear-filled eyes giving the night lights a kaleidoscope effect. With each blink, she saw herself betraying Vito and the Pope. She wanted to scream out and apologize to Vito for betraying him, but then the vision of Cardinal Lintzinburg would ask her, *Where is your daughter? Do you ever want to see her again? Then that hideous laugh.*

Genevie squeezed her eyes closed until it brought on a headache. She finally fell into a fitful sleep while Vito remained vigilant, his eyes open for any movement the agents might make.

Vito tossed the trash into the garbage bag that the flight attendant held, then smiled and woke Genevie. "It's time, girl, let's get ready. I'll call the Pope's secretary to see if he can squeeze us in this morning."

She smiled, yawned, and nodded her head. "Okay, sounds like a plan."

They felt the sun's heat as soon as they stepped out of the airport. The air outside seemed thick in their lungs. Vito was waving over his taxi from the Vatican when Genevie said, "I left my sunglasses in the ladies' room. Give me a moment."

Racing back inside, she pulled out her phone and tapped the first name on the list, "Cardinal Lintzinburg."

"We just landed and are headed for an audience with the Pope."

"Good, I will find a way to get you alone; it is imperative that we speak."

Vito watched Genevie put her phone away as she headed out the door toward the taxi. He also observed the other agents scurry about to find their rides. He shrugged. *Good luck. This will be a dull day for you.*

They got out of their taxi in front of the Vatican, and were escorted through St Peter's square and up to the Pope's chambers.

The Pope turned to greet them with a nod and took a seat in his chair while Vito knelt and kissed his ring, followed by Genevie.

"My son, how are you? And who is this?"

"I'm fine and have been busy, as you know from my reports.

This is Sister Genevie. I have known her for quite some time. She is stationed at the Simon College complex. We knew some of the same people, and she helped me decipher the codes. I hope to use her knowledge on the next set of clues."

The Pope nodded, but his eyes never left hers. "Sister Genevie, have you ever been to Vatican City before?"

Sister's gaze darted toward Vito then back to the Pope. She pulled nervously at the fingertips of one hand, "No, Your Eminence," she lied. "This is my first time here."

The Pope nodded as he turned to Vito. "I am aware of your movements and I know these matters are time-sensitive, so what can I do to help you?"

"Your Holiness, we'll need to get into the Vatican library to do some research."

The Pope waved his hand and his secretary walked over to Vito. "Whenever you are ready," he said.

The Pope lovingly put his arm around Vito and whispered to him, "Be careful, my son. See me before you leave. My secretary already knows to escort you in. Good luck."

Vito turned slightly and raised an eyebrow at the Pope, who winked back.

"Good luck, you two. Godspeed."

As they got off the elevator, Genevie realized she had never been down there before. She was like a young student on a field trip. The polished concrete floors mirrored her image and her amazement shone in her eyes. The large, squat V-shaped columns held up the massive Saint Peter Basilica above. Row after row of glass-enclosed chambers held the most delicate art and the rarest books, documents, and scrolls of the Church's history. The aisles were large enough in some areas to be a two-lane highway, and to enter the chambers, you had to go through a unique airlocked pod.

Each library chamber was a hermetic vault with low oxygen and a partial vacuum. This kept everything dry and mold-free. The only problem was that if anyone stayed too long, they would become lightheaded, and pass out. When handling the books, it was imperative to use gloved hands and tweezers to turn the pages. Small desks lined the outer walls that were adorned with beautiful, rare paintings.

"Okay, here we go," Vito said. "We need to find manuscripts, scrolls, and the Septuagint, and the Pentateuch. These documents will all have the Book of Exodus in them and the best translations, and the Pentateuch reflects the traditional Jewish grouping of these books together as the Torah."

Chapter Thirty-Three

HOURS LATER, VITO and Genevie still had not found anything in any translation to collaborate their thoughts about the Twelve Tribes or the altar. "We need to rethink this before we waste any more precious time," Vito muttered frantically.

Even though they had taken many breaks, they both were exhausted and felt faint from the low oxygen in the library. Genevie ran her hand through her hair and exhaled while Vito wiped the sweat from his brow. Stretching her neck up and down and rotating her head to diminish the stiffness that had settled in her shoulders, her eyes fell upon a painting on the wall. It was a Rembrandt portrait of Moses breaking the Ten Commandments.

Genevie straightened up, astonished. She shook Vito's shoulder. "Look, up there. We have been looking at this all wrong. The code and cipher have nothing to do with the Twelve

Tribes or the altar. It's about Moses writing down everything that God said."

"Oh my God, you're right. There was no known alphabet back then, so what type of language did he use to write down God's words?" It had to be the symbols on the picture of the Ten Commandments. These symbols and/or language must be recorded in the writings of the Jews.

"I don't know, but in that case, I doubt we will find what we're looking for here at the Vatican."

"You're right. We need to speak to the Chief Rabbinate of Israel."

"Great, but how are we going to do that?"

"Oh, ye of little faith."

Genevie looked at Vito with disdain in her eyes as he pulled out his phone and tried to make a call, but he had no service. He sighed and pocketed it. "We need to leave now. Sorry about the wise crack. It's been a long day, and we're tired."

"You're forgiven. At least I have my forgiveness to offer," Genevie said with a big grin.

When they left the Vatican Archives, the Pope's secretary was waiting just outside to summon Vito for his report. "Sister, please give us a few minutes. The Pope would like to hear Vito's update before he leaves. My adjutant will escort you wherever you wish to go."

"Oh my, that would be excellent. I'd love to see some of the artworks of Michelangelo."

"Follow me, Sister."

His secretary walked Vito back into the Pope's chambers, where the Pope greeted Vito with a concerned voice and a fearful look.

"Vito, my son, you will need to be extra careful for it has come to my attention that those working at cross purposes to us are getting nervous and possibly will try to eliminate you."

Vito pressed his lips together and shifted his body as he felt a chill run down his spine.

"I have been anticipating something like this."

"Be careful with Sister Genevie. I have been told about her visits to Vatican City, and she has met with Cardinal Lintzinburg."

"So, she lied when you asked her if she'd been to the Vatican before," Vito said in disbelief."

The Pope nodded. "Yes, my son. I'm afraid she did. I know nothing of her meetings with Cardinal Lintzinburg, but I fear they are up to no good."

"I have felt a tension between Sister and me, Your Eminence, but I thought it was because of our history. That said, she has made a couple of suspicious phone calls that made me wonder what was up, but I thought it was her personal business and none of mine. Little did I know."

While touring the Sistine Chapel, the adjutant was abruptly called away as Cardinal Lintzinburg stood behind a nearby column and discreetly spoke to Sister Genevie. "If you deem that you are getting close to finding the decipher code and relic, and we don't need him anymore, we will need to do something about him."

"I will not hurt that man, Cardinal."

The nun's impertinence raised the Cardinal's ire. He reached down and pinched her jaw between his stubby thumb and forefinger, looking her in the eye. "Now, now. We will have someone else do what is needed, and all you have to do is set him up. Take this. I want it activated immediately. Place it inside and on the collar of your habit. I'll be able to hear everything. No screw-ups if you want to ever see your daughter again. Do we understand each other?"

She nodded and walked away, looking for the adjutant.

"Vito, I know your love for God and I know your old training. We can only pray that God gives you the balance at the right time to protect yourself. In the meantime, watch your back. This will all fall out, and we will be on top. Go, my son. I will do what I can to root out the scorpions."

Vito smiled. "May I get a letter of introduction to the Chief Rabbinate and a helicopter ride to Israel?"

"You don't want anything easy, do you?

He shrugged. "I thought I'd ask for the impossible now and hope for the best."

Uplifted by anticipation, the Pope said, "Follow me; let's see what we can do. Will you need to keep the pilot?"

"No. We'll also need a car waiting for us. I prefer to travel alone with sister right now, thank you."

"All right my son, it shall be done. See my secretary; he'll take care of you."

When Vito stepped outside the Pope's office, Sister Genevie was waiting for him. "Did all go well?"

"Better than I thought. We have an hour to prepare ourselves. The Pope's secretary will get us a letter of introduction to Chief Rabbinate. And a helicopter ride to Israel. There is a shop outside the Vatican Museum where we can pick up fresh clothing; I believe they'll have the habit of your religious order. Mine will be a little easier to get. Let's go."

Chapter Thirty-Four

THEY READIED THEMSELVES to take off; Vito told Sister she looked good in her new habit and dress. Genevie looked Vito up and down. "You look good from the waist up. What happened to new pants?"

Vito shrugged and looked flushed, brushing down the pants. "They had nothing in my size or even close."

"They don't look too bad. People will only look at your upper body anyway."

The Pope's secretary escorted them to the lower level of Vatican City, where they picked up the freight line to St. John's tower and then the helipad's last stop. The brisk walk to board the helicopter. The weather was a beautiful, sunny 72 degrees.

This is great, we'll be in Israel before anyone notices that we're gone.

Cardinal Lintzinburg felt his phone vibrate and saw the

message, “Flying to Israel now on the Pope’s helicopter.”

“Damn.” Dialing Kristoff, Lintzinburg screamed, “That son-of-a-bitch put them on his helicopter to Israel. Get someone over there.”

“Don’t worry, I’ll have a team there waiting for them,” Kristoff said.

“How are you going to do that?”

“That’s not your problem.” Kristoff hung up, leaving Lintzinburg screaming over the phone.

Kristoff dialed Dean, head of the CIA. “I need you to check flights into Israel by the Pope’s helicopter. When you determine where and when, have a team there to follow them when they arrive. I’ll have them relieved by my men shortly.”

“Cersei, get Jake on the line, now.”

“Yes, boss.”

When the phone rang, she handed it to Kristoff.

“Hello.”

“Jake, do you know who this is?

“Yes.”

“Good. I want you to stand by for a call. They will give you information on the whereabouts of Vito and that nun. Send a team to Israel now on your private plane so you can change your flight path to whichever city they give you. Do you understand?”

“Yes, do I…”

"No questions, just get it done." Kristoff slammed the phone down.

As the helicopter banked to its left and headed towards Israel, Sister remembered to put the listening device in her new habit. "Turn around, Vito. I have a tag issue with this new garment." With trembling fingers, she grabbed the bug out of her pocket just as the helicopter hit an air pocket and jostled Vito right into her. *There goes the damn bug,* she thought, as it dropped onto her lap. Vito turned to apologize. Shooing him around, she reached and secured the bug and placed it in position.

A car was waiting for them at the airport in Jerusalem. As they settled in, Vito advised Genevie that he had readjusted his strategy. "I think it will take too much time to go through proper channels to get what we need even with the letter of introduction from the Pope."

Genevie didn't care about his readjusted strategy. Food was her first priority. "I need to eat something. We haven't eaten since we arrived in Rome, which was eleven hours ago."

"Okay."

"So, what's the plan?"

"I lived with a guy named Yefim…."

"Turn in here—Ha'Shamen. We'll grab something to go."

"All right, but you know that Ha'Shamen stands for The Fat Guy, don't you?"

"No, and I don't care. Just feed me."

Laughing he pulled up to the drive-up window and ordered for both of them. They ate greedily as Vito kept driving while trying to eat and dial his phone. He swerved wildly to miss a pedestrian who stepped off the curb in front of him as they pulled out of Ha'Shamen.

"What are you doing?" Genevie yelled. "You're going to kill us. Who are you calling anyway?"

"I'm trying to call Yefim. He and I were like brothers, and his father is one of the ex-High Rabbinate; he took a liking to me. He will have some or all of the information we need to get answers to our questions."

Lintzinburg called Kristoff with this information and the bug frequency so he could listen to everything they were planning. Kristoff smiled as he reached the agent in Israel, Aliyah Mustafa, who worked for the cabal.

Aliyah sat twirling her highlighted hair between her nimble fingers with one leg crossed over the other, bobbing up and down. Her high-fashioned dress did not fit a nine-to-five job. The sun that came through the window reflected on her bare sternum, and if she moved the wrong way, you could tell the color of her thong. She couldn't wait to hit the gym and do some damage to the kick bag when the phone rang.

"This is Aliyah Mustafa."

"Do you know who this is?

"Yes."

"Good."

"I want you to find this Yefim, the son of Elijah Blum. I want this Vito stopped from ever seeing Yefim's father. In fact, I don't want him to see another sunrise. Open your company e-mail and you will have the particulars."

"You got it. Sir, do I have permission for any resources I might need?"

"Use everything at your disposal. Just don't fail."

Kristoff already imagined the power from the relics; hell awaited anyone who failed now.

Winking, Vito looked down at his phone again, searched his contacts, and landed on the right one. He pushed the "Call" button.

"Hello."

"Yefim, is that you?"

"Yes. Is this Vito? Long time no hear. How are you?" He was looking at Aliyah with the gun pointed at his head, sweat dripping from his forehead.

"Hey pal, sorry to be short, but I need a favor."

"Anything, my friend. I will never forget what you did for my family and me."

"I need a meet-and-greet with your father."

"Wow, when?"

"I'm sorry. I would never ask if it wasn't a life or death

matter."

"Care to explain?"

"You know I can't. At least not now. Ask me in ten years. But I need to see him today. Besides, let your father know I have a letter of introduction from the Pope, if that'll help."

Aliyah poked Yefim on the shoulder and whispered, "Get him to meet you."

"Vito, give me a couple of minutes to make this happen; I'll call you right back."

"Thank you, my friend, that sounds good. Call me with the location.

Chapter Thirty-Five

YEFIM HUNG UP. *Shit!*

Aliyah backhanded him. "Keep it together, and you might make it through this. I want you to tell him that he can meet your father at your house."

"No, I don't want any bloodshed at my house." The next slap hit him before he saw it coming. "Shut up. But first, make him stop for a bottle of your father's favorite wine. What's your father's favorite wine?"

"Santinomi Reserve Motepulciano Cordano Abruzzo. It's only sold at the Avi Ben, the oldest wine store in Israel."

"I'll wait for him there and eliminate him."

Yefim called Vito back. "Come to my house. Papa says he is excited to see you. It would be best if you do not show up empty-handed. Stop and get a bottle of his favorite wine. Do you remember?"

"Of course, we sat and drank it together for many a night while you were out carousing. It is Santinomi Reserve Motepulciano Cordano Abruzzo, sold only at Avi Ben, if I remember correctly.

"Good, that's it. See you when you get here."

Aliyah, set up on the rooftop across from the shopping strip, lay prone with an eye to the scope and set her dial-in for wind and distance, then focused on the shop's doorway just as a skinny Tabby cat pranced by. She swore under her breath. *Damn cats. There are more cats than people here.* She lay motionless, calming herself and lowering her heartbeat with a couple of deep breaths. She didn't have to wait long before Vito's rental car pulled into the crowded parking lot. Places that would stay open on a Sabbath always filled up for the day.

Vito and Genevie found a spot two cars away from the entrance, hopped out, and headed for the door. Aliyah steadied her scope. Everything happened simultaneously. Vito reached for the handle on the front door just as the Tabby cat leaped out from under the car closest to the front door. Vito shoved Genevie toward the door as the bullet grazed him and shattered the glass in the door. Vito and Genevie fell through and landed at the foot of the display of two bails of straw with a picnic basket and a setting of dishes and wine glasses.

"Are you all right, Sister?" Vito asked, just as a case of wine exploded behind them. Straw mixed with glass and wine erupted all over. Vito pulled Genevie behind a pallet of crates and covered her with his body as he laid her down and ordered, "Don't move."

"My God, what is happening?"

"Stay here," Vito commanded. He rolled to the left, followed the counter down to the building's end, and went out the back door.

Aliyah screamed in her head, *Shit, this was supposed to be easy.* She left her gun lying on the roof, descended the back of the building, pulled her knife, and followed the alleyway towards the front of the building to better look at her prey. She ran smack into Vito.

She backed up, noticing blood on his arm. "So, I didn't completely miss," she said, nodding at Vito's wound.

Vito looked at his arm and saw the blood trickling down as Aliyah placed the first kick upside his head and spun him around. His head snapped to the left, and his body followed a tenth of a second later. She jumped about six inches to put more power into slamming her fist into Vito's face. Blood erupted out of his nose and lips. As he hit the ground, his mind went into action. He calculated four different strikes before he settled on the perfect move.

When she came down, his leg stretched out and swept her feet out from under her. She landed hard on her tail, and you could hear the crack of her wrist bone as she tried to stop her fall. Vito continued to swing the rest of his body into an upright position. Aliyah grabbed her knife and tried to strike with her good arm,, Her knife hit Vito's open bullet wound and ripped it wider. Blood gushed from it.

Vito saw stars but kept up his momentum. With a savage blow to the inside of her kneecap, he blew it right out of the socket using a slicing knife-edge kick. She screamed, and tears immediately followed, blurring her vision. As she looked up, he placed the last strike with such force to the upturned nose. He watched her eyes go vacant as she stared at him. Her head gave a slight bounce as it landed on the ground. Vito ran out of the alley and back towards the store to find Genevie in the car.

Sister reached over and swung the door open. "Let's get out of here."

Vito scrambled into the car while blood from his hand smeared the steering wheel.

"What the hell is going on?

"I'll let you in on everything in just a moment."

Genevie looked at him and cringed. "You look like you got hit in the face with a brick, and look, your arm is bleeding. Let me see that."

They could hear the police sirens getting closer. Vito put the car in drive and slowly pulled out of the alleyway into the street, looking for cops. The street was empty so Vito took of for Yefim's house while Genevie bandaged his arm the best she could and wiped his face with an antibacterial cloth.

"Shit, that hurts. Where did you get that?"

"Shut up, big baby, and pull over there for a moment."

Vito parked the car on the side of the road and turned to

her to ask again. Before he could finish, she clamped his nose between her hands and yanked it to one side, then back to center, setting his nose.

Vito screamed, throwing his head back. "Where did you learn that little trick?"

"I have two brothers, remember? And I borrowed the supplies from the wine shop."

Vito struggled to control his breathing, trying to ignore the pain in his body and the pounding of his heartbeat as he brought the car back onto the road.

When he pulled into the driveway of Yefim's home, the gate opened automatically. The gardens that covered the grounds had a particular color to them. It was all the hues of flowers, olive trees, and occasionally a fig tree here and there that twinkled in the sunlight. "Sister, you drive now. I'll meet you up at the door." He got out, and Genevie crawled into the driver's seat.

Vito kept low and disarmed the first man with ease. The second man started to pull his gun when Vito dropped him with a front kick and choked him out. He sprinted to the front side of the house.

Sister Genevie drove slowly, looking in all directions for any problems. At the end of the drive, she parked and got out. She was walking towards the door when Yefim suddenly opened it.

Yefim turned to face Sister as Vito started to close the gap between him and Yefim. Vito motioned for Sister to keep him talking. “Hey, what type of friend are you that sets his friends up to get killed?”

Vito crept up from the side of the house. “Don’t move, or you’re a dead man,” Vito yelled.

Turning towards the sound, Yefim yelled back, “Whoa. Boy, am I glad to see you alive. I thought that crazy bitch was going to kill you.”

“Oh, she tried,” yelled Sister Genevie.”

“I don’t know. She broke into my house and held me at gunpoint, waiting for your call. She knew everything in advance.

“So you tell me.” Vito grabbed Yefim, spun him around, and hit him square on the jaw. Yefim woke up tied to a chair. His father and Sister Genevie sat next to him while Vito paced back and forth, “Okay, sunshine, do you want to tell me your side of the story before I end this chapter of your life.”

Vito turned to see a mop of white curls swirl from Elijah’s head and a long Assyrian beard with spirals moving. “My son is telling the truth.”

“I already told you she broke in here and held me at gunpoint and told me that you would call. Then she laid out the plan for you to be at the Avi Ben store. That’s all I know.”

Vito quickly turned to Sister. “Give me your phone.”

“Vito, what are you accusing me of?”

“Who else could it have been? Give me the damn phone.”

Her face turned red. Her hands trembled and the phone

fell from her outstretched hand. Scooping up the phone, Vito held it out for her to turn it on. Her nerves were betraying her feelings as she entered the password. Vito scrolled through her phone contacts, calls, and messages. Nothing.

That was even worse; for now, he had to believe her and come up with why this person knew everything about his plans. Vito flushed as he handed her phone back to her. "I'm sorry, Sister, but I must find out how they knew."

"I understand your frustration, but you asked me on this wild chase, where people are dying, and we are getting shot at. So please contain your anger with me."

"Again, I'm sorry, and you are right. This has gotten too dangerous for you; you can and should leave and return to the college."

"I have started this with you to help you, and I will see it through to the end."

Vito jumped up, looked at everyone at the table, and headed out the door. Sister Genevie ran after him. She paused long enough to tell Elijah, "You can untie him."

Chasing after Vito, she hollered, "Vito, where are you going?"

"I'm going to check the car for any bugs or listening devices or anything out of the ordinary."

She watched Vito tearing apart the car. He started with the driver's side carpet and threw it out; finding nothing, he became more aggressive on the passenger side. Genevie moved out of his way, and as she passed the ripped-out carpet on the driver's side, she tossed the bug under it. Vito ran his hands inside the car seat and backrest, but still nothing. He pulled down the sun visors and checked the glasses compartment and glove box anywhere you could slide your hand in or out of. "Damn it." He sat down on the ground near the driver's side. Looking around, he ran his hands through his hair.

Placing the passenger side carpet down on the floor and trying to iron it out with her hands, Sister said, "We need to put this back together and talk to Yefim's dad."

The setting sun ripped the sky into a beautiful bouquet of color. Vito got up, copied Genevie's movements, grabbed the carpet, and placed it on the front floorboard; as he knelt to iron it out, he saw a glint of light. He quickly reached for it and held between two fingers a small bug. Vito swore in Sicilian, Figlio di puttana, son-of-a-bitch Genevie didn't know if he meant the bug or her. "What did you say" she yelled, Turning toward Vito, all she could see was him waving a small piece of electronic equipment.

Vito turned to run back to the house and Genevie gave a small, smug smile and followed.

Chapter Thirty-Six

"DID YOU FIND what you were looking for?" Elijah and Yefim asked.

Vito smiled and raised his hand, displaying the bug. "Yes, I'm sorry for getting everyone into this mess. Elijah, I need your help with this puzzle, and then I will be out of your life. Sister, please show them."

Genevie pulled back the front of her habit, found the secret pocket, and grabbed the paper with the symbols. She laid it out in front of the rabbi. The rabbi looked at it and shoved it back to her, shaking his head. "No one reads that anymore or even knows how."

"Elijah, I need this translated. I need it now because it is life or death for an entire nation."

"I'm sorry, but I cannot read this. I have never been trained to read this language—only a specific tribe of the Israelites was tasked with that."

"What tribe and where can we find them?"

"That's the problem. There are only three men alive that

I know of who can read this, and they are all in their upper eighties or maybe early nineties."

He stood and shuffled to his office, removed a portrait on the wall and opened the safe behind it. He rummaged through some papers and came out with the official list of the tribes and their associate land deeds, titles, and addresses. Turning, he handed it to Vito. "Please go now and good luck, my son. Pay attention to the tribe of Benjamin."

Excited and hopeful, Vito and Genevie hurried out. "Let me see that document," Genevie said. She examined the list. "Here, here is the temple where we must start."

"Are we sure that's the best place?"

"I'll double-check my phone maps."

"Good thinking."

After double-checking the location on her phone, she took a screenshot and sent it to Cardinal Lintzinburg.

Tapping her foot, she looked over at Vito. "It seems to be the best way."

Chapter Thirty-Seven

VITO ENTERED THE address into the navigation system and they were on their way. The location was forty miles north. They made good time with one stop for water and gas and soon parked in front of an ancient temple. Hustling up to the office door, Vito knocked. When no one answered, he opened the door and peered in. "Hello?"

"Come in." Around the corner came an older lady with glasses so thick you had to wonder how anyone could legally see out of them. Her old skirt, hanging down to her shins, showed off her nylon stockings in the color of vintage hospital beige, but her broad, genuine smile commanded all their attention. "How can I help you?"

Genevie took the lead. "Hello, we are looking for the Chief Rabbi."

"Oh, my. Come," the clerk offered, showing them to a large,

weathered table. "Please sit. Can I offer you a small beverage? As long as it's coffee or water," she said with a chuckle.

"No, we are fine," Vito said. "Is he available to speak with us?"

"Well, I'm sorry, no. Rabbi Zachariah fell ill last week and has not been able to speak since."

Genevie pulled out the sheet of paper with the clues and asked, "Have you ever seen these markings?"

The old clerk's eyes flashed between them, and she nodded. "Yes, I have, but it has been quite some time."

"Can you read them?" Vito interjected.

"I'm afraid only Rabbi Zechariah could read that language, as far as I know. But I have not seen him look at or study it in so long, I doubt he remembers it. It's a lost alphabet."

"Do the doctors know when he might recover?"

"Recover? He is just waiting for the Lord to take him."

Vito shot a look at Genevie. "We're sorry to hear that, please let him know we will pray for him, but we must be going."

"Where are you off to next?"

Vito laid out the document Elijah had given him and the lady's eyes once more betrayed her knowledge of it. "What do you know of this?" he asked, pointing to the paper.

"I know that it does not belong to you. How did you get it?"

"Elijah Blum gave it to me so that I might find someone to help me read this other paper."

"How is Elijah? I used to work for him many years ago. Till Yefim transferred me out here."

"Elijah isn't good. He is dealing with a personal problem," Vito answered honestly.

She sighed. "That's too bad."

"Would you be able to send us in the right direction?"

"Only two other rabbis can read this alphabet. Rabbi Nicodemus and Rabbi Hillel. The closest, Rabbi Nicodemus, is about an hour from here."

"Thank you for your kind help. We'll let ourselves out." Outside Vito paused. "Sister, our time is being cut shorter and shorter, and this feels like a fool's errand."

Pulling out of the parking lot, the gravel upturned and hit his car, sounding like a mini machine gun spraying bullets. They both flinched. Then, Genevie entered a new address into the navigation system. Looking over at Vito, "Checking my phone map," she said as she sent a screenshot to Cardinal Lintzinburg.

Chapter Thirty-Eight

JAKE FOLLOWED HIS men down the tunnel. When he heard something, he tapped both of them on the shoulder. As they quietly approached the chamber, they heard a chain rattle. Peering in, they saw Billy sprawled out in a net in blood-soaked clothes, sweat dripping down his bleak and colorless face. Billy's heart beat faster. *I can't keep moving to lessen the pain. Each move buries another part of me deeper into the slicing wire net.*

"Get over there and see if he is still alive."

Sam reached up and poked Billy with a gun. "Yeah, boss, he's still alive."

"So, Mr. Billy, can you talk?" Jake asked him.

"Get me down from here."

"Sorry, you look like you're dead already. Just tell me where my relics are."

"If I remember correctly, the package was mailed to me."

"Yes, but you see, I paid for those relics. I paid her handsomely to excavate them for me. So, as I see it, those relics belongs to me."

"I don't see it that way." I can't give in. I need them to release me.

"You, my friend, aren't in any position to bargain."

"That depends on how much you need those relics."

A diamond-shaped piece of skin bubbled up on Billy's arm, ready to be cut off and fall into the basket. Billy grimaced inwardly. Billy's hour was up and the demons could not take a chance on these humans seeing Billy being released.

"Lord Retribution, Master said not to kill him. We need to release him."

With a quick backhand, the lower demon flew out of sight. "He won't die; maybe get torn up a little."

Jake grinned. "I'm not the one hanging above the basket waiting for disaster to befall me. "Men, let me explain what this fool refuses to see. He is in a net that is made of carbon nanotubes, which can be up to 117 times stronger than steel and 30 times stronger than Kevlar. I know this because it was in front of my defense contract committee. His gravity will soon draw his body through that net, and since it's made in diamond shapes, his body and bones will be cut into diamond-shaped pieces. Granted, the bones will take longer." Jake looked back at Billy. "What will it be? My relics or your death?"

"As you pointed out, I'm a dead man, anyway I look at it.

So why would I give you what you want?" Billy looked around, the demons above waiting to pounce and Jake and his men wanting to see him suffer. Good lord, the searing pain of the wire net cutting into him brought on a freezing cold sensation that morphed into a hot burning of his body. His facial features changed slightly as the first diamond was cut and fell out of the net. Once it hit the bottom of the basket, it was consumed by its own celestial qualities.

"What was that?" Sam asked.

"Go look."

"Boss, there's nothing in the basket."

"What? Move out of the way." Jake looked down into the basket. "What the hell?"

"I need him alive. Damn it, Ben, get him out of the net, and Sam, keep your gun trained on him. Do it now."

Ben moved to grab the net. "I wouldn't do that if I were you," said Billy. Too late. Ben screamed with pain as he looked at his hand—the mark of a diamond slightly cut into it.

"Sam, grab the top where there's no net; now get him down, careful. Ben, here, tie this handkerchief around his hand," Jake said." Opening the net, they let Billy fall onto the table. With a loud moan, he rolled and tried to get up but fell back onto the table.

"All right, get on your feet. No more tricks. Take us to those relics, and maybe we let you and your friend Vito live."

Jake pulled Billy off the table. "Move it. I'm done playing with you. Take me to those relics. Let's go."

Billy straightened himself as best he could and shuffled down an incline stairwell until he came upon a door to the tower room.

"Hold up, what's in there?" Jake said.

It's rows of Internet servers stacked six to ten high. With fifteen towers in a row. "What you seek is in here." Billy opened the door and with every bit of energy he had left, he dove into a tuck-and-roll behind the tower's first row.

Sam opened fire on Billy.

"Stop! You idiot!" Jake shouted. "We don't know for sure if those relics are in here. All right, Billy, come on out, and no one will shoot you."

Jake motioned his men to go around to each side and put him in a crossfire. When they both got to the ends of the tower, Billy was no longer in that aisle.

"Shit, boss, this man disappears faster than a ghost. He's not here."

"What the hell are you talking about, Ben?"

"Just like Sam said, boss, he's not here."

"All right, spread out. Let's look for him and those damn relics."

Ben got to the last row of towers and found a cabinet made of glass. There sat the UPS package Joan had mailed to Billy. Ben smiled, opened the glass doors, and heard a click. Before the noise registered, he lifted the package only to have a blade swing across the front opening from left to right. Jake heard a scream and a lot of commotion and ran toward the excitement.

He saw Ben running around without a hand. Jake put a bullet in his head and told Sam, "Get those relics and let's get the hell out of here!"

Sam approached the relics slowly, looking on all sides and even peeking underneath them for more traps. He could find none. Gingerly, Sam picked up the package and it to Jake.

"Find us a way out of here," Jake demanded.

They turned to retrace their steps when everything went dark.

Chapter Thirty-Nine

As Vito pulled out of the parking lot, he noticed two cars following him. They were definitely novices. He followed his navigation system to Rabbi Nicodemus's location while he kept an eye on the car directly behind them. If any trouble was coming, it would be from Jake's men. Looking into his rearview mirror, he watched one of the occupants of the car pick up his phone and listen, then talk and hang up. Trouble's coming. Vito picked up speed, and both cars behind him did the same.

When they reached the temple parking lot, both cars peeled off.

Vito looked over at Genevie. "Let's get this done quickly. We've got company, and they're about to make their move."

Hurrying to the door, they used the heavy brass door knocker first and then rang the bell. Genevie laid her hand on Vito's arm. "Vito, relax. Say a prayer, and calm yourself."

Vito nodded in assent. “You’re right, Sister. I just have this ominous feeling.”

The door opened forward abruptly and hit Vito in the back, pushing him toward Genevie. She grabbed him. “Ominous? Like getting hit with a door?” They both groaned.

“Hello. May I help you?” The housekeeper looked to be about 5’3” and about sixty to seventy years old. Her wire-rimmed glasses framed her face perfectly and matched the powder blue shirt she wore.

“Yes, please, we need to speak to Rabbi Nicodemus.”

“And what is this regarding?”

“We have come a long way to speak to him about a matter that is life or death.”

“Hmm… I suppose you can’t tell me about this urgent matter.”

“Please, is it possible to speak to him?”

“Come in. I will ask him if he will talk to you.”

“Thank you.”

“Please understand something right now. If you upset him, I will shut down your conversation.”

Vito was surprised by her moxie. He had sized her up as a kindly little matron.

“We have no intentions of upsetting him.”

“Oh, I know that. But what you don’t know is that Rabbi Nicodemus has onset Alzheimer’s. We just got him bathed and changed his clothes.

Vito and Sister looked at one another and cringed. After a

few moments of waiting, the secretary returned. "Follow me."

They followed her into his private quarters. Vito and Sister noticed his long locks and a snow-white, untrimmed Herraic beard, a good ten inches long. He sat there with his Tallit, his fringed prayer shawl with Tzitzit (ritual fringes) attached to the four corners of the Tallit, but wore no head covering.

Vito started by pulling out his paper with the symbols on it. "Good afternoon, Rabbi. I am Cardinal Vito Rosario and this is Sister Genevie. We are honored that you would see us today. I need your help to decipher the alphabet on this page."

With a shaky hand, the old scholar reached for the paper. "Let me see that. It's been a long time." His voice was weak and it was clear that he struggled to focus his pale eyes. "We must read this…we must read this from the bottom—right to left. The first line says, "You have gotten this far, excellent."

Suddenly, all hell broke loose.

Gunfire erupted outside the building and inside by the office door. As bullets flew through the door, Vito threw himself in front of the rabbi to protect him. The two FEU agents put the final two shots through the would-be attackers, and all was quiet. Vito turned to see if everyone was okay when the secretary screamed, "Rabbi Nicodemus!"

They all turned to see Rabbi Nicodemus grabbing his chest but he was not moving. Vito bent down to tend to the rabbi, but there was no blood. His heart had simply stopped."

His secretary looked at Rabbi Nicodemus, pressed her lips together, and lightly struck her breast saying a prayer. Then she pushed Vito and Sister out the door to the rabbi's private quarters.

"Okay, it's time for you two to leave. I must call an ambulance."

Chapter Forty

BACK AT THE inn, Jake laid the Package on the table and told Sam he'd be right back. He slipped into the bedroom to call Kristoff.

Before he could dial, he heard a scream and ran out of the bedroom only to see Sam lying on the floor with a horrified look on his face. His death mask. Jake looked closer and saw the bone box on the floor. He picked it up and placed it back on the table, noticing scratch marks on the box. *You fool, you tried to open the box?*

Jake decided he would wait to hear from Ron before he called Kristoff. Then he'd be able to give Kristoff good news on two accounts: that he had the relics and that Vito was dead. Jake sat in a chair, poured himself a stiff drink, and exhaled deeply. He raised the glass to his lips, smelling the tinge of the alcohol. It tickled his nose and made his throat itch. He tilted his head back and swallowed. Then came the burning sensation as it always did.

Suddenly, his hotel door shattered open. Russell Carter and

two other FEU agents entered wearing full combat gear, their weapons raised and at the ready.

"Who the fuck are you?" Jake shouted, coming out of his chair.

"Shut up!" came from one of the men. "Where are the relics?"

"Get the hell out of here! Don't you know who I am?"

The butt of a weapon hit Jake in the head, knocking him off his feet. He scrambled to get back up, but a quick kick to his gut rolled him over onto his back. Raising his hands in defeat he said, "Over there…in that Package on the table." The soldier closest to the door picked up the Package, looked inside, and nodded.

"Okay, tie him up. Get him ready to travel," Carter ordered as he dialed the President. He answered on the first ring. "Mr. President, we have secured the package and will be en route to the Ravenna Arsenal momentarily."

"Your jet is standing by. We'll see you in a few hours."

Russell hung up the phone. When the President went to click off, he heard static on the line before he hung up. A second later, Dean Caputto, head of the CIA, also hung up.

"Get me the backchannel phone to the FBI," Caputto told one of his men.

"Yes, this is Bob," answered Caputto's counterpart at the FBI.

"Did you just hear that phone call?"

"I did."

"Do you have any men in the Ravenna area?"

"No."

"That's all right, we do."

"How the hell do you have someone there?"

"We've been watching the FEU for a while now. So, we'll take care of it from here. I'll keep you posted on their movements."

"Remember, *as its done,* not *after*." The FBI director hung up.

"Get Jake in the back of the van, and let's get out of here."

The FEU pulled into the Ravenna Arsenal, and stopped at the security gate. The CIA team swooped in at that moment, threw spikes under the tires, and surrounded the FEU vehicle—all before they could pull out their IDs.

The lead agent yelled, "Who's in charge? Slowly stick your hands out of the window, open the door from the outside, and get out."

The passenger in the front seat did as the agent instructed.

"Come to me," the operative said, waving his weapon toward himself. "Turn around. Good."

The CIA operative hit him from behind to establish his dominance but Russell shook it off. The operative inhaled deeply and played off his surprise. "Tell your men to get out and bring the package with them."

"All right, men, get out and place the package on the front seat." Seconds went by as they got out, leaving the package on the front seat.

"What's the matter with you? Get that package out here!"

"You get it," Russell replied.

Now came a more decisive blow to the back of his head but Russell was ready this time and swung around, grabbing the gun. Eight red laser points lit up his chest. Russell dropped the weapon and raised his hands. The soldier yelled for someone to grab the package. As another soldier retrieved the Package, he heard a muffled sound, looking in the rear of the SUV he saw Jake tied up in the back and set him free. "Follow us," he told Jake as the CIA soldiers dropped out of sight one by one.

Russell rubbed the back of his neck with his free hand and pointed. "You two, remove those spikes. We must get out of here before they realize they have the wrong Package. Glen secure the relics and let's go."

Kristoff picked up the phone. "We have boots on the ground with the intercepted package," he heard the CIA director say. "They should be arriving shortly."

"It's about time you earned your money."

The CIA director bit his tongue. "Yes, sir," was all he said.

Chapter Forty-One

"What have I done? Oh Sister, he could have been the only one to read these symbols for us. Now he's dead."

"Let's just get to Rabbi Hillel's temple."

"All right, set the navigation."

"Okay." Genevie set the nav, then sent a picture of the address to Cardinal Lintzinburg.

They pulled up in front of a sturdy old stone façade with oak timbers that reflected the character of the building. As they approached the door, a young man walked out of the office.

"Hello. May I help you?"

"Possibly," Vito said.

The young man opened the office door and realized that the family of Rabbi Hillel had taken over the rabbi's office, moving and packing stacks of books, papers, and knick-knacks. "Let's take a seat over here," he suggested, moving to the reception area outside the rabbi's office. The candles from a lit menorah cast their shadows through the temple. "I'm Rabbi Emanuel, the new rabbi as of two days ago. Sorry for the mess."

Sister looked shocked. Vito hung his head in utter dejection.

"Oh, my goodness, have I hurt you in some way? I'm sorry."

"No, no, we were hoping to find Rabbi Hillel. Is he here?" Vito said.

"No. I'm sorry to tell you he died last week. As you can see, they're loading up his possessions as we speak."

Vito pulled out the paper with all the symbols and showed the young rabbi. "By chance, have you been taught this alphabet?"

"No, I have not. I know that Rabbi Hillel was one of the only ones left in the world able to read it."

"Oh Rabbi, we must find someone to read this for us," said Sister Genevie. "The message contained in these symbols is a matter of life or death."

The agony and the disappointment on the rabbi's face said it all. "Have you tried…"

"We tried Rabbi Zachariah and Rabbi Nicodemus, but to no avail."

"Come with me," the young rabbi said as he ushered them back to a bench. "Please, wait here. Let me get you something to drink and we will discuss this further. I'll be right back."

Genevie looked at Vito as Rabbi Hillel's family carried boxes past them and into their truck. One young man, the grandson of the Rabbi Hillel smiled, and said, "Shalom."

Vito responded with a nod of his head. "Shalom."

Rabbi Emanuel returned with three cold glasses of water. "Please, drink. I called a friend in the Chief Rabbinate's office, and he has not heard of this language."

Vito could only sit and stare at the symbols on the paper. When his phone started to buzz, he handed Sister the paper and walked away.

"Hello."

"My son, I have not heard from you. Is everything well? Are you okay? I have heard of some dangerous things happening."

Vito hung his head in agony. "Your Holiness, I am fine., but I am sorry to report that I have failed you and the Church. I cannot get the symbols deciphered. The only three rabbis who know this language are dead or incapacitated. There is no one left who can help us."

"We are in the final hours, my boy. There must be something we can do."

"I will go back and examine my steps to see if I have missed anything, but I am not hopeful."

"I will say a prayer for your successful journey."

Vito bid the Pope a sad good-bye. Walking back toward the bench where they had gathered, he heard quite a commotion. *Wonder what's going on over there.*

Sister had laid out the paper with the symbols on it and started to explain what it meant to Rabbi Emanuel. "These symbols were used to hide the location of the Church's most sacred relics and now that Rabbi Hillel's is gone we are at the end of our journey to find the relics.

"Pardon me," said the young man who had greeted them earlier. "May I see that? It looks like something my grandfather made me learn."

"And you are who?" Sister Genevie asked.

"I'm David, Rabbi Hillel's grandson. Grandpa was concerned that there were so few Jewish people who could read this language that it would be lost to our people forever. Out of all his grandchildren, he picked me because I seem to have a knack for languages."

Practically shoving the paper in his face, Sister said, "Please, take a look at this and tell me if you can read it."

He nodded. "I believe I can." He started to read, but Rabbi Emanuel interrupted him. "No, wait, I'll be right back." He turned so rapidly that he almost knocked over one of the movers with a box in his hand.

A few minutes later, the rabbi returned, waving a pencil and paper. "Okay, let's try it now."

"Try what?" asked Vito, as he came in sight of Sister Genevie, Rabbi Emanuel and the young man.

The young rabbi grabbed Vito by the arm. "Praise be to God, this young man knows the symbols. He is Rabbi Hillel's grandson."

The smile that crossed Vito's face was bright enough to be seen in heaven. He realized then that this was the young man he had exchanged Shaloms with earlier. *The Lord works in mysterious ways, His wonders to perform.*

Sister Genevie scribbled furiously as David read. He occasionally had to pause his reading for her to catch up. When she was done writing down all she was told, she handed the paper to Vito, who began to read out loud.

You have gotten this far; excellent. I knew you'd get it. You will need to get inside the tunnels underneath Simon College. You will need a flashlight to get through some of them.

Go to the front of the auditorium. You will see an elevator to the left of the steps leading up to the double doors. Open the door to the elevator, but don't step in. You'll have to remove the steel floor. There are two ways to open it: use a heavy-duty magnet that will lift the portable floor high enough to get your hands under it and lift. Or slip something strong and narrow between the floor and walls and pry it up.

Take the circular stairs and be careful. On the left, you'll find the wall switch about fifteen feet in. You will see a steel door inside the tunnel wall. Look at the bottom of the door; you will see that it is on a track buried in the floor. A lever needs to be depressed, and the door will be released. Place your foot on the lever and leave it there until you secure the pedal with the latch. Otherwise, the door will spring closed and possibly cut you in half, so be careful.

Once on the other side of the door, you need to find another light switch to light the tunnel up. Follow the tunnel till you come to the fork. The right will take you to a chamber used for the underground railroad in the 1800s. Going to the left will bring you to a torture chamber used by a man who once worked for the college who was a sympathizer with the New Agers sect that was at Simon College a few years back.

Continue left and go through that chamber, and you will go down a ramp that leads into a section of towers. These servers were once used to broadcast hidden messages on a free game website for children. Go to the last set of towers and open the server's case. You will find two relics in one package. The thorn stolen from the crown of thorns of Jesus Christ. It will be in a golden box the size of a small matchbox. The other is a bone box that I did not have time to figure out how to open. I do not know what is in that box but I believe it to be the second relic—a drop of Christ's precious blood.

Good luck,

Joan

Vito grabbed Rabbi Emanuel, picked him up, and swung him around. "Praise be to God, thank you! You are the answer to our prayers."

The young rabbi gave Vito a wide smile. "You are quite welcome, but could you please put me down? I actually didn't do anything. It was Rabbi Hillel's grandson, David. He's the one who deserves the credit for deciphering the code. He's…"

Emmanuel turned to acknowledge the young man, but the boy was nowhere to be found. He had slipped quietly off to join his family before Vito even finished reading the letter.

Vito dropped the young rabbi and grasped his shoulders one last time for good measure. "Yes, yes." He nodded. "That's right. He was reading when I came up and Genevie was writing." He looked around for Sister Genevie, who had also disappeared, but was too distracted by the deciphered letter in his hand to ask where she had gone.

Genevie had slipped back into the church to pull out her phone and place a quick call.

"Cardinal Lintzinburg."

"We have the code, and it is deciphered."

"Okay, I will take it from here."

Genevie reappeared at Vito's side with a big smile. "We have it."

Cardinal Lintzinburg hung up and dialed a number.

"Speak."

"They have the code, and it is deciphered."

"I'll let Cersei take it from here."

Chapter Forty-Two

As Vito pulled the car out of the temple parking lot, he noticed something out of the corner of his eye. It was a car keeping pace with him. He drove a little faster. Then two other vehicles fell into a procession behind him. Vito felt trapped. Then two of the cars following him disappeared.

Vito entered a small village with cobblestone and narrow dirt roads that fit only one vehicle at a time. He drove straight up a street with only one turn, which was to his right. Vito tried to go straight, but a car was blocking the road. The car behind him stopped and blocked Vito from any movement except to turn right. As he turned, another vehicle was blocking his progress all Vito go do was then turn left into an abandoned parking lot with truck docks on all four sides, broken windows, and tagged walls, and a tiny alleyway that was only big enough for someone to walk through.

In his mind, Vito divided the parking lot into a grid. Vito and Genevie were in the bottom left of the square, and in the bottom right corner, to his delight, he recognized FEU agents.

In the upper left corner was a car with Ron's men in it and in the far-right corner was Ron.

Everyone sat still, staring out their windshields until Ron stepped out, impeccably dressed as always, and stood behind the car door. Everyone followed suit. "Listen, this does not have to be complicated. I want Vito. The rest of you can leave unharmed with my blessing."

"That won't be happening," said one of the FEU women. "Tell your men to stand down now, and I promise I won't kill you all."

Vito turned his head and looked at the woman. "Look, it's a fair trade. I can't have all this blood on my conscience."

"Listen to the man. He knows what is going to happen. You're going to be dead if you don't back off." As Ron started to get back into his car, his men aimed at Vito. Vito ran behind his vehicle, where Genevie was crunched down, ready to run. He looked at her in surprise.

Sister shook her head; she had not signed up for all this killing. She didn't even hate Vito anymore, which came to her as a complete shock. If it wasn't for Lintzinburg having her daughter, she could have possibly worked something out with Vito.

Jaqueline ran to the rear of the car, yelling to Samantha to open the trunk. "We really must thank Russell for all the goodies." She pulled out an M203 grenade launcher, attached it to the rifle, took aim, and let it fly.

As Ron watched Jacqueline take aim at his men, he turned

and pulled a M320A1 grenade launcher from the rear seat.

When Samantha and Jacqueline saw that Ron was about to blow them up, they dove for cover. The FEU vehicle's two front doors bent on their hinges and flew upward as they were ripped from the car, dancing around the two agents lying on the ground. Fire simultaneously broke out inside and outside of the vehicle. One of the headrests bounced off Samantha's chest. She felt a crushing pain radiating outward from her chest. Jacqueline screamed "Samantha" as she frantically patted down the flames licking at her jacket as the fire crept toward her.

"I'm coming," Samantha said.

"Hurry!"

Samantha inhaled, which caused her to grunt, and reach for her chest. When she exhaled, she hesitated a second even though she saw that Jacqueline did not have much time before the fire would be hitting her skin. Samantha wasn't sure she had enough breath to run to her but she couldn't forsake her team member and friend. With labored breathing, she ran to Jacqueline. Approaching her from the back, she grabbed the collar of her jacket, and ripping it down, she stripped her of the fire.

They looked at one another, asking, "Are you all right?" They both agreed that their heads were pounding like jackhammers, for sure. Other than that, they weren't sure.

Samantha gingerly touched her chest. "No one will be playing with these things for a while," she said with a faint smile.

Jacqueline showed Samantha her hands. "I won't be touching or grabbing anything hard for a while either.'" They each gave a tired laugh. "Thank you for your assist. It could have gotten bad quickly."

Samantha smiled at her friend. "Anytime."

With his two men dead, and Vito's team offline from their injuries, Ron's anger emboldened him to challenge this piece of shit. He got out of his car and yelled for Vito to come to the center and fight him one-on-one. Vito stood and saw a war zone in front of him. The smell of explosives permeated the air.

Ron walked to the front of his car and started to unbutton his suit coat and loosen his tie. "Come on, you little son-of-a-bitch. You have been a pain in my ass since we started this mission." Ron's blood pressure was hitting the stratosphere.

Genevie tugged on Vito's arm. "Vito, let's get out of here right now."

Vito shook her off. All Vito could see was Joan's beautiful face and the dark blood exiting her abdomen. Fueled by his anger, Vito crossed the parking lot to meet Ron while Samantha, Jacqueline, and Genevie watched.

Ron stood waiting—five-foot-eleven, two-hundred forty-nine pounds of solid muscle, and mean as a snake.

When Vito got within striking range, Ron lowered his shoulder and charged. Vito turned to his side and let Ron fly by but not without Vito getting clipped in the side.

Damn, he's fast for carrying all that weight.

Vito recouped and led with a roundhouse kick to the side

of Ron's head. Ron shook his head and laughed.

Shit, that would have put most men down on one knee, Vito thought.

Ron immediately turned half circle and landed a vicious blow to Vito's blocking arm, causing it to smash into the side of his own face. Ron continued with a savage left to the body.

Vito dropped to one knee, trying to shake off the blows, and regroup. He had only seconds.

Ron charged him, "You coward, stand up and fight," he yelled. "I thought you had more than that in you."

Just as Ron was about to make contact, Vito struck the right kneecap with a knife kick, and immediately swung it backward and struck Ron's left kneecap. Ron went down hard, but first, he landed an elbow strike to Vito's head. Vito's vision went blank for a second.

Ron dragged himself out of striking distance as they both tried to get up. With a renewed burst of strength, Ron limped over and lifted Vito's head. "Look at me while I'm putting your lights out for good," he said, following his remark with a deep belly laugh.

Vito touched Joan's necklace and heard a deep resonating voice in his head. ***You will not die.*** With an unexpected force, Vito lifted himself straight up and out of Ron's clutches and delivered a powerful slap to Ron's smug face.

Stunned, Ron turned back angrily, blood and spittle erupting from his mouth and nose before he could register what had happened.

Vito struck another vicious blow to his nose that caused it to flatten across his face. You couldn't even see his nostrils anymore.

Ron screamed, but as the adrenaline surged within him, he yelled, "Is that all you got?" He picked Vito up and threw him to the ground, then lifted his leg to literally stomp him into the pavement.

Vito shot straight up from his knees and hooked one arm into Ron's crotch, into a fireman's carriage, catapulting his body upward and over. Ron's free leg kicked out aimlessly as his head struck the ground, and blood appeared inside his ears and down the back of his head. Vito slowly stood and looked down at Ron before placing his foot on his neck and applying pressure. Ron tried to grab his foot and take it off of him, but he had no leverage. His face turned red, and his hand began to flail. Then the earsplitting noise of a gun going off brought Vito back to reality.

Genevie stood there, shaking and crying, the gun still in her hand. "You can't kill him."

Ron's other hand slipped out of his pocket and pinned a tracker onto Vito's inner pant cuff as Vito stood over him, blood dripping from his face and hands. He looked directly into Genevie's eyes, then bowed his head, forfeiting to her wishes. That was all Ron needed. He scooped himself up and took off running towards the open alleyway to the street.

Sister grabbed hold of Vito. "Let him go."

"That's all right. His adrenaline will only take him so far.

He's a dead man and doesn't know it."

"How do you know that?"

"I was once shot twice, and both bullets went clean through, but I was able to kill the two men before the adrenaline wore off and I went down. In my case, they weren't mortal bullet holes. Not like Ron's injuries he just sustained. He's done for."

Ron's running slowed to a stagger as he turned and yelled, "Next time, I'll kill you," and flipped them the bird. He slipped his phone out of his pocket and started to call someone as he wobbled out into the street. At that moment, a truck flew by, and Ron's large frame looked like a bug on its windshield.

Genevie looked at Vito in shock, then began to cry. He grabbed her and tried to comfort her but he was also in a rush. "We must get out of here before the police get here and try to detain us."

Sister sobbed. "I didn't know this would entail so much death and violence."

"Sister, I'm so sorry that you had to get mixed up in all this, but we are working for the greater good. Come on," he said as they hustled over to the two FEU agents. They both were maintaining a shaky stance as they checked themselves out for further injuries. "Are you all right?"

"We need a little patching up, but we'll be fine. Holding herself up with one hand on her knee, Samantha said, "Over there is Jacqueline, and I'm Samantha, Sam for short."

"I suggest we get out of here before we attract any more attention. The police are likely on their way already."

They headed for Vito's car. "Sister, can you sit in the back and see if Jacqueline needs help. Samantha, sit up front with me and tell me what the FEU will do next."

Samantha got in and sat on something, then jumped up and checked the seat. Before the light went off and the buzzing stopped, she saw an out-of-country number on the phone. It looked like a phone number in Rome. Samantha waved the phone in the air. "Whose is this?"

"That's mine," Sister said, and grabbed for the phone.

Jacqueline piped up from the back seat. "The quickest way back to the states and Simon Collage will be to get to the closest airport and grab a puddle jumper to Tel Aviv and then to the states."

Chapter Forty-Three

IT WAS COLD and stormy in Ohio as the CIA drove down the tarmac towards their plane at the Ravenna Arsenal. Jake took a glance at his phone and saw that Ron had called. *Great,* he thought. *Vito is dead, and I have the relics.*

"Who's in charge here?" Jake barked as he boarded the plane.

"That would be me, sir," a brash, young soldier said. The same one who had hit Russell. "What can I do for you?"

Jake smiled. "Transport me and that package to Washington, D.C."

"I'll speak to pilot about our destination sir."

Jake sat in the front of the G700 enjoying his drink. *Kristoff will be happy I have done all he wished, and I will become the next President of the United States. If only he would answer his phone...*

Jake became more and more frustrated with every unanswered ring. He wanted to impress Kristoff with his success in retrieving the relics and gloat over Vito's death. Instead, the answering machine clicked on, and Jake had to relay his rant of success to a recorder. "Kristoff, I'm already writing my presidential acceptance speech. You shall have your relics as soon as we land. Also, I have eliminated Vito."

The plane took a sudden jolt and bounced downward, then roughly pushed back up. Flying was not like driving a car and seeing the potholes to avoid. Air pockets were invisible and couldn't be prepared for. The inside of the plane flashed with a brilliant light before they heard the thunder; hail the size of softballs took them by surprise as it slammed the plane.

The pilot came over the intercom. "Please take your seats and buckle in. We have some rough weather ahead; I will be climbing to twenty-nine thousand feet for smoother air space, forty-one thousand if necessary."

Pointing the nose of the plane upward, the engines felt like they were stalling. The pilot took the plane off autopilot, choked the throttle, and evened out the engine. It was just in time to hear a scream and a loud explosion from the right engine as the flames lit the sky. The passengers were glued to their seats and staring out the window.

Rousing himself, the CIA agent-in-charge, a guy named Dunstan, started barking orders. "Be calm. We have enough parachutes for all of us." He walked up and down the aisle, tossing each person a parachute. He stopped by Jake to show him how to slip into his.

As Jake started to slide into his parachute, he wondered, *Is becoming President worth all I have been through? Killing people, getting shot at, beaten up, and possibly dying in a plane crash. To say nothing of having the woman I loved killed.* He continued to buckle up and strap his chute on.

They were over the eastern seaboard when Dunstan got hold of his superiors and told them the location where an extraction was needed. Jake grabbed the Package with the relics inside and got ready to jump. *In a tin can, on fire, and with only one exit into a frozen river. Shit.*

The door was released from its handle, and it popped out into the night air with a loud swoosh and a cold chill. The passengers jumped one at a time, with two agents sandwiching Jake between them. They landed in the Potomac River.

Treading water, Dunstan said, "Listen up. I have notified my superiors, and they'll have someone here in about twenty minutes."

In the low light of Kristoff's office, shadows bounced off the walls in front of his desk; the cherry leather furniture had an odd glow. Dripping water, Jake could not wait to tell Kristoff the excellent news. At the same time, the CIA agent Dunstan looked on.

"Jake, I received your message. I hope you have your speech in order. Now, shall we see what your rewards are? Let's take a peek at that package."

"Oh yes, sir, it wasn't easy getting these relics and having Vito disposed of, but it is done." Jake reached into his knapsack, produced the Package, and set it on the desk. They all smiled proudly.

"Well done. You did this all by yourself?"

"Yes, sir. Well, I had some help," Jake said, looking at the agent with a grin.

Kristoff went over and opened the Package. His massive smile abruptly turned into a hideous look, and the temperature in the room instantly rose fifteen degrees. Everyone in the room stepped back. Perspiration was already beading up on their foreheads.

Kristoff picked up the package and threw it at Jake. It nearly knocked him to the floor. With spittle and what seemed like foam coming from his mouth, he screamed, "You incompetent fool! You are worthless. And you," he said, looking directly at the CIA agent, "you were sent so Jake wouldn't fuck up."

With one quick stride, Kristoff closed the distance between him and the agent. His right arm struck faster than the stroke of a piston. He grabbed the agent by the throat, lifting him off the ground and squeezed hard. Dunstan's eyes bulged, then Jake heard the snap of his neck. The agent fell like a rock as Kristoff stared at Jake.

Trembling, Jake started babbling about how the agent gave him the package, how he didn't know that the FEU had switched them.

"Now, now, Jake, I believe you. I know that the CIA is a little incompetent." Grabbing him by the shoulder, Kristoff squeezed. Jake felt indescribable pain and tears filled his eyes.

"Now listen up, Jake. I'm going to give you one more chance to fix this. You will get to Garfield Ledges before anyone else and stake out the college. Be ready for them to bring the relics there to be picked up."

All Jake could do was bow. "Yes, sir."

"What are you waiting for?" Kristoff screamed.

Kristoff barked more orders at the surrounding peons. "Get that body out of here and get the director of the CIA in my office immediately."

"Yes, boss."

Everyone in the room scrambled; no one faster than Jake.

Chapter Forty-Four

WHEN HE ENTERED his office, the only light in the room came from the Resolute Desk. Everyone had made a joke about him bringing back that desk, but he just loved the history of it.

The "Resolute Desk" had been made from the oak timbers of the British ship, H.M.S. Resolute as a gift to President Rutherford B. Hayes from Queen Victoria in 1880. Every president since Hayes have used it, except Presidents Johnson, Nixon, and Ford.

He pulled the curtain to one side and stared out at the night. The amber-colored streetlights now shown through. He always felt like someone was watching him in this office.

Sitting down, he allowed himself to take a deep breath and stretch. He reached over and pulled on a gold chain. The soft light cast his shadow across the wall and windows. The constant espionage and treachery of the operation he had undertaken with the FEU was burdensome, but it had to go off without a hitch.

Forty-eight hours left before the election, he went through

his mental checklist again. He concluded that he was one step ahead in almost all areas, The only thing in doubt was the possession of the relics.

He heard some noise down the hall. A member of his Secret Service detail peeked his head in. "Sir, Johnnie is here with one of his friends."

"It's okay." He waved them in. "What are you guys up to?"

"Hi, Dad. I'm showing off your office," Johnnie said as both boys approached the desk.

Trent, Johnnie's friend, placed his phone down as he walked around the office. "This is unbelievable. I'm in the Oval Office."

"Yes, you are. So, what do you think of it?"

"It looks a little older than I thought, but it's still cool. Just think of all the great things done in this office."

"Indeed. John, take Trent to the kitchen and order any ice cream he wants. I'll be down shortly to join you for my favorite, chocolate and peanut butter."

"Okay," Johnnie said, taking off to the kitchen with Trent hot on his heels.

POTUS saw that Trent had left his phone and started to call his secret service agent to get it back to him when he stopped. He picked up the phone, shut off the light, and left his office. "Cliff, I'm going down to the kitchen. I'll meet you in my quarters," he told the agent at the door.

He felt something buzz, and retrieved Trent's phone from

his pocket. He swiped his finger to the left, and the phone lit up. As he did so, the call ended, but the phone stayed on, so he punched in a number. He looked around to ensure that he was alone, then pushed "Send."

When the other line picked up, he said, "This is a different number. Just say yes or no. Are you okay and clear?"

"Yes, we are good."

"Okay, listen, do you remember the last time you were in Ohio and how you got there and back?"

"Yes. Why?"

"Good, I suggest you do the same now. I believe my office communications are compromised."

"Okay, I will see you soon."

That will get them back safe, and it's coded enough that no one will ever know what the message meant even in the unlikely event this is found.

Russell called his agents together. "Slight change in plans. Do you guys remember the last time we went to Ohio?"

"Yeah, we rode in from vacation."

"Exactly. We're now going to rent some motorcycles and ride back into D.C. Boss says it's safer that way."

"Great," came the consensus.

"Closest bike shop in Garfield Township will be Mantua Harley Davidson about two and a half miles from Simon College. We can stay at the Garfield Ledges Inn and get there first thing."

When they reached the Inn, Russell remembered the first time he was there, the beauty of Simon College—like a storybook college. The old, glowing lamppost lights, herringbone and cobblestone walkways, blended into a beautifully mysterious setting. Then he thought about Billy Campbell, the only person to ever best him. *I highly doubt that man is human.*

Set up in the Dining hall Russell gave last-minute instructions to his men, I'll take first watch. Entering the cool night, he moved swiftly into the dark but seemed to hit a brick wall and bounced back. "What the heck?"

There stood Billy Campbell from Simon College. Russell looked at him with amazement. "I remember you. The last time we met was right here at this college when the New Agers were trying to send out their message years ago, and you outfoxed all of us. What are you doing here?"

"Hello, to you too," Billy said.

"Yes, hello. Now, what are you doing here?"

"I came here to get the relics. I know that's not what you want to hear, but I must return them to where they rightfully belong, and that's with Vito Rosario."

"I'm sorry, but you know I can't give those up to you."

"I thought you might tell me that, Russell, but you must look at the bigger picture. No government agency can lay claim to them. They are too powerful. They must be brought back into the Church or back onto holy ground."

"Right now, my men and I are on high alert, waiting for an

attack from the cabal to get those relics, and I know that you can handle yourself, but I would suggest you leave now before anything starts."

"I can't leave without those relics."

"We can talk about this later. Right now, I must prepare for their attack." Russell turned to leave and felt a gentle but unbreakable grip turn him back around.

Looking into Billy's eyes, Russell felt a comforting peace come over him as a blazing white light shone through the clouds. So bright he wanted to cover his eyes. But he could not move, and his peaceful smile turned into shock and disbelief. An explosion appeared before him, and his heart rate doubled. His body temperature continued to rise, rising hotter than 107 degrees and climbing. A nightmare of destruction appeared before his eyes. It looked like heaven and hell were at war. Then he saw the American flag go down covered by a mushroom cloud.

The sight became unbearable. Russell's body quaked. "No more," he screamed. "No more!"

Billy raised Russell's head and shook him out of his trance-like state.

Russell looked into Billy's eyes. "What the hell was that?"

"That will be the consequences if I do not get those relics back to where they belong."

"I don't know what just happened, but I know it was not of this earth." Russell cocked his head, hearing his men at the door.

"Come in," he said, his voice halting. "We've had a change in plans," he said, after they'd taken their seats.

"Has something happened?" one of them asked.

Russell looked at Billy. "You show them what you showed me. My team needs to see what I saw."

"You're making this a little difficult," Billy said. "You don't know the repercussions of me exposing myself."

"You know that we all took an oath to protect this country and these guys will take a stand no matter—win, lose, or draw."

"This is not the best way to tell them."

They all looked at Russell. "What are you talking about?" one of them asked.

"All right, close your eyes and bow your heads," Billy said. And as they did so, one by one, they started to sweat and tremble while making deep guttural noises. The temperature began to climb as each saw a different nightmare of a future in which those relics were released upon the earth by an ungodly force. After a long painful moment, Billy called each of them by name, and they slowly returned to normal.

When they looked at one another, they made different remarks to each other. "Look, Russell, your hair is a little white around the edges."

"Glen, you look like you aged in the face."

"Amanda, you have little crow's feet."

The group started to lament the horrific nightmares they had experienced, each of them feeling the burden of the knowledge weighing on them.

"You paid the price to see the future. You would not take my word on faith," Billy said.

"All right," Russell said. "Take them! Take the relics! Any chance you have a message for my boss?"

"Yes, just tell him that his Higher Power called on you to put them in safekeeping, He'll understand."

"Sure he will," Russell groaned. "Where are you taking them?"

"Back to Simon College."

"Good to know. Now get out of here. I've got work to do."

Kristoff raised his head and looked with a menacing eye across the eight-foot, cherry wood desk, locking on to the insolence of someone just walking into the office uninvited.

"My Master, forgive me. There has been a disturbance in the spiritual realm near Simon College, and I need to know what you would have us do?"

"It can mean only one thing," Kristoff said, his voice deep with vitriol. "The relics are there, and my demon lord has failed to keep Billy locked up. I want Cersei to follow up and keep an eye on Jake, that incompetent fool. Tell her I want him alive until I get my relics, and then I will dispose of him. Leave me."

"Yes, sir."

Kristoff hit the "Send" button on his phone, and when it rang more than once, he sneered as he waited.

On the other end, the Cardinal's hands started to shake.

"Cardinal Lintzinburg."

"Listen, I expect you to answer without hesitation when I call. Understood?"

"Of course, sir. What can I do for you?"

"That little bastard Vito is still alive and I don't have my relics yet. Neither you nor Jake got the job done."

Lintzinburg's throat felt as dry as sand. "I don't know how that happened. The old man is also still alive." The Cardinal jolted at Kristoff's ear-splitting shriek into the phone.

"The old man dies the day Jake becomes President, and I get my relics. Do we understand each other?"

"Perfectly."

"Now, let's make this happen. Vito Rosario must die or you will take his place."

"I will reevaluate the situation at once. Good-bye."

Within moments, Kristoff, stood behind his demon lord Retribution. It was already too late to react, as the demon lord suddenly felt his presence, and all he saw was a flash of red and black as his head fell past Kristoff's sword.

Chapter Forty-Five

"Dean, be seated."

Dean did as Kristoff ordered, feeling intimidated in the midst of the deceptively elegant and welcoming setting.

"Your agents have failed.

Dean swallowed hard, knowing how Kristoff reacted in the face of disappointment.

"Now I have a bigger mess to clean up, but I still need to retrieve my package and eliminate two obstacles." Kristoff slapped his hand hard enough to hear a crack in the wooden desktop. "And my time is up."

Dean's anger rose in his throat before he remembered who he was talking to. "What…what can I do to help you?"

"Let's start with my two targets."

"I promise you they will be eliminated."

"They had better be or the consequences will be devastating…for you, my friend."

"Where are they now?"

His nervousness eased for the moment, Dean leaned

forward and nodded. "Okay then, here is my plan…"

A devious smile appeared on Kristoff's face as he nodded. "So be it. Get it done. Wait, I have something special for them. Where will that drone take off from?"

"Tel Aviv."

"There will be a package there shortly with ammunition your men should use. Make sure you handle this?

"As you wish."

Vito and Genevie parted ways with the two FEU agents. They would all meet up later. Samantha and Jacqueline lingered to watch for any problems before last minute ticket purchases.

Vito and Sister purchased their tickets, then were escorted down the stairs to the tarmac and a vintage propeller plane that looked like it had been used in some dated movie from the '80s.

As they approached the aircraft, the airport alarms went off. Horns blared and security cars took off in all directions. Everything was in chaos. Hearing a loud buzzing sound, the passengers looked toward the sky, and pointed to a toy plane diving in on them. They ducked and screamed.

Having seen it first, Vito noticed that the flying object released something that streaked toward them. He shoved Genevie so hard that she hit the ground just as the object struck him in the chest right next to the heart. He felt a sudden sting and reached for his chest, growled from the pain, and staggered back and fell over Genevie.

Genevie felt her skin tingle and the hair at the nape of her neck rise as she rolled over and started patting him down. "Vito, are you hurt? Talk to me."

Vito saw the anguish in her eyes. "I don't know for sure, but I feel like fire ants are biting me in the chest."

Sister pulled open Vito's shirt. "Let me see." There was a small puncture wound on his chest next to his heart.

The drone started to circle back when something struck it and it exploded. Jaqueline and Samantha saw this and ducked back inside the airport.

Vito shook off Sister. "I'll be all right. Let's get out of here."

Before he could fully stand, One of Dean's men was there and kicked him in the ribs and Vito went back down.

Sister Genevie moved to attack the CIA agent who shoved his pistol in her face.

"I would think twice about your next course of action. It could be your last."

Samantha looked out onto the tarmac and watched Vito and Sister being captured.

Watching on video cam, Kristoff said, "Send your men down and grab them. Put them in an office and have them call me."

Dean nodded. "I have prepared a special office. It's the most secure room in the entire facility. Secure from all electronic surveillance and unauthorized people."

"Get it done."

"Immediately."

As Vito and Genevie looked up, they heard the slide being racked back on a .45 semi-automatic weapon and a voice saying, "Get up," and "Let's go."

The guard unlocked the door to the small office—army green walls, a steel-grey desk with two chairs, and a monitor on a table. He shoved them each into a chair, tied them up, and taped their mouths shut. A 40-inch hi-def TV monitor faced Vito and Genevie. Vito tested his bonds immediately by pulling and yanking on them to try and free himself. Genevie looked around in shock. Vito screamed into the tape; his shouts muffled beyond recognition.

The agent teased him by mouthing something, and then slapped him, telling him to "Shut up." The guard's watch suddenly started to beep. He shut off the alarm. "Hold on," he said as he turned on the TV monitor. "We have some late-breaking news for you."

On screen, Kristoff sat in full living color, obviously delighted.

"We meet at last, face to face, if not in person." The smirk on Kristoff's face and the burning red orbs for eyes was a look that would be forever burned into Vito's memory. "Now, officer, let's start this little game of ours. Pull your weapon and aim it at the pretty lady's head. Then, rip the tape from her friend's mouth."

His lips stinging, Vito yelled out, "You son of a bitch, let her go now. I promise I will kill you and this puppet of yours."

"Quiet now, and let me tell you how this game will play out. First, do you remember you got hit with something on the tarmac? Such a tiny little object. No bigger than a pin, was it? But it didn't kill you. At least it hasn't yet."

"What have you done, you sick bastard?" Vito spat, trying again to free himself.

"Tsk, tsk. Now, I have placed a capsule of a special material inside your chest. Does the dart that you stopped from hitting the Pope, the one with a drop of my blood in it, sound familiar? Now that capsule will go off at my command, or within the time frame I have set up for you. I will give you to the count of ten to answer my questions and save your girlfriend over there. Do we understand each other?"

Vito shook his chair violently, trying to escape. He yelled, "Please, leave her out of this! She is an innocent."

"Oh, but you brought her into this; how innocent do you believe she is? Officer, get your revolver out and empty it. Good. Now, Vito, where are my relics, and where is the key to deciphering the code? One."

"Listen, I couldn't get the key to deciphering them."

"Two. Officer, grab your revolver, and you may place a round in the chamber now."

"Wait, don't do this. She has nothing to do with our business."

"Three. You may cock the hammer."

The guard gave Vito a smug smile and pulled the hammer back.

Vito could smell a vinegary odor emanating from the guard, who truly enjoyed the fear in the room. "No! Don't do this; please listen. I want to help you, but you must do the right thing here."

"Four. Place the gun to her temple."

"What do you want from me? Untie me, and I'll help you get whatever you need."

"Five. Fire!"

Click. As Sister looked at Vito in terror, nothing happened as she cried into her tape.

The guard laughed.

"Please untie me, and I'll take you to the rabbi's temple to get what you need."

"Six. Spin the chamber. I believe she doesn't mean that much to him."

"You can't just shoot an innocent person."

"Seven. Don't think for a moment that I won't kill her."

"Okay, okay, we need to go back to Rome, where I have them hidden."

"Eight. Officer, give her a taste of what's about to happen."

The gun went off as both Vito and Genevie screamed. Genevie's ears were ringing, and an instant pain seared her brain from the loud explosion that went off right by her ear. The horror on her face told Vito everything he needed to know.

"Please, don't do this. You don't have to. Please tell me what you want me to do. I don't have the relics."

"Nine. Put another bullet in the chamber and spin it again. I don't believe you think I will kill her. Last chance."

"Okay. The clues have to be deciphered by a rabbi who knows…"

"That's enough lying. Ten. Shoot her."

Just then the door flew open, and two shots went off. Samantha leveled the agent as his gun went off, putting his revolver's round into the ceiling. Jacqueline started to untie Vito and Genevie as Kristoff went ballistic on screen. The two FEU agents, Vito, and Genevie stopped dead in their tracks as they heard the earsplitting sounds from the monitor and watched Kristoff morph halfway into his true, demonic self. There on the screen was hell itself. His head looked like a black fire, red hot coal with alternating black and white teeth in what seemed to be a jawbone of an ass with horns for ears.

"My God, what are we looking at?" Jacqueline gasped.

"That is what we are fighting," Vito said. "The ultimate supernatural being from hell. Satan in the flesh. And he wants those relics for their power."

"Vito," Genevie yelled, "We need to find a way to get that poisonous capsule out of your chest."

"What capsule?" Samantha asked.

Genevie rapidly explained what happened to Vito on the tarmac.

"I have heard of only two methods to get those out of the

body. One is simple. Just cut it out. Where is it?"

Vito turned around and showed her his chest. "The lump looks right on top of the pulmonary valve and right above the tricuspid valve. We can't cut near that without the proper equipment. Shit."

The other method is a lot more complicated. We need to get a current close enough to the capsule's ends and hit it with eighty-eight to one-hundred-and-eight megahertz at ten-second intervals. This will kill the "explode" signal and give you time to retrieve it from under the skin," Samantha said.

"But we don't have what we need here in this room," Jacqueline responded.

Genevie yelled, "Vito, what are you doing?"

"I need to get this out of me or render it useless before this guy Kristoff keeps his promise."

Climbing up on the chair, Vito tried to reach the ceiling light, but he was three inches too short. "Damn. Just wait. Samantha, I need you to take the back panel off that monitor." Climbing back down, he looked around and grabbed the monitor out of Samantha's hand. She looked at him as if he were crazy. "I need the table."

All of a sudden, he bent over and grabbed his head. His eyes narrowed as he moaned in pain. Then, it subsided just as quickly.

"That was the capsule moving," Samantha said. "We need to hurry,"

Vito hopped up on the table and pulled down the ceiling's

T5 fluorescent light and electrical conduit. The bulbs shattered. They were now working in the dark.

"Shit, Jac, shine your phone light on me," Samantha said.

"Do you have it opened yet?"

"Yes."

Vito dropped to the floor on all fours and started to moan. His eyes blinked rapidly, as he began to tremble.

"You better do what you're going to do now, or it will be too late," Jacqueline said.

Vito first took the monitor cord between his teeth, biting down and pulling it simultaneously, exposing the wires and ripping off the plug. Next, he pulled out the black and red wires from the light fixture, brought them over to the monitor, and spliced them into the CPU. He could only hope he was right and that his eidetic memory wouldn't fail him now.

Vito handed the wires to Samantha. "You can still see it sitting right under the skin. Just be careful not to go deeper than the wires that I bared. Now do it."

She nodded. "Sorry, Vito," she said as she jabbed both wires on either side of the capsule ends and counted to ten before pulling them out. Vito protested the pain. She repeated this three times. On the third try, there was an electric spark, and the smell of burnt flesh as Vito's body went into a seizure. He flopped like a giant fish out of the water, gasping for life.

Everyone in the room held their breath as Vito's body slowly emerged from the seizure. Jacqueline scooted over the top of his body and rolled him over to check his pulse. As they looked on, she shook her head. No pulse.

Genevie knelt above Vito's chest as Samantha got ready to give him mouth-to-mouth.

"On my count of five-one thousand, give him mouth to mouth." Genevie started pumping his chest with a count of one-one thousand, two-one thousand, etc., until she hit five-one thousand. Then Samantha expanded Vito's lungs with precious air.

"Wake up, Vito," Genevie yelled. "Breathe!"

They repeated the breathing and compression for several more minutes, after which Jacqueline looked at Genevie and shook her head.

Rather than concede, Genevie raised her arms high and shouted, "In the name of God, breathe, you pain in the ass." She slammed her fists down on his chest hard enough for his whole body to bounce. Samantha and Jacqueline looked on in surprise, but no life stirred within him. They all bent their heads as their eyes welled with tears.

Then they heard a cackle from the floor, and they all looked down at Vito. His eyes were wide open, and he was rubbing his chest. He clutched Joan's necklace and said a silent prayer as the others all grabbed and hugged him.

"Easy," he said, grateful. "I'm in pain here."

"Vito, I thought I lost you," Genevie cried.

They all breathed a sigh of relief, laughed, and hugged each other again.

Chapter Forty-Six

THE ELDER MAN refused a wheelchair as he used his crutches to pull himself along the gangway to take his seat in the first-class section. The group that came in behind him looked like a close knit group of friends. He smiled at each person getting on the plane; he loved to study people. He always wanted to have friends like that but was too much of a loner.

Genevie had found a new friend in Samantha, and they sat across the aisle from Jacqueline and Vito. The flight attendant's voice came over the mic with the standard pre-flight instructions.

"Please, everyone, take your seats. We will be taxiing to the runway shortly and dimming the cabin lights, but the floor will be lit for your safety."

The soft cabin lights helped them adjust their eyes to the darkened skies. Vito and Genevie each ordered a glass of wine while Samantha dozed off as soon as they were in the air. Jacqueline picked up the inflight magazine and flipped through the pages as the drone of the engines slowly put her to sleep. Vito and Genevie said a prayer for their narrow escape and laid back to rest.

As they disembarked at Cleveland Hopkins Airport, Samantha told Vito that Russell had a surgical team waiting. Samantha led them all to the VIP lounge and introduced Vito to the surgical team. “They’ll get that capsule out.” Samantha grabbed Vito and looked him in the eye. “Russell says, ‘First we do, then we trust.’” Vito nodded with a slight grin.

“Tell Russell he’s one of the only people I do trust.”

About an hour later they all met back up, and with warm hugs that could only come from experiencing a life-or-death moment, they said their good-byes. Samantha and Jacqueline had to report back to Russell and the FEU. Vito, patched up, felt relieved. He grabbed Genevie and they headed to Simon College.

He pulled the rental into the Derby and Sash Pub parking lot across the street from the backside of the college and directly in front of Garfield Ledges Inn. They sat and watched to see if they could detect anything different from the norm.

“I know the tunnels Joan was talking about,” Genevie said, “but I just can’t remember all the details of how to get in.”

“Okay, then how about pointing us in the right direction of a tunnel entrance rather than us using the front of the building.”

“I remember one was by the financial office.” Genevie pointed toward the far-right corner of the campus from where they were parked. “Joan used to say that’s where the Fat Man’s office was.”

Vito saw what looked like a tree resembling a witch's hand growing out of the ground and pointed to the herringbone walkway by the back door of the building.

"That's right. Joan said if you bounced a rubber ball on the brick walkway you could hear hollowness under the bricks."

"Let's go. We need to buy a hard rubber ball and some different clothes. We'll come back tonight under cover of the moonlight. Is there any way you can get hold of Billy?"

"Yes, maybe through the switchboard," Genevie said as she pulled her phone out and connected to Billy's voicemail. She left a brief, cryptic message. "I'm looking to find out how the Fat Man traveled around campus without being seen. Can you help? I will be in town soon." She hung up. "That should do it. It should be coded enough that no one but Billy will understand it."

The amber lights from the old-fashioned lamppost shone warmly across the street onto the Garfield Ledges Inn.

"You look good in jeans, and the baseball cap is a nice touch," Vito remarked.

"Thanks. You know you could have bought some new clothes yourself."

"I didn't have that much time. It took me over fifteen minutes to get a rubber ball. I'll be fine. Let's go."

Vito scouted the area, thinking he saw a familiar face at the inn but shook it off as impossible and moved on. They made their way back to the financial office and found the tree that looked remarkably like a witch's hand growing out of the ground. They followed the fingers to the herringbone walkway and started to bounce the ball as they walked.

Two gentlemen in suits walked towards them, and as they got closer, one of them reached into his inside coat pocket. Genevie suddenly grabbed the ball, laughed, and turned to Vito. "Give me my squeeze ball back I've been looking for that."

At the same time, the man in the suit asked for a light for his cigarette. Vito responded to the gentleman, "Sorry, we don't smoke." The men moved on.

Genevie started bouncing the ball again as they got closer to the financial office. They heard Billy whisper, "Listen, you two, follow my voice and get over here. Let's get those relics and get you guys out of here."

As Billy slid the door closed behind him, another set of eyes watched with a smile.

"Keep going. I need a minute to adjust these new shoes; I'll catch up."

"Be careful and hurry up," Billy said.

Bending on one knee, she quickly took her sock off and stuffed it in the door jam, "I'm coming."

As they stood before the elusive and highly coveted package, Billy said, "I just retrieved these from the FEU. They were reluctant, but they finally acquiesced. You must get these back to Rome."

"I hate to break it to you…"

Startled by the voice of an Israeli behind them, all three turned to see the older man with crutches who'd been on their flight. Only now, there were no crutches, just the gun he held on them. He was most definitely neither old nor disabled. "You see, my employer needs the relics he paid for. Now Genevie, collect them up and bring them along."

Vito turned to look at Genevie. "You know this man?"

"Not intimately like you know her. Maybe that will come." The man nodded to her and smirked. He waved her over to him with his gun as Vito looked like someone had just pushed him out of an airplane with no parachute.

"I thought I seen you earlier. And you Genevie I've had my suspicions," Vito said, "especially after I found the bug in the car, but I prayed that I was wrong, You set that up too, didn't you?

"We work for your friend, Cardinal Lintzinburg. As for the why, we have different motives. Mine is, as always, money. Sister's here is all about revenge. She never told you that you left her with a child, did she? Now that we are all caught up, hand over those relics."

Vito felt as though he'd been hit by a Mac Truck. "Genevie, I didn't know. Why didn't you tell me I have a child. His throat thickened and he felt his eyes beginning to well. Even so, he refused to let his emotions rule the moment. Instead, he decided to utilize a subtle move against his attacker that had gotten him out of similar situations in the past.

He focused his eyes just past the gunman, hoping to give

the gunman the impression that there was someone behind him. Then, Vito would twitch an eyebrow as though to signal this imaginary person. When the gunman whipped around, he brought the gun to bear on Genevie. Vito seized the moment and with a front kick he placed his captive against the wall and the gun went off missing Genevie altogether. He followed up with his best Krav Maga move which placed his foot at the throat of the attacker, their eyes locked for a nano second but all the gunman would ever see was a slight smirk before he felt the crushing of his neck.

Vito gathered up the relics. "Let's get out of here." He turned to Genevie, a sadness in his eyes that was not lost on her. "I'll get you out of here, then you're on your own."

Chapter Forty-Seven

ONCE AGAIN, JAKE sat at his desk in Washington, D.C., a fire crackling in his office fireplace, as he coordinated the attack at Simon College. Spotter One called in movement at the front of the auditorium, and Spotter Two called in motion at the side of the building. Two of the men closest to the disturbance moved into position. Jake's men waited for Vito and Sister Genevie in their designated places at all entrance and egress points to the college. "Be alert," was the message that came over their coms.

Billy made a commotion at the front of the auditorium to draw attention to his location. which left the roof unattended and the perfect place to escape. Vito and Genevie wiggled their way through the rooftop door.

As they lay on the roof, Vito raised his head to survey the area, then scooted across the top to check their escape route.

He nodded, and Genevie followed him to the edge as he lowered himself to the large balcony below. Genevie followed suit. Reaching upward, he grabbed her legs and directed them toward the window to avoid her jabbing herself on the balcony's wrought iron fence. As she continued to drop, he kept his hands on her sides and squeezed her slightly to keep her from coming down too fast.

When her feet touched the solid ground, Genevie looked into Vito's eyes. "Vito, I half expected you to drop me. I am sorry for hurting you and for all I have done to you."

"Please, stop. Now's not the time."

"Okay… well, if Billy did his job," she whispered, "we'll be able to get to the car undetected."

Vito nodded his assent. "Stay low and follow me."

Running for a short burst and ducking behind the campus foliage, they saw that the coast remained clear. Vito grabbed the car door and lifted the handle, only for it to snap back and out of his hand. He had been so intent on turning the inside light off that he had forgotten to unlock the car. The alarm went off, and the horn blasted, calling all the attention back to them. Vito punched the button on the fob, and he and Genevie jumped in and took off.

Spotter One yelled into his com, "They are across the street leaving the Derby & Sash Pub parking lot!" Jake's men rushed to their cars as Jake coordinated their rendezvous with Vito and Genevie. They gave chase.

Vito's car hit seventy miles per hour on Route 82 as he

headed west through Mantua. He took a left on Diagonal Road, part gravel, part asphalt, and the car fishtailed as his rear tires hit the gravel shoulder of the road. He was taking the "S" turns too fast for his car.

The lead chase car provided Jake their location and requested help. "We just crossed the city limits to Streetsboro and now we're turning down Frost Road." Their car was so big it kept hitting the front end on the bottom of each new hill. The hills were too close together for that speed. "Jesus, this maniac is going to get us all killed."

The other teams were responding, "We're right behind you."

The car behind Vito could not get enough of an airlift under the front of it on one of the dips, and slammed into the hill, spun wildly out of control, and died, blocking both lanes of traffic. The next car creamed into the first and cleared both cars off the road, allowing the last vehicle to continue their chase.

Vito turned into a warehouse district and tried to hide in the largest warehouse parking lot. A sign read in large letters, "Ogilby & Sons Distribution."

"Sister, let's just sit here for a moment and see if we lost them."

Jake sat at his desk, listening to his men crash one at a time until they lost Vito's trail. He started a tirade and threatened all of them if they did not find Vito immediately. He began to stare into space, wondering how he would tell Kristoff if they could not find him again.

That was when he saw a package on his desk labeled "Personal Effects." He ripped it open. The note inside read, *Here are the effects of one Ron Wolneski.* Finding this useless, Jake tossed the package back on the desk. His mind wandered to more important matters. *How can I get away from Kristoff?* He was distracted by a light glow from the box. The jolt from him tossing the box back on the desk must have turned Ron's phone on.

Scrutinizing the phone, he noticed a blinking that emanated from the top of the phone. After pushing a few buttons, he realized that the tracking program was working. *Ron must have planted the tracker on Vito.*

Jake called the one surviving car and gave them the coordinates to Vito's location.

Genevie felt the hair on her arms rising. Gasping, she pointed, "They're here."

"Okay, let's even the odds a bit. We won't make this easy for them. This place is big enough to hide in."

They scrambled to the door where employees were smoking outside. As they rushed in, one of the employees they passed said, "Hey, you can't go in there."

Vito and Genevie came to a complete stop and stared at the sheer awesomeness of the place. It looked like it had layers on top of layers of conveyor belts moving at a fast clip while towers of bins and shelves were driving by themself in all directions. Some turned to the left, others turned in complete circles, and then took off again. Containers were moving in all different directions. The vessels would be heading straight when suddenly an arm would shoot out and send them down a separate conveyor system. They would hit forked junctions and discreetly be shoved to one side or the other. Tiny red beams of light did all this work.

Mesmerized by the operation, Vito didn't notice the two men charging in on them until Genevie yelled, "Vito!"

"You go down that way," he said, pointing. "I'll try to make them follow me." He waited till the last second, then turned in the opposite direction from Genevie.

They both started after Vito when one of the men snapped. "You go get the girl, asshole, I got this one."

The two men split up and chased them down either side.

The first man drew a bead on Vito and cut him off. As Vito turned left, he tackled him. Both men fell two levels down, landing on a conveyor belt heading upwards. They started wrestling, and Vito dropped the relics. They bounced off one set of conveyors, only to land on another of the belts heading in the opposite direction at high speed. One relic followed the other.

Vito grappled with the man, finally putting him in a chokehold until he went silent. Pushing the man's body out of the way, he scrambled to find the relics. He saw the light reflect off the golden box that held the thorn and chased it down, trying not to lose sight of it as it disappeared into the jungle of conveyor belts, boxes, bins, and rollers that filled the depths of the two-and-a-half-mile long warehouse.

Genevie had taken off down a long corridor of shelves and bins and hid. The second man saw her running and pursued her. She could hear him coming and felt her adrenaline spike. The closer he got, the more she trembled in her hiding spot. Her heart pounded in her ears even above the loud noise of the distribution center's machinery. She ducked behind a stack of bins, holding her breath. The second man was almost upon her when Genevie pushed the containers on top of him and fled deeper into the warehouse.

The remaining henchman got clear and reported in. "Sir, we're in a warehouse in Streetsboro. Can you close it down?"

Jake made a phone call to the Mayor of Streetsboro, Ohio, promising her a political favor if she would send the police to close down Ogilby & Sons Distribution.

"Done," she said. "The police will be there shortly."

An employee pointed to the upper part of the conveyor belt. "Look," she said, "it's jammed and some of the parts are spilling out. *Shit.* Someone call Ken and shut down the conveyor."

"Damn, let's get some of these parts into new containers." The line workers were yelling back and forth that the pushrod was broken and holding up everything.

Ken came in yelling, "What the hell happened, Karen? Tim get over there and shut this line down now!"

"Don't know, boss," Karen replied. "Looks like something

jammed the belt."

Tim opened the emergency box with his key and depressed the red button. The conveyor would not stop. Fuck. He ran toward the main panel two machines over to pull the power lever.

Karen grabbed a hook and start pulling parts off the belt. Other parts on the line started to back up faster than Karen could pull them off the conveyor. Just then, the conveyor came to a screeching halt. All you could hear was the loud click of the pushrod trying to retract—CLICK…CLICK…CLICK—but it could not.

"All right, Ken, I'll have to go up there and free that pushrod." Tim tried to hold onto the end rails to steady himself, but the conveyor was too broad. All Tim could hear was the click of that damn pushrod calling his name. So, he held onto one side and pulled himself upward. As the man got closer to the box, he felt weak, sweat dripped from every pore as he pulled himself closer to the pushrod. He turned. "I…don't know…what's…happening to me. This thing…is glowing…."

Some of the ladies pointed at Tim. "Something's wrong," they yelled. "He's going to fall."

"What's wrong with you?" Ken yelled. "Are you okay? I can't understand a word you're saying."

"There's a glow…coming out of a crack…in one of the jammed boxes."

"Can you get to it?"

Before he could answer, Tim fell onto the conveyor, rolling

back down to the feet of his supervisor. Ken bent down, shook him, and yelled, "Tim." But there was no movement.

Whispers became loud shouts. "What's the matter with him.?" Some of the women covered their mouths to stifle their cries.

Ken bent down and looked for a pulse; there wasn't one. It took a long minute for that news to register with the employees. Then they were all talking and crying at the same time. Some stood silent in shock.

"Call 911," Ken yelled, as he stepped back from Tim's motionless body. Ken was at the boiling point but he had nowhere to direct his anger. He yelled for Lisa. "Go get the Raymond lift truck, I want you to lift me up there."

Karen yelled, "Ken don't go up there right now. We don't know what happened to Tim." The others all clamored around mumbling.

Ignoring Karen's warning, Ken climbed up into the lift truck basket. "Take me up but keep your eyes on me."

A loud booming voice echoed off the conveyor. "I wouldn't do that if I were you."

Everyone stopped.

"Who the hell are you? What are you doing in my warehouse?"

"Those two little things that you see are two small boxes that belong to me."

Spittle flew out of Ken's mouth as he went in circles in the basket yelling, "Look, you son-of-a-bitch, whoever you are, one of my guys is dead because of you. Karen, call the police. Lisa, take me up. This guy will never get those boxes."

"If I were you, I'd take my advice and leave those boxes to me. Your friend over there got really dizzy and then started to sweat, and finally, his heart stopped. That's what will happen to you if you get too close."

"The fuck you say?" I told you, you will never get those boxes."

Lisa had stopped the lift truck. "You should listen to the man, Ken. What if he's right? I'm not willing to risk my life by getting that close to whatever is radiating and I don't think you should either."

The employees yelled for Ken to leave it alone. "We don't want to die either."

"No one's going to die. Lisa, take me up. This man will never get those boxes."

Vito spoke softly. "Lisa. Listen to me. That is not radiation but something much more powerful if released by the wrong person. Bring Ken down and take me up.

"Lisa, you work for me. Take me up. I'm overriding your controls. I'll take myself up."

Vito shook his head and pleaded one more time. "Don't do this, please."

"Don't go up there. Listen to the man," some said, while others said, "Don't let him have those boxes."

Vito shot a glance at the crowd and shook his head.

The bucket started to rise. When it got within a few feet of the conveyor belt, Ken started to feel dizzy. Sweat poured down his face. The bucket started to wobble as did the conveyor belt. Ken raised himself up high enough to reach out and grab both small boxes, then fell back into the bucket. He toppled over and let go of the boxes.

Vito ran under the basket and caught the boxes, quickly covering them with his hands.

Everyone jumped back expecting Vito to fall over dead.

When he didn't, the questions started coming at him in waves.

He looked around and opened his hand and the boxes started to glow. Immediately the crowd felt a tingle and a healing of their sorrow for this evening's events.

As Vito started to back away, he saw the police coming in. "Remember this, you have seen the divine this day." He slipped away as the employees encircled the police officer telling them their story of what just happened.

Around the corner, Vito took a quick moment and knelt on one knee to say prayers for the dead and dying souls. He felt his phone vibrate as he slipped out of the building.

Genevie's attacker heard the clamoring at the end of the conveyor belts and ran down to investigate. After he watched Vito get the boxes, he saw Genevie standing two floors up in the corner. She was trying to get Vito's attention, but to no avail, so she turned and found a stack of bins that looked out of service and hid behind them. Her pursuer stood right in front of the containers that she hid behind. As she held her breath, he looked one way, then another, and turned to leave when the stack of bins that Genevie was behind moved straight for him. He jumped out of the way just in time to see Genevie squatting down against the wall. He stood above her and waved his gun. "Come on, get up, let's go." He took her out the back emergency door as the alarm went off, and was in his car and gone before anyone got to that door.

Vito answered his phone. "If you want to see your girlfriend alive, you will do what I say. I will text you a phone number to call and you will follow the instructions you receive to the letter.

Chapter Forty-Eight

JAKE INFORMED KRISTOFF that they had Genevie and had called Vito for a trade. Kristoff knew that it would be all over within hours, and he would finally be taking over the power of The Divine he had fought since the beginning of time. With this information, Kristoff summoned his war council.

Dean, the CIA director, stormed in, screaming, "Kristoff, I'm tired of you pushing me around! Do you know who I am? I am the most powerful person in the United States government, and I want that weapons system you promised me."

Dean stopped dead in his tracks when he saw what was before him, an image so grotesque and terrifying that his heart nearly burst in his chest. He froze.

Satan morphed back into Kristoff. "Dean, my dear boy. I'm sure you are the most powerful person in the United States. But as you can see, you are merely a very, very small, impotent creature." Kristoff's grin showed the wicked action that were to come, and with a flamboyant flip of his hand, he said, "As far as your weapons system goes, forget about it. You were never going to get it anyway. Those relics were meant for me. I know that tomorrow, November 4, your people have your election for your petty, little president. It just so happens that this November 4 is the day that all the realms in the spiritual world will be aligned for the first time since the beginning of time. This day will be the day I finish what I started."

All Dean could hear was hideous laughter coming from around the table. He turned here and there, frantic, but saw no one.

"I will storm the gates of heaven, dethrone your mighty God, and He will grovel at my feet for all eternity. He looked Dean in the eye. "So, you see, Dean, you were never meant to get those relics or that weapons system, but I can help you a little. I can put you out of your misery right now." Kristoff morphed back into Satan and grabbed Dean by the head. When Dean felt Satan's hand, he screamed. His body started to melt as if molten lava had been poured over him. Within moments, Dean was a puddle of magma. Satan turned back to his war council. "Now where were we?"

"Go ahead and make the call," Russell said.

Vito whipped around to see Billy Campbell and Russell Carter standing behind him. They looked Vito up and down and saw that his white collar was ripped and barely hanging in position. His face bruised and battered, Vito bowed his head, then pushed the call button on the pre-dialed number. The phone rang twice before he heard a voice say, "You will go to the southwest terminal of the Akron Canton Airport. Ask for your ticket; it will be in your name. Take that flight to Dulles Airport. There will be a black SUV with government plates on it. Get in and tell them you want to see Jake Howard. They will know where to go. Do not deviate from my instructions. And tell no one, or you will never see your girlfriend again." The line went dead.

Billy looked at Vito and nodded. "I will see you when you need me." Then he turned away.

Vito looked at Russell. "How and why are you here?"

"You have good friends in high places. So, what is your plan?"

Vito shrugged. "I must get her."

Russell nodded. "But first let me make a phone call. Sir, there have been some difficulties with the packages, and I will need further intel and transportation." Russell went on to tell POTUS his situation.

Vito watched as Russell listened intently. "Oh sir, one more thing. This will be on CIA territory. Would you like me to declare ourselves to Dean at CIA Central?" Russell hung up and nodded to himself.

"Vito, as of late last night, Dean Caputto of the CIA has gone missing, and even his security team can't reach him. What have you gotten yourself into? Yet everyone is still on high alert for those boxes. So, listen up. The road you will be on turns into a fork. At that junction, my unit and I will be waiting to see if he takes you to the right of that fork. If so, that road goes to the empty ammunition depot."

Vito and Russell shook hands and went their separate ways. "I'll see you at that fork in the road," Vito yelled back at him. "Be ready to rain hell down on them."

Russell chuckled. "Who does this guy think he is—*Rambo?*

Vito walked into the Akron Canton Airport, retrieved his Southwest Airlines ticket, took a seat, and waited for his plane to board in forty minutes. As he sat there, anger welled up inside him as he had never felt it before, arousing something primeval deep inside. He had thought he had given this all to God, but it was bubbling back to the surface. The betrayal of Genevie and the child he never knew about. Cardinal Lintzinburg.

The Pope must be warned.

Vito looked around and found a doppelganger of himself. The man was dressed in high-fashion clothes and toted a high-end bag and luggage. Vito got up and followed him into the empty executive club. He greeted the man and then choked him out until he fell unconscious. Then he dragged him into an empty dressing room. He took the luggage and garment bag into another changing room and pulled out a black shirt and pants with a sport coat. The pants were too short, but the rest fit him to a tee.

Placing the sport coat on, he looked into the mirror. Damn, the shoulder pads did not fit his larger physique. The two relics sat on the table next to his old clothes. He sat and thought for a moment, then took off the sport coat, grabbed the nail cutters in the shaving kit, and cut a small opening in each shoulder. Wrestling out the padding, he covered the top of each box with a small amount and replaced them. His shoulders would hold everything in place; he checked himself in the mirror. *Not bad. This will work unless they grab me by the shoulders.*

He came out dressed in all black and proceeded to board the plane, with hopes of resting for the fifty-five-minute flight. Once he deplaned, he walked directly to the black SUV waiting for him.

As they checked him for weapons, the man stuck his hands inside the coat and patted him down. Vito shifted his weight from one foot to the other. At the same time, sweat appeared on his brow. "Hey, Max, look at this guy. He's sweating like a kid who got caught in a lie."

Max walked over, spun him around, put a hood over his head, then sucker-punched him in the gut. Vito doubled over and grunted. Then Max cuffed Vito's hands behind his back.

Using this time to calm his mind, Vito was reminded of having his eyesight taken away when Enzio tried to trip him up during his training session. Now, as Max pushed him into the back seat, Vito decided to sit back and say nothing, focusing instead on the road, the sounds, and the turns.

The driver laughed. "This schmuck didn't even bring a gun."

"That's because I plan on killing you both with your own guns."

They both laughed.

When they came upon the fork in the road, the driver asked, "Which way?"

"Right."

Vito catapulted his head into the driver's head. All you could hear was the crunch of bone-on-bone as the driver passed out. The front passenger reached for his weapon before he realized he needed to grab the steering wheel, and it was too late. His gun hit the floor as the SUV hit the tree and bounced backward with the driver's foot still on the gas. The SUV slammed back into the tree again. The front seat passenger's head went through the windshield. Both henchmen lay helpless and injured.

Vito's mind slowly came into focus. All he could hear was the motor running and the wheels churning in the dirt. Bending at the waist, he lowered his head between his legs, squeezed his legs together, and wiggled the hood off. He raised his head, surveyed the damage, and kicked the back door open. Clumsily he searched both men for the key to the handcuffs, luckily found it, and released himself. Then Vito took their guns and knives.

Canvassing the area, Vito heard a movement. He crept up behind the man. Recognizing him as one of Russell's, he placed a gun to his head. "Take me to Russell."

"Hey, Rambo." Vito turned to see Russell, getting out of an

SUV. "Leave my guys alone, and let's get Sister so we can get out of here. The ammo depot is about three clicks up the road. Let me break it down for you."

"No need. I've been here before."

Russell and his men looked at Vito with new appreciation.

"All right, take this com. It will keep you and the rest of us in direct communication. Let's head out."

Harsh winds appeared out of nowhere, shaking the trees as the foreboding clouds rolled in. They moved straight through the woods, up to the ammo depot. Within five hundred feet of the building, Russell gave a silent command with his fist to hold their positions.

"Hey, number one," came over Russell's com. "This place looks deserted."

"I know, be extra careful." He nodded, and they all took up their positions. Four went around back while Russell and the other three, including Vito, took the frontal attack position.

Within minutes everyone was in a position to breach. Everyone checked in. "All right, on my command of three. One… Two… *Now, now, now.*"

All the doors flew open at the same time. It was a perfect military strike. They all looked at one another. Why was there no resistance? Broken windows and an old, rusted warehouse racking system with one wall entirely made up of loading docks was all they found. The second floor held a roller conveyor with some unworthy casings spilled about. The 200,000-square-foot building was a picture of the past.

Russell, his team, and Vito were the only ones in the empty 5,000-square-foot office space except for one person—Sister Genevie, tied, mouth taped, and head down. One lone light bulb hung above her. The dim light seemed to cast a long shadow over the floor. The only sound was the creaking of old metal expanding.

Lightening flashed across the broken windows creating strange, grotesque shadows. The thunder vibrated some of the broken glass out of the window frames.

Vito ran towards Genevie while seven other voices yelled into their coms, "No!" and "Stop!" But it was too late. Vito had gotten within three feet of her, and without warning, Genevie and Vito were encased by a set of lights that formed a grid all around them.

Samantha yelled, "Don't move! That is not a regular photo sensor light." She walked up to the light grid, reached into her pocket, and threw something at the light. As soon as it hit, flames appeared, and it disintegrated. "This is a laser field. Any movement on their part will cut them to pieces."

Vito stood perfectly still, looked all around and took a deep breath. God help us. He felt a slight vibration in his heart.

Russell called out. "This is a first. Chung, find the power source, and let's see if we can defuse it. The rest of you, secure this depot. Let's remember that we have only minutes until Vito meets Jake."

Genevie sat slumped over. Exhausted, a tear rolled down her cheek.

"I'm so sorry for getting you into this, Genevie."

She didn't answer.

Vito tried to twist his arm to maneuver between the lasers. The upper part of his arm touched the laser and burned the loose part of his coat clean through. He yelled for Genevie to wake up.

She brought her head up, but quickly dropped it again.

"Sister, wake up. It's me, Vito."

Sister groaned and tried to speak but was slow to realize that the tape on her mouth held her back.

Chung came back into the room and marched straight up to Russell. "The power is being brought in from underground, and it's too deep for us to get to."

"Listen up. There has got to be a way to get this grid down. I want answers and suggestions now, and need I remind you that time is not on our side." The team had no doubt that Russell was in charge and expected answers.

"Wait a minute," Chung said. "That much power being used to keep those lasers on in a wireless setting needs some sort of booster, and even a small booster box would be able to do it. Let me check the walls."

"Check for what?" Russell asked. "Tell us. We'll all help."

"I can't tell you, but I'll know it when I see it."

"Okay, go. Vito has to be..." He paused to look at his watch, "at his meeting with Jake and Kristoff in eight minutes."

Chung took off as they all zoomed in on Vito. He was wiggling out of his coat. "Sister, I'm going to wrap my hand and arm with this coat. Then I'm going to take that tape off your mouth." As he reached toward her, everyone held their breaths. They could smell the burnt coat and flesh as Vito ripped the tape off her mouth. He started to wobble from the pain and almost fell over, but caught himself.

"Vito, stay still, damn it," Russell screamed.

Sister nodded her head and mouthed, "Thank you."

Chung returned. "What the hell smells so bad?" Though no one answered, they all looked at Vito. "I found it. But there is no way to short-circuit this type of box. It has a tiny hole that only allows for a unique tool to stop the lasers."

"All right, we need to get Sister Genevie out of here and Vito to his meeting in a few minutes. Let's get out there and look for the underground electricity."

"Vito," Genevie said in a raspy voice. "Listen to me." They all turned to hear what she had to say. "Do you still have the relics?"

Vito nodded and gingerly pulled his coat up, turned inside out what was left of it, and squeezed them out.

"Give them the golden matchbox with the thorn off of Christ's crown of thorns."

Vito looked puzzled for a moment; then a smile crossed his face. "Russell, come get this."

"What's that going to do?"

"This relic has the properties you need for opening that unique box. Come, take it."

Russell tried to reach in without cutting himself, but his

arms were too bulky. The smell of flesh reminded them this was *impossible.*

Samantha took her coat off and told Russell to move. "You can't do that. You will cut your arm off or close to it. I have the longest and the skinniest arms. I've the best chance of doing this."

Russell growled, "No, stand down."

"Sorry, but we're out of time. It's now, or we pack up and leave," Samantha said.

Russell hated when he was boxed in a corner like this and had to watch one of his team do something dangerous that he should be doing. He reluctantly nodded his agreement.

Samantha looked at Vito. "Are you ready?"

Vito nodded and positioned himself to twist and reach out as far as he could. Sweat dripped down his face and hit the laser, which sizzled. Samantha reached between two of the cross-like beams of the laser, to the point where she could no longer reach, and Vito stretched out all the way and touched her fingers.

"Okay, Vito, now move the golden matchbox to the tips of your fingers, and I will try to pinch it between my fingertips."

"Okay, here goes..." The box balanced on his fingertips and wobbled back and forth. Samantha hit the box with the end of her fingertips, and it fell back into Vito's palm. "Try it again," he said.

"I'll have to try to grab it when it tips to the front of your fingers. Otherwise, I won't be able to reach it."

"All right, ready…go."

They both reached out simultaneously, and as she reached for the wobbling relic, she hit the top of the box. Time froze as everyone watched it start to tumble downward. The air was sucked out of the room. But Samantha, quick as a snake, reversed her hand into a cup and caught the box. Vito had also moved reflexively to catch the box but froze again when he saw that she had recovered it. They all saw something hit the ground, followed by a few drops of blood. Vito grimaced and pulled his arm back, immediately starting to wrap the part of his skin that had been sliced off. He grabbed the necklace around his neck and said a silent prayer of thanks for keeping him safe.

Sister Genevie yelled, "Hurry and use the thorn to turn off these lasers!"

Samantha handed the box to Chung, and off he ran.

A moment later they all stood in darkness. The field was gone as fast as it had appeared.

Samantha stood next to Chung. "What happened using that relic?

"All I know is that when I brought the tip of the thorn close to the circumference of the hole in the power box, it felt like it was being drawn in like a magnet to steel. I know that I was under pressure. It felt like my hand started to tingle, and I thought I saw a soft glow of light for a quick second, but I couldn't swear to it." He shrugged his shoulders and caught up to Russell, shook his head, and returned the relic. "Don't ask," he said and walked away.

Russell grabbed Vito. "Are you all right?"

Vito nodded.

"Good, we need to go. Here, take the relics. You only have two minutes before they send someone here to kill her." Turning to his men, Russell called out, "All of you, get out of here before they get here. I'm sure we had to have set off some alarm."

Vito looked at Russell. He had seen that look before in every one of his team members' faces—tired, aggravated, hurt, and physically and mentally pushed to their limits. It was time to bring it! To end it now.

"Russell, stay here with them. I'll take it from here." Vito tucked the relics away. Trudging through the woods, he came upon an open area surrounded by trees. The rain glistened in the moonlight.

As Vito got closer, he froze in his tracks, his mind captivated by horrific memories. This was where the nightmares took place. All the lies from Enzio. He remembered Enzio bringing him to this facility for the training, the beatings, and the waterboarding. He dropped to his knees with such force that it rattled his bones. He brought his hands up and squeezed his head to stop the memories of the pain. In his mind's eye, this was the worst of it—the gruesome deaths of his family.

There they were again, his beautiful family, his father coming out from the trees screaming something he couldn't understand, but he saw the gun in Stefano's hands, and Vito quickly shot him, and he went down. Vito had run over to investigate when he heard his Momma yell for him. "Vito, why did you kill your brother and sister? Look at their beautiful bodies with bullet holes in them." Vito started to scream, "Momma, I can't understand you. Your face is gone. What is happening to me?"

Vito blinked his eyes and, in a flash like changing channels on a television set, it brought him back to reality. Vito opened fire. Then collapsed.

Two soldiers from the warehouse spotted Vito down. They came up from behind him, grabbed him and yanked him up. What the hell had happened here? He killed all of these men, and there was not one scratch on him.

Chapter Forty-Nine

THE SOLDIER YELLED, "We have been looking for you since you killed our driver and his partner. They slammed open the door to the warehouse and threw him in. "Grab that chair by the table," another soldier ordered. One of the soldiers struck Vito from behind, causing him to wobble on his feet.

Then a booming voice came out of the darkness. "Leave that man alone and leave us. Now. All of you." The command was so authoritative and resonating that the soldiers retreated immediately. "Jake, tie him up in that chair."

Pointing his gun at Vito, he coaxed him into the chair, then duct-taped his arms and legs to it. Now that Vito was secure, Jake taunted him with a grin.

Kristoff came out from the shadows. "Jake, where are my relics?"

Vito interjected, "Where's Sister Genevie?"

Kristoff yelled at Jake, "Search him."

"First, you and I have some business here, Kristoff. I know what you want. You want the relics, but now I'm concerned with getting what I want. I'm after the Presidency. I'm way down in the polls. How do you propose to make this happen? I want to know this, and I want to know it now."

"Don't worry. I have the cabal ready to release the right technology and turn things in your favor. With the strength of the relics, people will easily be persuaded to vote for you." Kristoff relieved Vito of the relics and placed them on the table.

"But how can that be?"

"Come here, Jake." Kristoff reached out and put his arm around Jake's shoulder. "That's a good boy. Listen, Jake, I'm in charge of the software in every voting system globally. Did you think that you were the first that the cabal did this for? Oh no."

Jake looked into Vito's face and mouthed, "There is nothing I can't do."

A wide grin broke out on Kristoff's face. "In the interest of complete transparency, I need to tell you something though. I did not have you steal those relics for me to use them in your puny election."

Jake broke free from Kristoff but couldn't turn away from his eyes that glowed fiery red. Shaking, Jake yelled, "What the hell are you talking about? You make that phone call and have those polls turn in my favor."

"Now, now, Jake. Hell is what we're talking about, and it's where I will be sending you shortly."

Jake's face turned ashen; he clenched his fists till they turned white. He finally exhaled and took out his pistol.

Kristoff stood there and laughed. "Oh, this is good. Those

relics were never intended to do anything for you. They are for my warriors. We will use the power of the Heavens against itself, and we will, at last, accomplish the plan which was mine from the start. So, be a good boy, and I'll let you watch."

Jake was shaking uncontrollably when he fired six shots at Kristoff. Kristoff looked at his chest with the holes in it, then raised his head and looked Jake in the eye, laughing. "Tsk, tsk." Kristoff morphed into Satan and marched straight up to Jake, grabbed him by the throat, and raised him three feet off the ground. Jake clutched his throat and kicked his feet as life drained from him.

"You are a weak and pitiful man."

Vito yelled out, "Jake, do you believe in God?"

Satan turned like the wind at full speed and tilted his head, looking Vito directly in the eye.

Jake nodded. "Yes, I do."

Satan's glare turned into a murderous rage and with blazing eyes he grabbed Vito with his free hand. He stood with Vito and the chair in his right hand and Jake in his left hand and quaked in anger.

"Are you sorry for your sins?"

The warehouse erupted from a host of demons with an inarticulate noise that sounded like "Do not lose that soul."

Jake screamed, "Yes! I'm sorry I ever went against God for this… this horrific beast."

Satan shrieked in anger as more demons started to appear and hover about, bellowing "kill him" as hysteria took over.

Satan tilted his head and looked first at Vito. He smiled in his arrogance. Then he looked at Jake.

Vito yelled out, "Your many sins are forgiven! In the name of the Father, the Son, and the Holy Spirit!"

Satan's eyes went wide. "Nooooo!" he screamed.

A chorus of unadulterated screams could be heard. "No, that is our soul!" Satan thrashed Jake's body about until he finally squeezed the life out of it and dropped it to the floor.

Throwing the chair and Vito back to the ground, Kristoff scoffed, "You think you're clever, don't you? You just made your own death so much worse. I may have lost Jake's soul, but I'll have yours. A sanctified priest's soul is worth so much more. Ha!"

Satan went to pick up the relics.

The skies swirled black, the silence of the Heavens deafening before that celestial command from the Almighty, "Help my prodigal son, Michael. Go."

Michael, the Archangel, and Billy Campbell stood behind Vito.

"Well, well," Satan sneered, "look who showed up."

Michael regarded Satan. "If you open that box in front of your demons, they will die."

Satan sneered. "So be it."

"No, Master. No," yelled the chorus of demons.

"I will open it when it is my time, not yours. I still have

unfinished business with Billy for my two overlords. But first, watch what I do to this puny human.

Looking down at Vito tied in the chair, Satan reached his hand out to draw Vito's heart from his chest. Vito cried out in pain. His shirt began to swell. Satan cackled. "My, my, this is a true believer. He's a tough one," he said as he applied more pressure to Vito's heart.

Vito clutched at his necklace, his thoughts burning with the knowledge of God's merciful nature.

Now, in the throes of what was to be his long-awaited triumph, Satan screamed at Michael, "This can't be." Satan applied more pressure.

Vito screamed as Satan ripped some of his shirt away.

Satan howled in triumph. Michael extended his hand outward toward Vito as if in comfort. Just then, Joan's necklace ripped through Vito's shirt and flew into Michael's hand, instantly transforming into the Archangel's mighty sword.

In a fury, Satan raised his fist. "No. Not this time," he screamed. He swung around, eyes blazing like fire, as Michael brought his sword down, and with a single swipe, sent Satan flying across the room in a lifeless heap.

For a long moment, all was deadly silent. Vito, slumped in his chair, slowly raised his head as Billy removed his ties.

The sound of thunder swelled in the room. "You know by now that I am gone only for this moment in time. Like you, Michael, I am made for eternity. I will see you again! But on this day, I will not go empty-handed. I have the bone box along with its precious contents, fools. And a little something else."

Everyone looked about in confusion. What was he talking about? Only then did they notice Genevie's lifeless body.

"No, no," Vito yelled. "He's taking her soul." He looked up. "Lord, no, please."

A blast of air blew through the room, knocking things over. Papers flew everywhere, and chairs slid about, hitting the walls before a great golden swirl spun upward from the place where Genevie's body rested.

Satan's disembodied voice screamed as if from the abyss. "No! She is mine. This one is mine!"

But once again, the might of the Archangel prevailed.

EPILOGUE

The crisp cool night had called him out. Vito walked halfway through Saint Peters square and turned around to see its majestic beauty cast against the only thing more beautiful, the starlit sky. He felt humbled and blessed to be alive for all the near-death experiences he had survived in the last few days.

He walked on and shook his head. "Thank you, God, even though no one will ever know how close we came to a catastrophic end to civil nations of the world, the United States in particular."

He wondered if he would ever see Cardinal Lintzinburg again, after the Pope had defrocked him and set him back home to Germany for a sabbatical. Or, for that matter, he wondered if he would see Billy again. Had he gained a relationship with a celestial being, or was this a one-time deal? He secretly hoped to see him again.

Even the FEU discreetly celebrated with awards for Russell and his team's foresight and bravery in dealing with unknown entities. For all his gratefulness, there was still the loss of Genevie, which touched his heart more deeply than he had been prepared to acknowledge.

Something moved in the shadows. Vito moved with purpose toward the square's entrance. The shadow followed.

Vito swung around a column and waited.

A few moments later he stepped out, grabbing the person with his right arm, ready to strike. In the scuffle, he heard a breathless squeak. "Father."

He stepped back and released his grip. "Genevie?" Impossible. He looked closer at the face of a young woman.

"I'm sorry for following you but I needed to talk to you. My mother told me to find you."

Vito saw the puzzled look on her face, which appeared slightly familiar.

"The letter," the woman said. "She gave it to you. Haven't you read it?"

Vito shifted his weight, remembering that there was a letter. What had he done with it?

She looked into his eyes. "My mother made me promise to give you this copy just in case."

He reached out and took the letter, his eyes never leaving hers, his mind settling on a long-ago memory of Genevie. "You…you called me Father."

"Yes."

About the Author

Fred Gray is a two-time award-winning novelist. While

his first fantasy adventure, "Cloud Kingdom," is a captivating tale of two youngsters who become warriors in another realm, it is also a values-driven story dealing with real-life issues such as bullying—perfect for young readers and parents alike. When Fred isn't writing, you can find him at the gym, on cross-country motorcycle trips, or helping others change their lives. In addition to being a successful author and life coach, he is also a talented magician and professional dog trainer. Look for his "Cloud Kingdom" sequel, "Warous, Son of Stous," soon to be released.

Fred's books are available
online and in local libraries,
at Amazon.com and on Kindle Books

Visit his website:

www.FredGrayAuthor.us.

Scan QR Code

For Easy Review